THE ZERO
AND THE ONE

RYAN RUBY

Legend Press Ltd, 107-111 Fleet Street, London, EC4A 2AB
info@legend-paperbooks.co.uk I www.legendpress.co.uk

Contents © Ryan Ruby 2017

First published by Twelve, an imprint of Grand Central Publishing.
1290 Avenue of the Americas, New York, NY 10104, USA
www.twelvebooks.com

The right of the above author to be identified as the author of this work has
been asserted in accordance with the Copyright, Designs and Patents Act
1988. British Library Cataloguing in Publication Data available.

Print ISBN 978-1-7871988-7-6
Ebook ISBN 978-1-7871988-6-9
Set in Times. Printed by Opolgraf SA
Cover design by Gudrun Jobst I www.yotedesign.com

Ryan Ruby was born in Los Angeles in 1983. He has written for *The Baffler, Conjunctions, Lapham's Quarterly, n+1*, and the *Paris Review Daily* among other publications, and has translated two novellas from the French for Readux Books. He lives in Berlin.

Follow Ryan at
www.ryanruby.info

To Lisa

Since I completed it, I have been ambivalent about the advisability of offering this book to the general public Members of the general public expect a book that is *written for them*—for their edification or entertainment—with these ends in mind, in a comely and hospitable style. But mine is an unsafe book, and not just anyone will emerge from it unscathed. This will explain why it is written the way it is written. If I have not lain out truths before the reader in the straightforward manner to which he is accustomed, it is not because I wish to shock, offend, or puzzle him. In fact, I have only his safety in mind. In my style—cryptic, paradoxical, at times nonsensical—will be found the best evidence of my compassion for the general public. Its very *inhospitableness* is a *cordon sanitaire* intended to protect a certain type of reader from understanding what I have written and thus from becoming contaminated by the wisdom that has been coughed into each of the following pages. Thus, I must candidly warn the reader that whoever desires a straightforward presentation of What I Think will not possess the strength to survive an encounter with it; such a reader is advised to close the covers now and thoroughly disinfect his hands. For I mean to take those who have the audacity to turn the page on a lengthy journey of interpretation through many dense, humid, and pestilential jungles of thought. The journey and it alone will provide them with the necessary training to withstand their understanding of my book and, should they have the endurance to reach the end, not to be annihilated by the vision I have set out before them there.

— Hans Abendroth
From the "Author's Preface to the First Edition" of
The Zero and the One

REPETITION.— If something happens once, it may as well have never happened at all. Unfortunately, nothing ever happens only once. Everything is repeated, even nothing.

A British Airways jet, high above the coast of New England. The captain has turned off the fasten seatbelt sign, but mine remains strapped tightly across my waist. My fingers clutch the armrests, knuckles white. The air hostess evens her trolley with our row and bestows a sympathetic elevation of her eyebrows on me as she clears minibottles, plastic cups, crumpled napkins off my tray table. The other passengers regard me with caution. When I stumbled back from the toilet, I found that the young mother in my row had exchanged places with her tow-headed, round-faced toddler, who now stares obliviously at the white fields outside the window, in order to provide him with a buffer zone in case I were to do something erratic. Perhaps I'd been mumbling to myself again: a dangerous perhaps.

I tried to apologise to her, to explain that I rarely drink so much, it's only on planes that... but no luck. She doesn't speak English.

It's true, flying terrifies me. I can count the number of times I've done it on one hand. Twice with my parents. Once with school. Most recently, to Berlin with Zach during the Easter holiday. None of which has remotely prepared me to endure this seven-hour trans-Atlantic torture. Nothing — not a book or an inflight movie or even three minibottles of whisky — helps me to relax. The least bit of turbulence, every unexpected dip in altitude, signals The Beginning of a Crash.

On the flight to Berlin, Zach noticed my anxiety and argued that this was precisely what was *so interesting* about air travel. It was to be regarded, he said, as an exercise in *amor fati*. As soon as you stepped through the doors, you were forced to resign yourself to the possibility that your *conveyance will turn into your coffin*. Your fate was no longer in your hands, no longer under your control. In fact life was always like this, but only in special circumstances were we made aware of it. *If to philosophize was to prepare for death he could think of no better place to practice philosophy than on an airplane.*

His words were no comfort to me then. They're even less of one now. The *last* thing I want to think about are preparations for death. And coffins. How does one transport a body across the ocean? On a ship? Down in the hold with the rest of the luggage? Maybe on every flight there's a coffin going somewhere. At this very moment my t shirts and toiletries could be nestling up with the dead.

When it is time, the air hostess helps me firmly lock my tray table and return my seat to its upright position.

We're beginning our final descent into New York, she explains.

No Miss, I am tempted to reply. Not our final descent.

The customs officer is a candle stub of a man with a damp, fleshy face that seems to have melted from the dark hairline of his crew cut into the wide, unbuttoned collar of his uniform. He flips through every page of my mostly blank passport, looks from me to my photo and back again. The photo, I remember, was taken at a booth in the Galleries, three or four years ago, in the thick of my rather dubious battle with puberty, right after one of those visits to the hairdresser, which, because I no longer live with my parents, I am no

10

longer obliged to make. I neutralise my expression and remove my glasses, as I had been instructed to do then, but it is only when my left eye, which has astigmatism, wanders toward my nose that the resemblance finally becomes clear to him. He asks me to confirm the information I had written on my declaration form.

Student. One week. 232 West 113th Street.

Business or pleasure?

Funeral.

The stamp falls with a dull, bureaucratic thump: Welcome to the United States.

I know what New York looks like from the establishing shots of countless films and television shows. But there the city is only as large as the screen you watch it on. A safe size. Contained. Manageable. Odourless. Two-dimensional. With clearly marked exit signs, if you're watching at the cinema. With a volume dial and an off button, if you're watching from the comfort of your living room.

These taxi windows offer no such protection. On the motorway, my driver slices through traffic, steering with one hand on the indicator and the other on the horn. When a removal van tries to pass us, he closes the distance at the last moment. The driver leans out the window of the van, his face red, spit flying from his mouth as he tries to shout over the siren of the ambulance behind us. Not one to allow an insult to go unanswered, my driver rolls down the passenger-side window, letting in the foul breath of late afternoon. I probably shouldn't have pushed my luck by getting off the plane.

Can you believe this shit! he bellows a few minutes later. He's been trying to engage me in conversation since he first pulled me from the middle of the taxi queue at the airport, not sensing from my mumbled one-word answers that I'd prefer to be left alone. Our eyes meet in the rearview mirror, which is wrapped in the black beads of a rosary; the silver crucifix dangling from the end bobs and sways as he speeds round a double-parked car.

Can I believe what, then?

What this world is coming to! It's been all over the radio this week. This brawd in Texas drowned her five kids in the tub.

I sigh with resignation and ask why a person would do such a thing.

Because she's crazy, that's why! Post-pardon depression or some shit. Said God told her to do it. God of all people! Now you tell me, boss — would God ever tell somebody to kill their own child?

If I'm not mistaken, I say, clearing my throat, God ordered Abraham to sacrifice Isaac. And the Father himself offered up his only begotten son to —

What? What was that you said? he yells, although he's heard me perfectly well. The taxi screeches to a halt. This is your stop, buddy.

At the airport, I changed all the money I'll have to live on for the week. It was the first time I'd ever held dollars in my hand. Green-and-black pieces of paper, no nonsense notes, dour expressions on the portraits of men called Grant, Jackson, Hamilton — presidents presumably. I take a Grant and a Hamilton from my wallet and press them through the square opening in the plastic screen that separates me from the driver. Plus tip, buddy, he says. I hand him another ten dollars.

He remains seated as I take my luggage out of the boot. As soon as he hears the door shut, he speeds off again, leaving me, I soon realise, far from the address I'd given him. Not an hour in New York and already I've been ripped off.

My hostel is located opposite a primary school in the middle of a short, derelict street in Harlem. I'd spent most of my savings on the flight and this one was the cheapest I could find at short notice. On my walk here, three different beggars asked for money in tones ranging from supplicant to menacing. I dropped the two quid I happened to have in my pocket, shrapnel from the carton of cigarettes I bought at the duty-free shop, into the outstretched cup of the one I passed as I turned onto 113th Street. I moved on, head down, hoping he wouldn't notice until I was well out of shouting range.

I ring the doorbell. Open the door. Approach the large desk in the lobby and say, My name is Owen Whiting, I have a reservation. At the other end of the room, an elderly couple is sitting on an exhausted brown couch, watching a game show on the telly. Another guest is typing an email at the ancient computer in the corner. Next to him, there is a plastic display for tourist brochures and pamphlets and a table whose dusty surface supports a metallic coffee dispenser, a stack of paper cups, and a basket filled with pink sachets of sugar, plastic stirrers, and jigger pots of milk and cream. Framed photographs of the Manhattan skyline have been hung unevenly and seemingly at random on the beige walls.

My room, up three flights of stairs, proves to be equally spartan. A pair of bunk beds. A bank of lockers for valuables. A grated window that looks out onto a fire escape and down into a dark alley, which is separated from the road by a barbed wire fence. The ceiling fan spins slowly, straining to circulate a dainty handkerchief of tepid air on the slab of dusk that has also taken up residence here.

My bed must be the one on the top left — at least that's the only one that's been made. I strip down to my underwear, stuff my clothes into my rucksack, and place it into the locker with the key still in the hole. Book in hand, I climb up to my berth and lie down on the thin pillow and starchy sheets. The reading lamp clipped to the metal bedpost splutters a few flashes of yellow light before it shines a paltry neon cone on the cover of Zach's copy of *The Zero and the One*.

On the black background, the white circle of the titular Zero intersects the white circle of the titular One, forming an eye-shaped zone the jacket designer coloured red. Beneath the title, also in red, the name of the author: Hans Abendroth.

From the earliest days of our friendship, Zach and I sought out philosophers whose names would never have appeared on the reading lists we received before the beginning of each term. To our tutors, such thinkers did not merit serious consideration. Our tutors were training us to weigh evidence, parse logic, and refute counter-examples; they encouraged us to put more stock in the rule than the exception and to put our trust in modest truths that could be easily verified and plainly expressed. Whereas the philosophers who interested us were the ones who would step right to the edge of the abyss — and jump to conclusions; the ones who wagered their sanity when they spun the wheel of thought; the ones, in short, who wrote in blood. In counter-intuitiveness we saw profundity and in obfuscation, poetry. With wide eyes, we plucked paperback after paperback from the shelves at Reservoir, the used bookshop opposite the entrance to Christ Church Meadow, our own personal Nag Hammadi, hunting for insights into the hermetic nature of the universe and ourselves.

Zach had seen an aphorism from *The Zero and the One* cited in Lacan's seminar on Poe, a reappraisal of which had appeared in *Theory*, a London-based journal of continental philosophy whose back issues Reservoir kept in stock. Subtitled "an essay in speculative arithmetic," *The Zero and the One* (*Null und Eins* in the original German) is Abendroth's only book to have been translated into English. For a whole month we searched every bookshop we passed and came up empty-handed — not a negligible failure in a city that must be one of the world's largest markets for used and rare books. Even Dr. Inwit had never heard of Abendroth. The Bodleian had two copies, naturally, but the one that was permitted to circulate was on loan that term. Zach placed a hold on it, only to be told, when he returned to the Philosophy and Theology Faculty to collect it, that it had been reported missing. Despite his insistent pleading, the librarian, citing a recent act of Parliament, refused to divulge the identity of the borrower. When he finally found it, on Niall Graves' shelves

14

at the *Theory* launch party, he yelped, alarming some of the other partygoers, who must have thought he had just done himself some serious injury.

Though he was quite generous with his money — he picked up the tab wherever we went and never once turned a beggar away — Zach wouldn't let me borrow the book. It was, you might say, his prized possession. He quoted from it often and sometimes read whole passages aloud when he wanted to prove some point. The first time I held it in my hands was four days ago, when his father and I were cleaning out his rooms. Save for the travel guide I bought at Blackwell's, it is the only reading I've brought with me to New York.

I flip through the collection of aphorisms, looking for one in particular. The book shows all the signs of intense study: broken spine, wrinkled edges, dog-eared pages, creased jacket. Inside, the margins are heavily annotated in black pen. The underlining consists of lines so perfectly straight they must have been traced there with a ruler or with the edge of a bookmark.

On my first search, skimming all the dog-eared pages, I fail to find the passage I'm looking for. It was something about *The Possessed* he read to me that night. Something about Kirillov. Kirillov's suicide. The aphorisms all have titles, but there's no table of contents; nor is there an index of names in the back. I'll have to be more meticulous, examine every sentence Zach found worthy of comment. I turn back to the beginning, but I'm only able to read a few pages before the light bulb splutters again, this time fatally, and the room goes dark. I flick the switch once, twice: the light isn't coming back. I take off my glasses and slip the book under my pillow, giving what remains of my waking attention to the vague, slow circles of the fan and the dim lattice of orange and black the streetlamp has cast on the ceiling.

I've just begun to fall asleep, for the first time in a week, when I hear someone, one of the other guests, struggling with the door lock. Two shadows, one male and one female, stumble into the dark room. From how loudly they whisper to each other not to make any noise, it's clear they're both totally pissed. They fall into the bunk beneath mine; the bedsprings shriek under their combined weight. I cough into my fist, to let them know someone else is in the room, but they remain oblivious or indifferent to my presence. Rather than embarrassed silence, the rustle of fabric. Lips on bare skin. A moan — hers — escapes the fingers of a muffling hand as the bedframe begins to sway. Beneath the small of my back, my mattress elevates slightly. The palms of her hands or the balls of her feet, I wonder.

Outside the window, there is a dull pop. Then another three, in rapid succession. The bedsprings stop contracting abruptly beneath me.

What was that? the woman whispers, petrified.

What was what? Her lover sounds deflated. He knows exactly what she's referring to, and can already tell that he's lost her attention.

That *sound*.

Nothing, baby, he says. It was nothing. Just a car back-firing.

I never learnt where Zach found those pistols. Where does one buy a handgun anyway? Estate sale? Antique shop? The black market? I hadn't asked, and if I hadn't asked it is because I'd rather not know. When Bernard told me that the Inspector from the Thames Valley Police had managed to trace the pistol (he said pistol, *singular*, and I certainly wasn't about to correct him), I let it be understood with a wave of my hand that I preferred to be kept in the dark about certain aspects of the case. Still, this hasn't prevented me from speculating. Whoever sold the firearms to Zach would surely have told the Inspector about the second pistol. Unless he bought them from two different people. Unless: he stole them. It wouldn't have been the first time, after all.

The pistols were small and old. Their black barrels were

no longer than my outstretched index finger, the sort of weapon my grandfather might have stripped off the corpse of some Nazi officer during the war. They looked ridiculous to me, but Zach was quite serious about them, as he was about any technology the rest of us considered antiquated. When I asked him if they even worked, his expression soured. *Of course they do!* He'd *tested them* to make sure. Yanks and their bloody guns. Whatever else they may feel about them, they're all obsessed by them. Even Zach, the latchkey kid born and bred in downtown Manhattan. When he collected me from Prelims, one pistol weighing down each pocket of his dinner jacket, he must have been the most heavily armed person in all of Oxfordshire.

RITUALS OF SUSPENSION.— The ritual that can withstand the deadening weight of its own unbroken repetition has yet to be choreographed. Any ritual so rigid that it fails to include the means of its own periodic suspension is bound to go extinct.

Pembroke is one of the smallest and poorest of Oxford's colleges. The Cotswold stone buildings seem to turn inward, away from bustling St. Aldate's, as if ashamed of the plainness of their features. The Old Quad, where I was given rooms, lies quite literally in the shadow of the fairer sister over the road. Tourists would come from round the world to visit Pembroke Square, only to turn their backs on our Porter's Lodge so they could have a better angle from which to snap a photograph of Tom Tower, the lavishly ornamented gateway to Christ Church.

The college was old enough to have produced a few notable alumni, but the most famous of them, Samuel Johnson, was sent down after a year for a lack of funds. Today, its students are better known for the speed of their oars on the Isis than the speed of their pens in the Exam Schools. It is largely made up of those like me, who have what the Student Union euphemistically calls *non-traditional backgrounds*, and who were only able to attend the oldest university in England by grace of what the Bursar called, rather less euphemistically, *hardship grants*. (Mine in particular were financed by the sale, a few years previously, of *Man in a Chair*, an early painting by Francis Bacon, a poster of which was the only decoration on the walls of my rooms.) Rounding out the Junior Common Room were the thicker products of the public schools, Erasmus scholars from the continent, and Americans on their year abroad.

Of this last group there were around twenty, paying American tuition fees to add English polish to their CVs. The reason for their presence at Pembroke was nakedly economic, a way for a college whose endowment consisted almost entirely of subsidies from its wealthier neighbours to generate a bit of additional revenue. They were lodged in the back staircases of the North Quad, on the main site, with the rest of us first years. Though they were only two years older than I, and though they were living, many for the first time, in a country not their own, this slight difference in age lent them an air of cosmopolitan sophistication; I certainly wasn't the only one to regard the *visiting students*, as they were called, more as elders than as peers. For better or worse, they generally had the run of the place.

Zach was not long in distinguishing himself, mostly through skirmishes with various members of the college staff concerning the finer points of college etiquette. The first time I recall seeing him, he was being reprimanded by Richard Hughes, the Head Porter, a lean and sallow-faced man in his fifties, whose fingernails were worn longer than his sense of humour. I remember looking out my window to see what the fuss was about below. Zach, it seems, had walked across the immaculate square of lawn in the Old Quad on his way to the pantry. Not content to defer to authority — or local custom — he was demanding, in those flat syllables I'd come to know so well, the explanation for such an absurd rule. The one he was given ("only fellows and newlyweds are permitted to walk on the lawn of the Old Quad") didn't satisfy him. He demanded another. The exasperated Head Porter told him that it was "out of respect for the sleep of the dead monks who are buried there." To this he nodded, convinced and perhaps a tad impressed. But whenever he walked through the Old Quad, he made sure to toe the cobblestones near the edge of the lawn, not seeming to care, now that he had been reprimanded, that he was liable to pay a fine if he lost his balance.

A fortnight later, I was sitting alone at what had already become my regular seat at my regular table, reading whilst I waited for Formal Hall to begin. I was dressed subfusc— jacket, white bowtie (in my case poorly knotted), black commoner's gown— the requisite attire. Zach arrived in the company of Gregory Glass, in the middle of a heated political debate.

"I can't believe what I'm hearing!" Gregory was saying. The other visiting student from Columbia, Gregory was short and barrel-chested, with long curly brown hair that was held off his face, no matter what time of day, by a sporty pair of sunglasses. I'd already seen him several times at macroeconomics lectures, furiously scribbling away in the front row. That term, not a single lecture would conclude without Gregory raising his hand to ask a question, or rather, to give a meandering observation in an interrogative tone.

He asked me if they could sit at my table and, without waiting to hear my answer, continued talking to his friend. "Don't tell me," he said, in a voice that could be heard from one end of the hall to the other, "you're going to throw your vote away on Nader!"

"I'm not throwing away my vote," Zach replied, perfectly calm.

"I'm *not voting*."

"But it's your duty to vote! You complain about the government all the time, but when you're given the chance to actually change things, you throw it—"

"See, that's where you're wrong. My vote doesn't actually change anything. Nor does yours, Greg. You and I are registered in states that have already pledged their electors to Gore. And anyway, on the major issues there is a consensus between the two parties that differs only in rhetorical emphasis. During the presidential debates, the questions are never *How should we organize our economy?* but *What flavor of capitalism would you like?* Never *What role should the United States have in the world?* but *How blatant should we be about our empire?* Third-party candidates like Nader, who at least would give the election the veneer of choice, are marginalized into irrelevance by unregulated campaign finance laws and" — here he pointed a finger at Gregory — "the bad-faith scare tactics of pseudo-leftists and lesser-evil socialists like you."

Fuming, Gregory tried to respond to this accusation, but Zach sped to his next point before he could get a word in. "So don't tell me it's my *duty* to accept this state of affairs. It's not my duty to give legitimacy to this farce we call democracy. Under the present conditions, voting is one of those customs more honored in the breach than the observance."

Gregory looked like he was going to lean across the table and grab Zach by the bowtie to get him to stop talking. To make sure he wouldn't be interrupted again, he almost shouted his rejoinder. "Man, you're so full of shit! I'd rather be a 'pseudo-leftist' than the beautiful soul who's scared to get his hands dirty in actual politics. You think of yourself as a purist, but you're just a cynic with a trust fund. You talk about not being able to opt out of capitalism? Why would you even want to? You're its beneficiary! I've never met anyone more bourgeois than you."

"As Marx defined bourgeois, maybe," Zach said, with a dismissive twirl of his wrist. "But not as Flaubert defined it. Speaking of cynicism, *Comrade Glass*, let's say for the sake of discussion that your socialist dream is realized on earth. Poverty is eradicated, exploitation rooted out, war declared a thing of the past, and total freedom of thought is granted to all. That's the idea, right? Now, will mankind hunt in the morning, fish in the afternoon, raise cattle in the evening, and criticize after dinner, as Marx predicted?" he asked, counting off each activity on his fingers before answering his own question. "No! They'll shop in the morning, fill their prescriptions in the afternoon, watch TV in the evening, and die of boredom after dinner! Stupidity is not just the result of false consciousness and organized oppression. It's the natural condition of the vast majority of mankind. It's the one thing that is equally distributed among the rich and the poor. Solving our political and economic problems will do nothing to answer the question, *Why bother?* In fact, all evidence suggests that it will only make *that* question more difficult to answer."

Meanwhile, the hall had filled up with students and the fellows of the college had taken their places at the High Table. In a slow roll, the current of conversation ebbed and the hall flooded with the sound of bustling chairs as we all stood to hear the Classics Tutor recite the Latin Grace. All save Zach, that is, who remained seated. He took the opportunity to slide my book close enough to him to get a better view of the cover. He tapped the title with two fingers — I was reading *The Birth of Tragedy* — and nodded with approval. Grace concluded, the sound of conversation and sliding chairs and clanking cutlery resumed. The waiting staff appeared and began to place the starters on our plates.

Gregory returned to his seat and gave Zach a stern look.

"I bet you were the kid in homeroom who refused to stand for the Pledge of Allegiance."

"We didn't have homeroom at The Gansevoort School, Greg."

The Hall Manager had also noticed the sole seated student and went to enquire into this breach of conduct. The Hall Manager was called Mr. Stroop, a squat man well past middle age, whom I couldn't stand. Stroop had worked at Pembroke for over a decade, but was far less convincing than the Head Porter in performing his role as the guardian of the college's traditions and values. It was precisely in his comical assiduousness that he betrayed his working-class origins. No one who belonged at Oxford, who was slated to go there from birth, from before their birth, cared half so much for the college's traditions and values as he did. This confounded and perplexed him, but as he did not understand why it was the case, he was undeterred in his mission. Queuing up at the pantry one day, I heard him correct the pronunciation of an American who had ordered his sandwich without tomato. "It's toh-*mah*-toe," he said. "Not toh-*may*-toe. You've come all this way to receive a proper education. You should at least learn how to order a sandwich." A proper education. One he himself had not received. A fact that was not lost on the American, who sneered at this bit of servility and told him to bring the sandwich "without toh-*mah*-toe. Right quick!" Which Stroop did, causing me to wince.

Implying he couldn't hear what was being said over the general din, though he must have known quite well what the Hall Manager was there to discuss, Zach motioned him closer to his ear. Stroop stooped as he was told and the whole table quieted down to listen to what promised to be a duel of insincere politeness.

"Mr. Foedern —"

"How may I be of help, sir?"

"I couldn't help but notice that you — and you alone — were not standing during the recitation of Grace."

"Yes, sir, you'll have to forgive me. You see, I don't speak Latin."

"Don't speak Latin? I'm afraid I don't see what that's got to do with it."

"I'll explain. To stand means to assent, no?"

"To stand? Yes, I reckon..."

"Well, there you have it. I can't assent if I don't understand what's being said. And I can't stand if I don't assent. So perhaps you'll be so good as to translate the Grace for me so I can decide whether I assent or not."

Zach batted his eyelashes with feigned innocence and, receiving no response from the flustered Hall Manager — whose only Latin, needless to say, was *Veni vidi vici* and *Dominus illuminatio mea* — tucked into his prawns. Mr.

Stroop interrupted him to escort him to the High Table so the Classics Tutor could translate the Grace for him. I watched Zach listen gravely, exchange a few words with Stroop, and return to his place at the table. But he did not sit down. He poured himself another glass of wine and drank it in a single swallow.

"Now that I understand," he told us, "I definitely do not assent."

"Where are you going?" Gregory demanded.

"To Hassan's," Zach said, referring to the kebab van on Broad Street. "I'm sure *they* will agree with my position on the Latin Grace."

I never again saw Zach attend Formal Hall, but I noticed that during every subsequent Grace, one or two students remained seated, small acts of rebellion that would plague Mr. Stroop until the end of the year.

THE FEAR OF THE INEXPRESSIBLE.— Language doubles: it transforms the physical into the metaphysical, the specific into an instance of the general, the particular case into an abstract idea. Naming marks the creation of an entirely new ontological region that shadows the old one, coextensive yet distinct. Access to this doubled world is what makes transcendence possible, but this access is never total, nor is it ever complete. This is precisely what is so terrifying about the inexpressible. The *inexpressible* is the sliver of the material that resists all colonisation by signification; it is the remainder *par excellence*. Greek mathematicians, for instance, were so intimidated by the inexpressible that they did not hit upon the simple solution of making nothingness disappear by assigning it a number.

At seven in the morning, the receptionist is the only person in the lobby, and even he is still asleep. His hands are folded on his heaving chest; his feet, crossed at the ankle, hang over the corner of his desk. Doing my best not to disturb him, I reach over the top of the desk to pull a strip of paper, on which the computer's login and password are printed, from the pile he keeps in a blue-and-white cup that says WE ARE HAPPY TO SERVE YOU in ochre pseudo-Hellenic font. I manage nonetheless to knock the cup onto his lap. His eyes fly open and he straightens in his chair, giving me a glazed and irritated look. Sorry, sorry, I say, backing slowly away from the desk, palms in the air. The receptionist smacks his lips and stretches, then starts to put the slips back into the cup.

I sit down at the computer terminal, type the address of Oxford Nexus into the browser, and scan my inbox for new messages. There is one from the editor of a London poetry journal informing me that the sonnet *"Eadem, Sed Aliter"* I'd submitted with Mr. Zachary Foedern has been accepted for publication in the Autumn issue. Had I received it only a month ago, this news surely would have made me swell with pride — it's the first time my name's going to appear in print, after all. But the knowledge that my co author isn't here to celebrate with me renders the editor's congratulations more bitter than sweet. I look at the other address in the recipient field and think of Zach's inbox, filling up day by day with emails like this one, messages that will go forever unread.

There is one from my father, confirming receipt of the email I sent yesterday informing him I had arrived safely at my destination, and requesting, with typical curtness, that I ring him or Mum as soon as I was able to purchase a phone card.

And there is one from Claire.

In the short time we'd known each other, how many hundreds of emails had I exchanged with Claire? This is the first that has ever filled me with dread. The subject line meant that she was no longer in Oxford, but had gone with Tori to the latter's parents' house in Greenwich. Yesterday, whilst I packed my luggage, she quietly slipped into Tori's bedroom, where the lights had been off for days, to check on our grieving friend. She came out again to kiss me goodbye when it was time for me to walk to the bus station at Gloucester Green. Her face was pale with worry; we kissed like we'd never see each other again.

FROM: clairecaldwell@st annes.ox.ac.uk
TO: owenwhiting@pmb.ox.ac.uk
SUBJECT: From Greenwich

Writing to you from Tori's. We took the train and arrived last night. The mood here is grim. No change from when you last saw her. She slept fourteen hours yesterday. When she's awake she's absolutely inconsolable. She's lost half a stone in the past week and it shows. Her parents are alarmed, but none of us know what to do with her. Mrs Hardwood suggested she see a therapist, but she wasn't having it. Last night, before we went to sleep, she told me she feels guilty, that she's responsible for Zach's death. She would have liked to have gone with you to the funeral, but she felt it wouldn't be appropriate, because she thinks she's the cause of it. All she talks of is Commems. How she wished she hadn't pressured him into going. Anyway, the point is moot. She's in no condition to travel.

I know it's absolutely horrid of me to say, but Tori's grief is becoming overwhelming. It's as if no one is allowed to be sad but her. I know your relationships with Zach were much closer, but I loved him too and I haven't been able to show it. I can't keep it in all the time. It amazes me that you have so far. I had to tell someone this and you're the only person who would understand. We carry other people's burdens and then there is no room to carry our own so we drop it off on someone else. I'm sorry it had to be you, darling, because you're carrying the heaviest burden of all.

Take care of yourself there. Try to take a moment to enjoy yourself if you can. I know that sounds blasphemous or somehow disrespectful of the dead, but we still have lives to live. Never forget that. Never ever forget that.

I'll keep you posted on what's happening here.

All my love,
C

Some response is necessary — but what? All that comes to mind are empty formulae. Chin up. Hang in there. I'm *here* for you. I type them into the message body anyway, to see how they look. They seem to drown in the white field, their meanings no match for what ought to be said. Double-click, delete. Maybe no response is better than an insufficient one, dashed off just like that. Claire really *was* the best of us: the most thoughtful, the least self-centred, the kindest. How could I presume to comfort *her*? She who was only a second away from being in Tori's position. Carrying the heaviest burden of all? If she only knew.

The lobby is stirring with the other guests, some of whom are waiting impatiently to use the computer, preparing themselves, I sense, to invoke the 15 Minutes Only clause handwritten by The Management on a piece of paper taped to the wall above the thick beige monitor. When I close the browser and stand up from the office chair, no fewer than four pairs of vulturine eyes dart in my direction.

What I need is a walk. Some fresh air. To clear my mind. To think of what I'll write to Claire. According to the map at the end of my travel guide, if I turn left and make another left at the nearest crossroads, I should find myself before long at the entrance to Central Park.

Outside, Manhattan is fully conscious, an infernal orchestra of pheumatic drills, car horns, rowdy schoolchildren, and disputation that is well into the overture. Already the sun is out and blazing. Pearls of sweat form on my forehead; I can feel the backs of my arms slowly turning pink. The shadows of street signs and newspaper kiosks look like petrol that's been spilled on the pavement.

At a corner shop, I buy a coffee, a croissant wrapped in plastic, and a phone card. The man who sells them to me has dark copper skin and wears a succinct black moustache set between a bulbous nose and a row of white, straight teeth. The nearest phone box, he tells me, is just down the road. Near the door are stacks of various local tabloids, all of which lead with the story about the Texas mother whose behaviour had so outraged my taxi driver. I feel rather sorry for her. Above indignant headlines in large white letters, the lurid cover photos show a bespectacled brown-haired woman, her arms handcuffed behind her back, her chin sunk into her chest to avoid looking into the cameras that surround her, trailed by a press of police officers in light blue uniforms.

My mother answers up the phone. Dear, is that you? Owen? Speak louder. I can hardly hear you.

Yes, Mum, it's me, I shout into the black receiver. I'm at a phone box. Dad told me to ring when I'd bought a phone card.

Daddy said he got your email. He's got quite good at it, hasn't he?

Is he there?

No, dear, it's one o'clock here. He's at work.

Yes, that's right, of course. Would you tell him that that's the best way for us to communicate whilst I'm here?

Of course I shall, she says. There is a long pause. The funeral is tomorrow, isn't it?

Yes, tomorrow. Somewhere in Brooklyn. Or maybe it's Queens. Is that far? Are you all right? Do you need anything?

In what I hope is my most reassuring voice I tell her everything's fine.

On the telly it said that it was beastly hot in New York, she says, to fill an awkward silence with idle talk. High of thirty-three degrees! Hard to believe it could get that hot anywhere in June. Though it's better than all the rain we're having here, mind.

A robotic voice interrupts to inform me that I only have twenty-five cents remaining on my phone card.

What was that, dear? I didn't —

Listen, Mum, I think my time is running out. Everything's fine here. I'll ring you if there's an emergency, but meantime just keep checking your —

Three beeps. The line cuts out.

Though I doubt she'd fancy New York, Mum would probably appreciate Central Park. Years ago, en route to my eldest
cousin's wedding in Sheffield, she insisted we stop, despite
Dad's grumbling, in Derbyshire to see Chatsworth House, the
basis for Pemberley, Mr. Darcy's estate in *Pride and Prejudice*,
her favourite novel. But for my mother, the surprise hero of
our excursion turned out not to be Jane Austen, but Capability
Brown, who designed the house's gardens.

I'm as keen on landscape architecture as my father is, but
Zach, an outspoken partisan of the unnatural, might have
seen something in it. One of the aphorisms he underlined
in Abendroth's book describes a walk the philosopher took
through Berlin's Tiergarten during the last year of the war,
at the height of the Allied bombing campaign. Abendroth
thought parks and gardens belonged in the same conversation
as novels and paintings. *They are all*, he writes, *triumphs of
artifice*. The landscape artist alienates nature from itself by
planting trees and flowers and lawns in picturesque patterns
and designs. Nature fights back, of course, doing what it
always does, growing and decaying. Gardening is the art of
forcing nature to conform to our image of how it ought to look,
which is a *victory for consciousness*, even if, as Abendroth
acknowledges, the ways human beings have thought nature
ought to look have usually been *frivolous* and *sentimental*.

I find a shady spot beneath a tree and sit, swallowing my
croissant more out of duty than hunger, washing down the
dry pastry with the burnt coffee. Out on the lawn, a formation
of men and women are floating through a series of Tai Chi
postures. I watch them for a few minutes, trying to interpret
the choreography. They push forward an invisible wall with
their palms. Curl them around an invisible ball. Hang an
invisible lantern on the air behind them. I watch until I am
exhausted by the slowness of the movements, exhausted by
the harmony with which they execute the postures, exhausted
by their faces, tranquil and empty.

After hours of aimless wandering up and down the endless avenues of Manhattan's west side, I am back in the lobby, last in the queue that has formed for use of the computer. I have to write something to Claire. It's been too long already. No doubt she's begun to worry. Whilst I wait, I open *The Zero and the One* and continue from where I left off earlier in the day.

Next to the last aphorism on page 32, Zach had written:

Critique of Moralism
Tragedy as critique
of faith in moral knowledge
i.e. faith that problems have solutions
But Life ≠ Math

Having run out of space in the margin, he continued the thought on the bottom of the page.

Freedom caught between
Scylla of EM (determinism of the solvable)
& Charybdis of T (determinism of the unsolvable)
WITBD?

In the context of the passage, EM clearly stood for "everyday morality" and T "tragedy," but what of the acronym, if that's what it was, at the end? My guess, after concentrating on the letters, wondering what they could possibly stand for, is that Zach was asking What Is To Be Done about this situation, how such an antinomy could be resolved. *Introduce T into EM?* was the answer he gave here, ending with a tentative question mark that a few months later would evolve into a dreadful full stop.

When my turn to use the computer finally comes, I write a short note to Claire, forcing myself to use all the formulae, and one to my parents, repeating what I said to Mum over the phone. Then I log off. The anchorman on the telly is announcing today's winning lottery numbers to an empty room. Standing, I begin to make my way upstairs: tomorrow will surely be a long and difficult day. But as I reach the foot of the staircase, I have an idea. What if there were a way to get into Zach's email? I dart back to the computer, fall into the chair, type *zacharyfoedern@pmb.ox.ac.uk* into the long rectangle, and begin trying out passwords.

I type: *abendroth*. I type: *zeroandtheone*. I type: *zachandtori*. I type: *kirillov*.

Each time a message in red letters says: *You could not be logged on to Oxford Nexus. Make sure that your user name and password are correct, and then try again.*

UNIVERSAL HOMELESSNESS.— Thought exiles man from being, being exiles him from his self, his self exiles him from the external world, the external world exiles him from time, and his tomorrow will exile him from his today just as surely as his today exiled him from his yesterday. Never and nowhere is man truly at home. In order to experience this all he needs to do is to return, after even a short absence, to the city of his birth.

We didn't officially meet until the first week of the following term. We passed each other in the quads, collecting letters at the pigeonholes, ordering books from the library and pints at the pub. In a city as small as Oxford, in a college as small as Pembroke, it is impossible not to cross paths with someone all the time — and Zach was particularly hard to miss. Still, I saw him less often than I might have done. That term, he kept mainly to the other foreign students and I kept mainly to myself.

The day my parents dropped me off in front of the Porter's Lodge, they each took me aside to dispense a few pearls of parental wisdom. My mother told me whom I knew was more important than what I knew. She encouraged me to overcome my *native shyness* in order to befriend people who might one day prove useful to me. Despite wincing when I first heard it, during Fresher's Week I made a sincere effort to follow her advice, only to discover how little I had in common with my classmates. We couldn't swop stories about the exotic locales we'd visited on our Gap Years because I'd gone straight to uni; we couldn't compare notes about the cultures of our respective public schools because I hadn't attended one; we couldn't debate which was the best neighbourhood in London because my knowledge of the capital was little better than that of a tourist; we couldn't bond over our shared loyalty to this or that football club because I didn't follow the Premier League.

So we talked about the weather and did the one thing we all knew how to do: get pissed. I watched stupendous bar bills turn into group song and shoving matches and urine and vomit well before the pubs closed their doors at eleven. One day, I thought, standing outside the toilet of a dodgy dance club, waiting for one of my new acquaintances to finish retching, one of these tossers is going to get himself elected to Parliament.

My father's counsel had been more to the point: best not to indulge in any vices I couldn't afford.

It was just like them to give me contradictory advice.

For a brief period of time, I sought out the sort of company neither of them would have approved of. If I'd had no luck making friends at college, I would surely better my chances amongst like-minded individuals whom I'd select myself from one of Oxford's many student groups. On Cornmarket, a militant of the Revolutionary Worker Student Alliance sold me a copy of the broadsheet *Permanent Revolution* and informed me of the state of the many struggles for liberation from imperialism and class domination taking place around the globe. It was the first time I'd heard phrases like *surplus value* and *determinate negation* and *international flow of capital* and *mode of production* — which I'd encountered reading the books by Marx and Lenin I checked out from the Central Library and hid from my father's censorious gaze when I ought to have been revising for my A levels— spoken aloud.

The militant, Arjun Patel, of Balliol College, invited me to the Alliance's next meeting, which was held every

Thursday in the basement of a Presbyterian church near the University Parks. I attended two of them, and the drinks that followed, mostly keeping silent whilst the same four or five students debated the tactics of forming a provisional affinity groupuscule with the Oxford Socialist Workers' Union, from which they'd splintered last term. I volunteered to sell *Permanent Revolution* with Arjun, put up flyers in pubs and bookshops around the city centre, and joined a march protesting top up fees and one in solidarity with the Al Aqsa Intifada.

But before the third meeting, I was taken aside by Mary Chapman, a Wadham College third year with a dagger's swipe of dyed-red hair, a stud gleaming atop her nostril, and a keffiyeh around her neck, who informed me in BBC English that it would be best if I stopped coming. "You see, some of the comrades... not me, mind... but some of the comrades," she attempted to explain, "believe you're with the filth. And as we may or may not be planning a major action at the moment... some of the comrades reckoned that... that it would be for the best if you were not around... whilst it's being discussed."

I wondered whether it was my native shyness or my still-untamed accent that had aroused their suspicion; either way, I was too offended by the accusation to protest my innocence. I walked back to college in a huff, my lip upturned, my fists buried in my pockets, making speeches that were alternately piqued (the theme being: *none of these people is worth my friendship!*) and self-pitying (the theme being: *why then don't they think I am worth being their friend?*) under my breath. The glow of anticipation that had suffused the days between my acceptance to Oxford and matriculation — the sense that I was on the verge of great adventures, love affairs, making lasting connexions with kindred spirits — had already begun to slip away. The future that now stretched before me looked lone, level, and deserted. What had been the point, I wondered, of coming here in the first place?

For the rest of Michaelmas I shuffled between lecture, library, hall, my tutors' rooms, and my own. Invitations charitably offered to bops and clubs and pub quizzes were at first refused, then no longer forthcoming. I requisitioned from my savings five quid a day for drinks at The Bear, where I sat alone, my eyes searching the cases of regimental neckwear for the tie of my grandfather's battalion or scanning the pages of a novel. Once or twice a week, I went without my two pints of porter and took myself instead to concerts at the Sheldonian or movies at the Pheonix Picturehouse in Jericho. My studiousness earned me words of praise and concern from my tutors, who predicted that if I carried on like this, I was sure to graduate with a double first and a head of grey hair.

I would have preferred to stay on at college to study for Collections during the holiday, but our rooms were being used to house interviewees, and anyway, my parents insisted on having their only child at home for Christmas. My father picked me up from the bus station and drove me back to our back to back on Ruby Street, where I passed an interminable five weeks.

It had occurred to me to wonder how my parents were getting on in my absence, but my mother's weekly phone calls detailed no significant alterations to their usual routines. Mum kept busy with her book group, her gardening, and her work at court. Dad came home from Somerdale and installed himself with a lager in front of the telly to watch the pundits dissect Tony Blair's political future in the wake of the failure of the Millennium Dome. Politics in the age of New Labour hardly made for interesting television, I thought, but as a member of the loyal opposition my father wouldn't miss a single argument.

"What a fiasco," he said to me when I joined him on the couch a few days after Christmas. "The Tories shall be back in power come June. Mark my words."

It was his way of making conversation. He would say something calculated to offend me; normally I would rise to the bait, arguing the point with him, sometimes for hours, until I got so frustrated that I would walk off in a rage, slamming my bedroom door behind me. Dad would calmly return to doing whatever he was doing before the debate started, usually watching the news, satisfied that he had, for a little while at least, made some connexion with his son.

This time, however, I merely shrugged and said nothing. As a young man of the Old Left, I knew I was meant to condemn Third Way centrism as a smokescreen for venal neoliberalism. But the politics of the Vicar of St. Albion — like the man himself — struck me not as evil, but as inconsequential and rather banal.

Only once did my parents ask me what I'd been studying, probably just to get me to say something, anything at all. I would have preferred to have read Philosophy and French, but they thought it important for me to learn something useful, like Medicine or Law or Economics. So we split the difference and I wrote down *L0V0*, the course code for Philosophy, Politics, and Economics, on my application.

Selecting a topic at random, I explained Gini coefficients and Lorenz curves to them, with no attempt whatsoever to make my words comprehensible to the layman. When I came to the end of my little lecture, my mother, who had been nodding blankly, turned to my father and said, "Well, then." They never brought up my studies again.

Nights I would take the bus into town, to see whichever band — the louder, the better — was playing a set at The Chatterton. Two storeys of former warehouse near the harbour, The Chatterton was where I had spent the part of the last few years not devoted to sleeping and studying doing permanent damage to my hearing and my liver. The venue had opened its dingy doors a few years before I was born, quickly establishing itself as a fixture of the local punk scene. The Cortinas and The Zeros had been regulars there, as had Disorder and The Undead. Even The Clash had played the club on their Out of Control Tour, shortly before they broke up. I once saw Mark E. Smith play a set there and nearly died from awe.

The club was now in decline, but it had enough history that performing there was considered a rite of passage for every upcoming punk and hardcore outfit in Southwest England and Wales. The rest of my peers may have preferred the Carling Academy and The Thekla, where they could dance to house and trip hop, but I remained faithful to the power chords on offer at The Chatterton.

On New Year's Eve, after a quiet dinner at home, I stood far from the stage on the second floor, drinking whisky, surveying the dance floor. I watched three punks collide like quarks in a particle accelerator until the sound of distortion and feedback flattened into a high-pitched and hollow ringing. Just like not-so-old times.

In the lull between the first two acts, I went downstairs to get another drink and recognised, at the bar, someone I knew. John Simms, my childhood friend. Simmsy, as everyone called him, lived nearby, in Ashton Vale. Between the ages of thirteen and sixteen we spent a great deal of time in his attic room poring through his elder brother's record collection, drinking cans of lager, and professing our common alienation from the rest of our schoolmates, which we documented with an EP's worth of songs, whose lyrics I wrote to the accompaniment of Simmsy's fierce strumming. The songs were all about the glories of doing drugs and stealing from shops and evading the filth and dying young — all of which, needless to say, I'd then had no actual experience.

We'd seen each other less and less, of course, since I'd gone on to the lower sixth and Dad had got him a job at the factory, the same one he'd made me take as a character-building exercise that summer, and which I vacated when I returned to school. We hadn't spoken once since I went up to Oxford, but seeing him now I felt for the first time in my young life the fondness of recollection known as nostalgia.

I waved to get his attention. He was standing on the other

side of the curved bar, with one arm around the shoulder of a chubby, green-haired bird, whose ears, from the top to the lobe, were silvered with rings.

"Simmsy! How the hell have you been keeping?"

"Um, yeah. Right as rain, fanks. Ow long've thee been ohm, then?"

There was an awkward silence. In Simmsy's question, I detected a reproach. "Two weeks," I admitted. He was right. I should have phoned. The girl with him was glowering at me. "Well," I said, in an attempt to change the subject. "Aren't you going to introduce us?"

"E eve," she said flatly. "Coupla times now, mind."

"Christ, Peg. Is that you? I hardly recognised you. Didn't you used to have blue—"

"Orange," she corrected me.

"Lissen, Owen," Simmsy said, collecting the pair of pint glasses the bartender had placed before him. "Some peepaw upstairs is wayten on dese. Wish yer dad a Happy New Year fer me, won't thee?"

As I watched them leave, I saw how na.ve I'd been. There was no denying it: things had changed. My accent was becoming different, as were my interests and, perhaps most importantly, my future prospects. I couldn't just come back home on holiday and pretend to be his mate again. But nor had I been accepted by my fellow students at Oxford, who looked at me and saw the likes of John Simms. For them I would be forever marked by my so-called background. I found myself between two lives. Two camps. Two worlds. And to be in between is to be nowhere at all.

I didn't stay to hear the band count down the New Year. By midnight, I was at home, in bed, with an open book and the bottle of sparkling wine my parents hadn't finished. The first year of the twenty-first century was ending, not with a bang, but with a whimper. As might have been foreseen.

A few days later, I received an email from each of my Hilary Term tutors. On the email from my tutor for the

Plato paper, the other address was: *zacharyfoedern@pmb. ox.ac*.uk. This, I recall, I noted with ambivalence. My initial impression of Zach, intriguing though I found him, was not entirely favourable. From what I'd seen of the way he'd treated Richard, Gregory, and even Mr. Stroop, he struck me as domineering and arrogant, qualities that would make him difficult to work with.

At an Internet caf. I printed out the list of reading I'd be responsible for in the coming term. The thick stack of pages, which I fanned with my thumb before the eyes of my parents, was enough to convince them of the necessity of my immediate return to college. Dad drove me to the bus station before work, at six in the morning. There he handed me a cheque. Compared to what I'd seen spew out of the wallets of my new classmates, it wasn't much, but as he'd never before given me a present without some occasion or purpose, the gesture was worth far more to me than the number he'd written there. "I'm giving you this because you've demonstrated your ability to live frugally," he said, implying that I had somehow earned the gift, perhaps in order to cover up his embarrassment at what we both understood was uncharacteristically sentimental behaviour. He cleared his throat. "Don't spend it all at the pub."

I nodded silently. Two hours later I woke up in Gloucester Green.

IN THE BELLY OF THE HOUR GLASS.— Beneath each of us shifts the sand of a desert vaster than the Sahara, the desert of our past, over whose dry dunes memory can only skim, blowing temporary patterns of recollection and reinterpretation across the surface of a noumenal landscape wherein the ever-changing is indistinguishable from the eternally-the-same.

My second-best suit is a charcoal-grey double-breasted with peaked lapels, made in a Pakistani sweatshop for an off-brand designer, in a style and cut that have not been in fashion since my father was my age. The jacket was always ill-fitting, foreshortening my arms and widening my chest and shoulders all out of proportion. On top of that, it travelled poorly. The shirt and trousers wrinkled in my luggage and one of the jacket's side vents is visibly creased. Worst of all, it isn't black.

Not a very fitting tribute to Zach, who was always so smartly turned out. His clothes always fit him perfectly. There were, I remember, several suits, including a dinner jacket, a grey flannel three-piece, and even a tweed blazer with brown elbow patches. An equal diversity of flamboyantly patterned French-cuffed shirts occupied his wardrobe, when he bothered to hang them up, that is. The dinner jacket he wore quite frequently too, even when the occasion called for less formal attire — yet another of his eccentricities. I wonder if he'd always preferred to err on the side of the overdressed, or if this was only an affectation he'd developed since his arrival in England. One often got the sense that he regarded his days at Oxford as a long series of costume parties, where he was not so much studying as playing the part of an Oxford student.

Nothing to be done about it, though. The only other suit I own is now hanging somewhere in the back room of the dry cleaner's not far from Claire and Tori's flat. I took it there in a state of panic to have the mud washed off it. The bloodstained wingtip and white bowtie I wrapped in a plastic bag, which I stuffed into one of the black-and-gold bins on Cornmarket. Then, overwhelmed by nausea, I veered into The Cellar to vomit. The suit has probably been cleaned by now, but I doubt I'll ever go back to collect it. I never want to see it again.

I slip my passport into the breast pocket only to be reminded that something is already there. The envelope with Zach's name on it. Had I really brought it with me? I've not looked at it since I recovered it from his pidge as soon as I stepped foot in college and brought the other envelope, the one with my name on it, to the attention of the Head Porter, who in turn gave it to the police. Here, in my hands, the last evidence of my participation in our pact. I bring it to the rubbish bin, ready to begin tearing. Any rational person with the most minimal instinct for self-preservation would have destroyed it ten times over by now. Yet I can't bring myself to do it. Save for this black pearl, his copy of *The Zero and the One*, and my memories of our time together, it's all I have left of him.

I roll the object between my thumb and forefinger. He had placed it, without telling me he was going to do so, in the envelope along with his letter to me, an envelope I was never meant to open. What in God's name were you trying to say with this, Zach?

To arrive at the cemetery, I'm to take the 2 or 3 train at Central Park North, transfer to the J at Fulton Street station, and exit at Cypress Hills station. In order not to think about what will be waiting for me there, I find myself a seat somewhere in the crowded carriage and do my best to pay attention to *The Zero and the One*. But the subject of the next aphorism Zach had annotated does little to distract me. It concerns the death of Socrates in the Phaedo, a dialogue we had studied together. Abendroth takes issue with Nietzsche's famous interpretation of the passage. According to Abendroth, Socrates did not believe that death was a cure for the disease of life, as Nietzsche says, but rather that there really is no answer to the question of whether there was life after death. Socrates' last words were not really *Crito, I owe a cock to Asclepius; will you remember to pay the debt?* but rather the active and ironic silence with which he answers Crito's final question — *The debt shall be paid; is there anything else?* Plato's narration reads, *There was no answer to this question.* Abendroth thinks both Crito's question and Plato's narration are double entendres.

I close my eyes. Once again, Zach's face, after I pulled the trigger. His eyes expanded a millimetre and began to glaze. Then they flattened into a squint. I saw his cheekbones rise, his eyebrows arch. Meaningfully it seems to me now. But what meaning? Regret? Repentance? Or even shock at my betrayal? Was he trying to recall the eloquent phrase he had prepared to deliver before his plans went awry?

He tried to tell me, I think.

I crop the image in my mind, zooming in on his mouth. Concentrating on the movement of his lips. Attempting to read on them the phrase he was trying to utter, the last words that were lost, not to an active and ironic silence, but in a gurgle of blood. His lips opened slightly, of that much I'm certain. But now I seem to remember that, just before they parted, they expanded into his cheeks, revealing a brief glimpse of red teeth. The uncompleted phrase must have begun with two syllables. A long vowel sound. Followed by a short one.

Suddenly I feel warm sunlight on my eyelids. We are above ground again, crossing into Brooklyn over one of the bridges. It's a spectacular view. Standing up, I press my

43

hands to the windows of the train doors and feel the magic for the first time, that breathless combination of awe, wonder, and sublimity people convey when they attempt to capture in words the Babelian hubris of downtown Manhattan. To my right are alpine ridges of blue glass and grey steel culminating, at the far end, in the white, quadrangular peaks of the Twin Towers. Shooting out from the side of the island are two more bridges, two arches suspended over the silver river, each lifted at two points like the hem of an evening gown whose wearer must elegantly ford a puddle. Through the shimmering warp of their steel cables, I can just make out the Statue of Liberty, no larger, from my vantage, than a chess piece presented to my eye by the palm of the harbour.

Manhattan, like Oxford: a city of dreaming spires.

The train suddenly banks around a curve, throwing me off balance. I do a ridiculous dance down the aisle until I am finally able to stabilise myself against one of the metal poles that runs from the floor to the ceiling of the carriage. Several faces turn contemptuously in my direction, their wordless scowls telling me I don't belong, that here I am out of place.

It's not long, however, before they resume their indifferent expressions. Now that no one is looking at me, I search for a new seat. There is one at the end of the carriage, but I discover, as soon as I approach, that it is being occupied by a polystyrene box, opened at the hinge to reveal a pile of small white and grey bones.

**SYMPTOMS OF THE DISEASE PHILOSOPHY.—
Philosophy does not begin in wonder. It begins in
anxiety, with the disquieting suspicion that things are
not how they should be and are not what they seem.**

My tutor for the Plato paper was Dr. Marcus Inwit, fellow
of Magdalen College. When I returned from holiday, I did
some research, and learnt that his interpretation of ancient
philosophy, as a guide to the art of living rooted in the
cultural and political institutions of fifth-century Athens, had
revolutionised the field, no small feat for a discipline that was
more than two thousand years old. His argument that ancient
philosophy was a series of what he termed, after Ignatius of
Loyola, *spiritual exercises*, had had a decisive influence on
Michel Foucault's "Greek Turn" in the three volumes of his
History of Sexuality. Like most English academics, Dr. Inwit
was positively indifferent to continental philosophy, but it
was undoubtedly because of Foucault that his tutorial was in
such high demand. To have been randomly assigned to it as a
first year was an incredible stroke of good luck, sure to excite
awe and envy from the many DPhil candidates who packed
out his lectures and clamoured for his attention during the
long Q and As that followed.

Having taken extra care to finish my first paper early, I
spent the last Sunday before the first week of Hilary Term
reading his monograph on Heraclitus' aphorism *Nature loves
to hide*, only to oversleep my alarm. I might have bicycled to
make up the time, but in the morning it was pouring icy rain. I

45

found myself at the Porter's Lodge completely drenched and with only a few minutes to spare, which time I then wasted trying to find Dr. Inwit's rooms in that large, labyrinthine, unfamiliar college. It wasn't clear which of the lawns was the Deer Park I had been instructed to keep to my left, and, starting to panic, I looked round to find someone I could ask for help. At that moment, there was only one other person in the quad, a student in a superbly cut black suit, a coffee-brown leather satchel hanging from his shoulder. He was waiting at the entrance to one of the staircases, standing beneath a wood-handled brolly, exhaling smoke, a dark purple crescent beneath his eye.

He recognised me before I recognised him.

"I'm glad it's you," Zach said, holding out the umbrella to me, which I accepted, and a cigarette, which I declined. "Last term I had one of these double tutorials with a kid named Christopher Pomeroy. Know him? Why would you? A second year. Dumb as a brick. I even tried to get a one on one with Dr. Inwit, but the Dean of Visiting Students said it was impossible. That's what he said: *impossible*. But now that I see it's you, it's a different story entirely."

I didn't respond to his observation about the intelligence of his former tutorial partner, whom I knew only by reputation, as a member of Pembroke's vaunted boat club. Nor did I enquire how he had formed his judgement of mine. Presumably it was from the book he'd seen me reading that night at Formal Hall. Instead, after a long pause, I asked him how he'd got that shiner.

"I insulted the sister of one of the drunker patrons of The Cowley Arms."

"What on earth for?" I cried, a question that could equally have been asked of his presence in that pub. It was unheard of that a posh Yank like Zach should have wandered so far east of the city centre.

"To tell you the truth, I don't remember. She may have cut in front of me in line. Or I may have remarked on something stupid she said, or maybe she remarked on something stupid I said, and it escalated from there. It's all a blur. I guess two nights ago I was also one of the drunker patrons of The Cowley Arms."

Zach dropped his cigarette into one of the urn-shaped planters that flanked the entrance to the staircase. The cigarette extinguished with a hiss as it pierced the pea-green skin that had formed on the layer of brown water. We watched it float there for a moment, in silence. "Well, it's time," he said finally. "Let's go up."

From the thick frames of his spectacles to the brown patches on the elbows of his blazer, Dr. Inwit looked every bit the Oxford don. He had a full head of silver hair and mangled, tobacco-stained teeth. For all that, he was also a tall, robust-looking man, who was said to have been an excellent batsman in his day. He greeted us warmly and asked us how we took our tea.

Inwit's rooms smelled of pipe smoke and dust. Books were scattered everywhere, according to an organisational principle no doubt apparent only to the eye of their owner. On the door hung a framed poster from a 1989 conference on the Pre-Socratics at Freie Universit.t in Berlin, and on the walls were reproductions of various famous paintings, mostly Old Masters, including *Aristotle Contemplating a Bust of Homer* by Rembrandt, *Bacchus and Ariadne* by Titian, and Holbein's *Ambassadors*. There were two large windows above the lumpy sofa on which we'd taken our seats, but on a day like this, when sunlight was scarce, his two green desk lamps did little to enliven the rather gloomy atmosphere.

We stretched out our hands to receive the plain white cups of tea, each balanced precariously on a saucer. Dr. Inwit sat in his wing-backed armchair and began to load his pipe.

"Now," he said, taking a puff. "I trust you've both received your reading lists and assignments from me over the holiday and have prepared a paper on the *Symposium*. Which of you fancies reading first?"

Zach and I looked at each other and with a string of overly deferential babbling invited the other to have the honour. Dr. Inwit interrupted us with bemused resignation and took a silver coin from his trousers pocket.

"This happens every term. Why I bother asking, I no longer know. A formality, I suppose. Mr. Foedern, you'll be heads." He showed us the side of the coin with the profile of the Queen. "And Mr. Whiting, tails," he said, showing us the side with the lion and the unicorn. We watched it spin through the air and fall into his broad palm. He flipped it onto the back of his hand. "Heads. That means you, Mr. Foedern."

Zach passed a copy of his paper to me and to Dr. Inwit, who waved it off, explaining that he preferred to listen. Zach notched his cigarette in the ashtray, took a sip from his tea, and began to explain the troubling implications of Alcibiades' description of Socrates as *atopos* in the prelude to his speech in the *Symposium* for Plato's characterisation of the philosopher and his conception of justice in the *Republic*.

"Often translated as *bizarre* or *strange*," he read, "the word literally means *without place* or *out of place*. When Paul and the Evangelists use the term centuries later, people or actions that are described as *atopos* are considered not fitting, wicked, and even harmful. All of which would perfectly describe Alcibiades himself, Socrates' most famous pupil — after Plato, of course — one of the youths whom the philosopher could be accused of corrupting. Especially," he added parenthetically, "when we compare Alcibiades' description of their relationship with the sexual mores of the time." With the help of a concordance, Zach had tracked down the appearance of the term in the other dialogues and found that in the *Republic*, the word was used to describe the sophists, whom Socrates considered out of place as educators. "If Plato's definition of social justice — doing one's job and not meddling in anyone else's — can be construed as everyone occupying his rightful place in the *polis*," he continued, "then,

I will argue, it is precisely Socrates — philosopher and sophist, gadfly and busybody — who is *out of place* in the ideal city he himself constructs."

At this point, I too stopped following along on the copy he'd printed out for me. I could feel my eyes slowly and involuntarily expanding with an amazement that quickly modulated into competitiveness and an admiration that quickly became nervousness. My cheeks, I'm sure, were bright red. The argument I had made in my own paper, about the concept of identity presented in the myth Aristophanes tells about the origins of love, which I had spent the whole week perfecting, and of which I was, until that moment, quite proud, sounded mundane and amateur by comparison.

When Zach finished reading, Dr. Inwit yielded his paper a moment of respectful silence — at least that's how I interpreted it — before going on to question him thoroughly about his thesis. Then it was my turn to read. Next week, I thought, as I handed Zach a copy of my paper, I would make sure to read first. There was no way, I vowed, I'd ever let this bloody bastard get the better of me again.

WE DO NOT EXPERIENCE OUR OWN DEATH.—
This is well known, well remarked upon. We only
experience the Other's death; from this we infer
that our death will only be experienced by the Other.
Death is not so much a fact as it is a recognitive
status. Immortality requires the aspirant to convince
the Other that, *all appearances to the contrary*, he
is not really dead. Immortality is thus an audacious
conjurer's trick performed in plain view of the
Other which annihilates this very inference through
dramatic projects of total misrecognition, the most
obvious of which is Death itself.

From the clover-shaped gate on Jamaica Avenue, a road lined
with cypresses leads deep into the cemetery grounds, where
it intersects a motorway, then narrows into a footpath and
snakes up a hill. Manhattan is still visible in the distance, but
by a trick of perspective the skyscrapers seem to have been
truncated and foreshortened; their crowns appear to be resting
on the peak of the hill, interspersed with the headstones
and mausoleums. Before long I arrive at the address of the
squat building Zach's father, Bernard, had given me when
he requested my presence at the funeral. With its square,
crenellated tower and its thin window slits, it looks more like
a crusader's fortress than a mortuary chapel.

I first met Bernard during our stay in Berlin. He was there
on business, attempting to scare up some financing for the film
he was co producing. It was not going well. The details of the

production were being kept under lock and key by the director, who was demanding total control over script, cast, crew, and location. With so little information to go on — all Bernard was allowed to say was that the film was an adaptation of a beloved Russian novel — it was difficult to persuade potential investors to part with their Deutschmarks. He was there for a week or so, working from dawn 'til dusk from his suite at the Adlon, on Pariser Platz, the finest hotel in the city. Though he paid for both of our flights and for our accommodation, he had little more than a few hours to give to his son and his son's new friend. We spent them at a restaurant with a view of the two churches on Gendarmenmarkt, listening to his frustrations with the investors, who were in his estimation risk-averse, overly rule-abiding, and lacking in vision. German, in a word. All too German.

A compact, well-built man, Bernard was bald, with a salted moustache and lines that had been permanently chiseled into his forehead by a lifetime of impatience. He spoke rapidly with the traces of a New York accent. To my eyes, he had the look of someone whose childhood had been a string of petty thefts and back-alley brawls; the sort of man whose every step up the ladder of financial success had come at the expense of someone softer, more principled, advantaged from birth; the sort of man who might play at refinement when he visited his old neighbourhood and a working-class tough at board meetings or on conference calls. Though this might have alienated me from the somewhat aristocratic affectations of his son, it only endeared the two of them to me more. To me, they represented the possibility of generational progress. My child, I remember thinking wishfully, as Bernard handed his credit card to the waiter without looking at the bill, would grow up with all the advantages Bernard had provided for his.

Are you here for the Foedern interment? a woman asks as I walk through the doors into the foyer of the building. The name badge pinned to her white blouse identifies her as

51

Darlene Jackson, Assistant Funeral Director. When I nod, she solemnly collects a wicker basket that had been lying on a sideboard between stacks of colourful brochures with advice on how to cope with loss and grief and a large arrangement of flowers. Please take one, she says. Inside the basket is a pile of semicircles made of black suede. I must have looked rather puzzled, because she immediately recited, They're kippahs, also known as yarmulkes, a skullcap or head covering worn by Jewish males during prayer services.

Jewish. It had never occurred to me that Zach might be a Jew. I'd heard Zach refer to himself as a devout atheist and a secular freethinker, but never as a Jew. These things aren't incompatible, I suppose. Look at Marx and Freud. Maybe he hadn't considered himself a Jew and that's why he never mentioned it. Still, he never mentioned it. Wasn't there something in that? Though he frequently presented himself as a proponent of radical openness and total honesty, as a person willing to discuss any subject, no matter how sensitive or taboo, he could also be closed off about things like that. About family things. Childhood things. Things that touched, as they say, too close to home.

I place the skullcap back into the basket. Had it been anyone else's funeral, I might have worn it, out of the same respect for a foreign culture that obliges a person, say, to take off his shoes when entering a Japanese home. But my uncovered head would be a tribute to the memory of Zachary Foedern, who refused to stand for Latin Grace.

The small chapel is only half full. On either side of the carpeted aisle are rows and rows of empty pews. I would have expected a much larger gathering, a room crowded to capacity with people who had come to pay their respects to a person whose life had touched theirs as deeply as it had touched mine. The mourners are all dressed in black, but somehow they give the impression that this was what they usually wore, that the clothes they put on today would be taken out of the wardrobe again the next time they had to attend an opening at an art gallery or spend a night at the opera. Almost no one here is under thirty. Where were all of Zach's friends from Gansevoort and Columbia? What Gregory Glass had told me — could it really have been true?

In the front row, Bernard sits silently, rigidly, paralysed by grief and by the sense, which I was coming to share with him, that what we were witnessing was completely unreal. His right arm is wrapped tightly around his wife, who has buried her face in his chest, no longer able to watch.

Leaning on his left shoulder, then, must be Zach's sister, Vera. Of Vera all I can see is the back of her neck, framed between a ragged line of black hair and a black necklace, her quaking shoulders, encased in black cotton, and the fistful of tissues she presses to her nose and mouth. The openness with which she expresses her sorrow is in pointed contrast not only to the anodyne eulogy being delivered uncomfortably over her sobs, but also to the stoicism I am desperately attempting to perform in the back pew. My fingernails are dug into my palms, my teeth are clenched, and every cell in my body is conspiring to forbid my eyes a single tear for fear of what else I might let out if I allowed myself to cry.

For there, in front of the family, is the coffin. A simple, closed pinewood box, flanked on either side by flowers. Far too small and fragile a thing to contain a personality as outsized as Zach's. Suddenly, an idea takes hold of me. An insane, ludicrous conviction is drawn like a satellite into the orbit of my brain. *Zach's not in that bloody box*, I think. *No one is! He's faked it! Faked his own death!* It'd be just like him, after all. The sort of grotesque prank he'd be likely to pull. Wildly, I look around the chapel to see where he's hidden himself, from what perch he's been listening to the eulogies, with what impish grin he's been taking in the proceedings. I want to dash down the aisle, rip the lid off the coffin, topple the empty box from its dais, and shout at the stunned mourners, *See! He's not really dead!*

But then, who knew better than I did how dead Zach really was? None of the eulogists is going to allude to the circumstances of his death, of course, whether out of ignorance or out of politeness. The present speaker, a woman with a long braid of yellow hair running the length of her back, whom the rabbi introduces as Hilde Gwynn, Zach's English teacher at Gansevoort, lists his academic accomplishments and speculates about who he might have become had he lived. (She does not say: *Had he chosen to live*.) Remembering his frequent contributions to classroom discussions and the lively cast of mind that revealed itself in his papers, she said he would have made a fine lawyer or a brilliant professor. Indeed, I thought, whilst she spoke, offended by the rather conventional life she had imagined for him, so different to the one I would have wished for, he might have had a wife and family, served his country, been a leader in his community. All outcomes as likely as not, if things were otherwise than they are. Which they never will be.

I wonder what would happen if I were to take my turn behind the podium and read his note — *our* note. Somehow I doubt anyone here would understand it. The way Zach died will always be unfathomable to these people, impossible to tally with the person they thought they knew. A person who had so much talent, so much promise, who'd been given every advantage, and had willingly thrown it all away. The simple fact of his death refuted all their hopes for his future. It showed that he had considered their reasons for living and found them wanting. This was the very thought that had to be passed over in silence, if only to put to rest the worry that they were mourning a perfect stranger. Or worse, that he may have been right.

The rabbi invites Zach's uncle to the podium to deliver the next eulogy. In the story the uncle tells, by contrast, I do recognise the friend I knew. Ten or eleven years previously, Vera and Zach spent the summer at the cabin in New Hampshire he and his wife owned. Zach would go roaming through the woods in the company of the family's two dogs until night fell. But when it was time for supper, he never remembered to leave his muddy shoes outside. His room was always a shambles and his bed never once was made.

That's pretty typical for a ten-year-old, the uncle admits. But the funniest thing was that he had an argument for it. When his aunt attempted to get him to clean up after himself Zach said, *What's the point? It's just going to get dirty again.*

Here, finally, was the child the father of the man. Zach's slovenliness did not go unjustified without reference to some higher principle. When he told me his reasons for dismissing his scout, something unprecedented in the history of Oxford, one would have thought he was discussing the futile labours of Sisyphus rather than the simple, quotidian tasks of hoovering the carpet, tidying the bed, emptying the bin, and scrubbing the sink. Unlike the rest of us, he spent the year in filthy rooms. But for him, this was nothing so much as a tacit acknowledgment of inescapable mortality.

The mourners march slowly behind the coffin, following it up to the gravesite at the top of the hill. It is almost noon and nearly all of them are wearing sunglasses. At the gravesite, Bernard pulls a rock from his trousers pocket and places it on a headstone. Mrs Foedern takes a few flowers from the bouquet she is holding and hands them to Vera, who leaves them at the base. They observe a moment of silence before walking slowly, arm in arm, to the edge of the gaping hole less than a metre away. The names carved into the stone are Meyer and Rita Foedern.

As the coffin is lowered, a Hebrew prayer is said. A spade is passed from hand to hand. The community will bury its dead. When the spade is handed to me I want to protest: I won't throw dirt on my friend! But hadn't I already? Hadn't I pressed his body into the muddy bank of the river? Unlike those present, I shall not only suffer his loss, but also the image of his death. An image I'll never see the end of. An image I'll never be able to unsee. An image I'll always carry with me, his life forever imprinted on my own, his death also mine in some way. To stand here at his gravesite, shovelling dirt on his grave: Doesn't that make me a murderer somehow? Yes, a murderer. For not stopping him. For going along with his plans. Rather than saying, when he first told me of them, *That's the daftest thing I've ever heard*. For lacking the courage to tell him no. Until it was too late. People are responsible not only for what they do, but what they fail to prevent. I hadn't felt the shot, but I felt the report. I feel it still.

For dust thou art, I hear the rabbi say, and to dust ye shall return.

Death and Birth, Nothingness and Being, the Zero and the One. The same things, as the title of our poem had it, only different.

ON THE MEETING OF TWO MONADS.— The biographical explanation for so absurd an idea as pre-established harmony should be sought in Leibniz's particular susceptibility to the vice of friendship.

On Saturday of third week, Hilary Term, I awoke to the sound of the frenetic peppering of knuckles on my door. It was only half nine, but already I'd fallen asleep in my chair, a novel upside down on my chest. I stretched and yawned, but made no attempt to answer the door. It was not that I thought I'd only dreamt the sound; it was that I was certain the knocking wasn't intended for me. Barring my scout, who always gave a single, polite warning rap before she entered my rooms every morning, no one had intentionally knocked on my door in months.

Probably it was Martin Montcrift, the boyfriend or lover or whatever of Susanne Knottsby, whose rooms were next to mine. Martin had already bothered me twice that term, pissed crosseyed, confusing my door for hers. The knocking grew louder, more urgent. Finally, I lay the book face down on my bedside table and lifted myself from my chair to once again direct Martin to the proper door. On behalf of my ability to fall back asleep I gave an audible sigh. The walls in my staircase were very old. And very thin.

Instead it was Zach. He flew across the threshold without waiting to be invited in, as if he had been expecting me to be expecting him. All I saw was the flash of a figure in a camel overcoat and a red scarf passing into the room. I didn't realise it was him until he was already sitting in my chair, legs crossed, excitedly twitching his foot, touching his fingers together, talking away:

"So this is what the rooms in the Old Quad look like. Much nicer than the ones in Staircase XVI, which, I assure you, are positively institutional, what with the neon light and the carpet from the 60s and the sink and those goddamned metal shelves sticking out of the wall. I bang my head on them every time I try to brush my teeth. And you can't even open the window without letting in a whole Luftwaffe of flying insects—"

"I was just going to put on the kettle," I said calmly, hoping to bring Zach to whatever point he had come to make. As this was the first time he'd visited my rooms or shown any interest in me outside of our tutorial, I was suspicious of his motives for being here. I suppressed another yawn. "Fancy a cup of tea?"

"Tea? No, we don't have time for tea."

"We?"

"Nope. No time. You see, I've dropped by to ask you a favor. Which is not to say this isn't a social call. But it's also something of an emergency. For a place as small as Pembroke, you're a hard man to find. Richard wouldn't tell me where you lived — out of spite, of course. So I had to go rushing around trying to find someone who knew you. Finally, I managed to track down what's his-name, you know you know, the president of the JCR —"

"Martin Mont —"

"Yes, him. Martin Montcrift. He told me where you lived. Said he only knew because it's next door to the girl he's been, how would you say it, shagging."

"Listen, Zach. This wouldn't have anything to do with the paper that's due Monday for Dr. Inwit?"

"Paper? What? I finished my paper *hours* ago. This is what I'm trying to tell you. Hear me out for a second, alright?"

Earlier in the day, he had been putting the conclusion on his paper for Dr. Inwit in the Lower Reading Room of the

Radcliffe Camera, when he'd locked eyes, not just once, but *three times*, with the student sitting opposite him. "A girl," he said, blatantly relishing each feature as he recalled it, "with long waves of blonde hair, limpid blue eyes, bow-shaped lips and..." Here he placed a hand on his chest and allowed his rather purple description to fade away into an ellipsis. Distracted from study, he ripped a page from his book, wrote her a note, folded it in two, and slid it across the table. He produced the paper from the pocket of his overcoat and handed it to me. I opened the fold and saw

PERENNIAL CLASSICS
PLATO
PHAEDO

Translated by
BENJAMIN JOWETT

With an Introduction and Notes by
DR. MARCUS INWIT

MAGDALEN COLLEGE, UNIVERSITY OF OXFORD

I saw this done in a movie once. When are you free? I'd like to take you out for a drink.

Funny you should ask. I'm free tonight, as it so happens. Do you know Freud?

The psychoanalyst? Or the bar in Jericho?

Is that an attempt at wit?

Of course, the bar in Jericho. 10 o'clock?

10 it is. But be warned. I'm bringing a friend in case you're not as charming in person as you are on paper.

Fair enough. I will also bring a friend, so yours isn't bored when I find myself lost in conversation with you. Tell me what you'll be wearing so I'll be able to recognize you in a crowded bar.

If you can't recognise me by the eyes you've been staring into for the past half hour, you don't deserve to find me in a crowded bar.

THE PLEROMA PRESS
London— New York— Sydney

And that's where I come in," I said flatly, when I finished reading. I pictured the scene to myself: Zach flirting well into the morning with his blonde-haired, blue-eyed Venus, whilst I struggled to exchange more than a sentence or two with her homely friend, counting the minutes until I could get back to exactly where I was.

"That's where you come in."

"Well, Simmias," I said, quoting the text whose title page he'd appropriated for his flirtation. "Do you think it befits a philosophical man to be keen on the so called pleasures of, for example, food and drink... and sex... and the other services to the body? Do you think he values them highly, or does he disdain them, except in so far as he's absolutely compelled to share in them?"

"That depends, my dear Socrates, on whether it is possible to release the soul from its connection with the body, which is in turn contingent on whether the soul is immortal, the four proofs you offer in favor of which are all thoroughly risible. Now," he said, standing up. "Let me help you into your overcoat and your smart shoes and all of your other bodily adornments —"

"What about Gregory Glass? You lot are mates, right? Why not ask him?"

Zach looked disgusted. "Greg? *Please*. I can't spend the evening getting into infantile debates about trivial matters of American politics. It will put our dates to sleep and me on edge. I've come to you because you're the right man for the mission."

"I'm sorry to disappoint you, Zach. It's just that I have so much work to do."

"Bullshit."

He didn't try the usual mode of persuasion, the one that had been tried on me before, the one that was most likely to make me dig in my heels. He didn't tell me that he had just as much work if not more than I had and he was going out anyway, a rhetorical strategy I have always regarded as an attempt to make someone feel guilty based on a false equivalence between the work habits of two different people.

Instead, he picked up the book I had been reading and said, "I see you're in the middle of *Against Nature*, which, unless you've been lying to me, isn't on the list for any of the papers you're reading this term. From this, one can infer that you've already finished your assignments. I happen to know that you never go out, unless it's to the library. Martin whatever-his-name-was said as much. Now, I know you're not straightedge or a recovering alcoholic, because I've seen you at The Bear. I've watched you. You get a table by yourself, drink two pints of Guinness, and go back to college, where there's nothing to do but schoolwork and reading. All of this I suppose is commendable compared to the other students here, whose only reading this term has been of the labels on the taps at the pub. But think of it, Owen. At some point in the near future you're going to look up from your reading and realize that your only experience of life is made out of paper. Now, you're smart, you know this how? Because you're reading a book about a man who shuts himself in and reads books. But the difference between you and Des Esseintes is that he's an old man remembering a life he's wasted, whereas you're a young man wasting his life in such a way that when you're old you'll have nothing to remember. I can only assume that the reason you don't go out is because you can't afford to. Well, not to worry. Since you're doing me a favor, it's only fair that drinks should be on me."

As I sat in stunned silence at this astonishing bit of presumption, the sound of caterwauling breached the walls. This time, Martin — or someone else quite possibly — had found his way through Susanne's door without any help from me.

"C'mon," he said. Mission Accomplished was written all over his face. "Just imagine how little *work* you're going to get done if this ridiculous opera continues all night."

Once I had accepted that the evening had placed itself out of my control, that what happened would happen, and that I should just sit back and watch it happen, I was swept up in Zach's expansive mood. On the way to Freud's, he walked quickly, with purpose, slicing through the oncoming crowds without breaking stride, firing observations at me at the same volume and speed regardless of whether I was by his side or if I had fallen a few steps behind because, unlike him, I'd politely allowed someone to pass. Neither the stride nor the speech was impatient, exactly. He didn't move or speak with the look of someone who was late for an engagement, although, as it turns out, he was. It was clear that this was his normal pace, which I now understand is the speed anyone must keep to escape trampling when walking in New York.

From the first three weeks of our tute, from the papers I had heard him read, it was evident that Zach was clever. But it was heartening to discover that, at least as far as our tastes were concerned, we had a great deal in common. Of course, as I would soon learn, we didn't come down on the same side of all the controversies, but we agreed which controversies were the important ones. This left us enough common ground for friendly argument and perpetual conversation. Taste is often dismissed as a superficial foundation for a friendship, fitting only for the young. That two people enjoy similar things, the argument goes, is not a reliable indicator of a fundamental compatibility of disposition. To me, though, our shared interests implied shared experiences and shared opinions about the value of those experiences. Such commonality was not impossible, but it seemed exceedingly rare, all the more so considering he and I had been born thousands of kilometres away from each other, in different countries, in unalike cities, to different families. I had long imagined such friendships existed (hadn't I read about them?), but until that night the person for one of my own had eluded me.

The particular subject of our conversation that night was, I'll never forget, Walt Whitman. Zach didn't like him, he told me, as we made a left onto Little Clarendon Street, a quaint line of boutiques and restaurants between St. Giles' and Walton Street, illuminated at night by strings of Chinese lanterns. This puzzled me. All Americans, I thought, liked Walt Whitman. That's why I had mentioned him in the first place. The freedom that pulsated through his ecstatic exclamations, the chaotic diversity of the worlds he catalogued with them, the potential for unlimited self-invention that echoed in his every barbaric yawlp represented to me what was so attractive about Zach's native land, where no one had the misfortune of being saddled at birth, as we were in England, with a thousand-year accretion of what was considered good and proper. As I came to know him better, these were the very qualities Zach seemed to exemplify in his own words and actions. They were precisely what I liked about him. Zach, however, found Whitman's earnestness particularly grating. "Only Russians have earned the right to use that many exclamation marks," he remarked pithily. Which American poets did he prefer, then? "Ezra Pound and T. S. Eliot," he told me, much to my surprise. Those two were as un American as you could possibly be, elitist and pessimistic and inaccessible. Both had turned their backs on their country, the one to embrace Italian fascism, the other to become a classicist, a royalist, and an Anglo-Catholic. Still, I couldn't begrudge him his choices. *The Waste Land* and *The Pisan Cantos* were both books that had places of honour on my shelves.

With its Ionic portico and columns, supporting an un-adorned pediment made of Cotswold stone, the Freud caf. could have been a Roman temple. The entrance of the door was painted light blue, above which the name of the bar had been painted in gold, substituting the Latin *V* for the English *U*. Really, it was a deconsecrated church. Besides the name, this is what Zach said he liked about it. As his argument to Gregory at Formal Hall had made clear, he didn't quite care when the last priest would be hung in the entrails of the last boss, but he longed for the day when every church would be converted into a bar, or at least a cinema. Houses of dissolution and spectacle, in his view, were the only suitable futures for the former offices of illusion.

When we arrived, the two girls were waiting for us at a circular table at the end of the room, near what had once been the apse, but was now being used as a stage. A jazz quartet had just finished its set and was in the process of packing up its instruments, whilst the next act, a DJ, was setting up his turntable and records. I was half expecting them not to be there. Despite the note Zach had showed me, his story was indeed too much like a scene from a film to be believed. It may well have been an elaborate pretext for something else, though what exactly I couldn't say.

My excitement had dampened as I followed him through the door to the bar and watched him scan the room on his tiptoes. It was restored again when he said "Aha!" and walked in the direction of their table, with the confidence of a man who knows that provoking doubt in his audience is necessary for his conjuring tricks to be taken for genuine magic.

"But you're American!" Victoria exclaimed when he introduced himself. His hyperbole aside, she looked more or less as Zach described her. Her friend, Claire, was also a pleasant surprise. She had dark eyes and a wide, welcoming smile that was enhanced rather than impaired by the fumble of teeth it disclosed. She wore her auburn hair in a bob and her long, oval-shaped face possessed the sort of feminine beauty usually found in young boys. So Zach had gone for a stroll in Bodley's garden and picked himself a pair of English roses.

"Please don't hold it against me," he replied. "I assure you it wasn't my fault. As compensation, I've brought along

Owen Whiting, an honest-to-God Englishman, who will be my translator for the evening."

They declared themselves charmed to meet us and mock-imperiously sent us to the bar with their drink orders so they could, in Victoria's words, whisper their first impressions to each other.

At the bar, waiting for service, we did the same. He tapped a cigarette out of a blue pack and offered me one, only to finally remember, after several such offers, that I didn't smoke.

"No, I'll take one," I said. I desperately needed something to do with my hands. He lit it for me and I puffed without inhaling, so as not to cough in front of him, letting the smoke rest for a moment against the back of my teeth before dozing it from my mouth with the blade of my tongue.

"Well?"

"Not bad, Zach. I was worried that my, uh, date was going to be a bit of, well, a bit of a minger."

"Me too!" he said, with a laugh. He put a hand on my shoulder and smiled affectionately. "I'm very glad you decided to — Ah yes, barkeep. We'll have two Stolichnaya and tonics, each with a twist, and one Plymouth martini, dirty, dry, and stirred." He turned back to me. "What are you having?"

"Double whisky, please. On the rocks."

"What *brand* of whiskey? It's important to specify, otherwise they'll just give you the well. Jameson's? Are you sure? And a double Jameson's on the rocks, please."

The toast, proposed by Victoria, was to chance meetings and new friendships. It was to be the first of many that evening. At some point each of us took a turn to raise a glass and praise something of equal abstraction and ideality. The precise subjects of these subsequent toasts, however, have been forever lost to my memory thanks to the drinks that accompanied them.

We learnt that Claire and Victoria were in their second year at St. Anne's College. Claire was reading English and

French and Victoria was a PPEist like Zach and me. They met during Fresher's Week the year before, on the dance floor of Filth, when a timely intervention from Claire had saved Victoria from the unwanted attentions of a townie. The two had been friends ever since. They now shared rooms in one of St. Anne's brick flats on the Bevington Road, a few minutes away from the bar.

I expected Zach to dominate the conversation. As I'd seen at hall or in our tutorials or earlier in my rooms, he was certainly capable of it. He could easily unleash an avalanche of words, spoken at a volume and a speed with which it was difficult to compete. But that night, he merely directed it, preserving the flow of conversation with a series of well-placed questions and observations, calculated to allow each of us to humbly display our best features and place us at an ease that would enable us to share confidences normally reserved for friendships of much longer standing. Once or twice, after making some particularly witty remark, he'd immediately turn the conversation over to me, giving the two girls the impression that we knew each other better than we in fact did. The impression, in turn, rubbed off on me.

When, for example, Claire told us she was taking the paper in Nineteenth-Century French Literature, he said, "God, earlier tonight I had the hardest time convincing Owen to come out. He was just *too* absorbed in this book he was reading. What was the name of it?" he asked me, though he knew very well what it was called.

"*Against Nature. À Rebours*," I answered, irritated at first by this conversational gambit. But Claire, on cue, exclaimed, "I love Huysmans! Have you read *Là-Bas*?"

And so the conversation split in two again, just as he'd intended. Claire and I discussed decadents and symbolists at a perpetually rising pitch of enthusiasm, whilst Zach whispered to Victoria about things I suddenly found myself too engrossed by Claire to eavesdrop on. Every so often, when our eyes met for long enough to make the subtext of our words apparent to us both, I'd look over at Zach and Victoria, ostensibly to check in on them, only to discover that they were talking with hushed animation, their faces only a few inches apart.

Only once, sometime between the third and fourth round of drinks, did he usurp the conversation. The DJ had put on a record he liked. When he heard the opening notes of the song, he straightened visibly.

"Oh! I'm terribly sorry," he said. "But whenever I hear this song I *have* to dance."

The song was a pop number from the last decade, the sort of song I assumed he would have considered as naff as I did. But Claire and Victoria shot up to join the others who were beginning to congregate in front of the DJ booth. I hesitated, making a gesture to Zach to indicate that I would just stay and watch.

"Owen!" He was practically tugging at my sleeve. "It will be fun! Don't you trust me yet?"

"It's just... I look ridiculous when I dance."

"Of course you do! Every white man looks ridiculous when he dances."

"What's the trick then?"

"The trick?" He laughed. "The trick is *not to mind* that you look ridiculous. Not to give a fuck. To dance for yourself and not for other people."

"But I've not got any rhythm."

He grabbed me by the shoulders. "It's the music that has the rhythm. You just have to have the music, okay? And that's easy. Having rhythm isn't physical, it's psychological," he said, impatiently prodding his temple with his index finger. "You have to submit to it. Allow yourself to be *possessed* by it. Once you do that, you'll realize you're having too good a time to care about how you look. C'mon c'mon, they're already playing the first chorus!"

It was as he said. He flailed and gyrated like a complete fool and no one seemed to mind. He displaced the energy around him so that, by the time the second chorus was played, some of his motions were being adopted by me and then by the others on the dance floor. Lesson learnt: you can get away with anything, no matter how daft, if you can do it without flinching.

We stayed on the dance floor for one song, then another, and then another, until our sweat-darkened fringe stuck to our foreheads and our breathing grew heavy, pausing in the transitions between the songs to take quick, regenerating sips from our glasses. At first there were four of us dancing around each other, twisting and spinning at a distance. But as the music continued, Victoria permitted Zach and Claire permitted me to put a hand on her waist, and then to dance closer, thigh to thigh, tessellating until we were two.

For the first time since coming to Oxford, I had a good time on a Saturday night. A minor achievement, it's true, but before it happened it seemed like an impossible hurdle, a hurdle so tall that it discouraged all jumping. We stayed at Freud's until the lights came on at half one, then we slipped into the damp, cool February morning. We walked down the centre of the empty streets, laughing and smoking and talking loudly, until we reached the door of their flat on the Bevington Road.

Victoria was quite drunk but she said she was not yet ready to finish having such a lovely time. Zach hesitated at first in front of the open door, as though he was about to politely excuse himself and return to college alone. With one foot already on the staircase, I looked back at him in panic. Surely this was what the whole night had been leading up to, after all. Surely *this* was why he'd convinced me to leave my rooms. He couldn't have brought me this far only to leave me now. "Be a dear and close the door behind you, Zach!" Victoria called from the top of the stairs. He looked up at the voice, then down at his shoes for a moment, before finally relenting. He patted me reassuringly on the back and together we charged up to the top of the staircase, where the girls were waiting for us. We stayed for another drink and didn't leave until late the next afternoon, he without his red scarf and I without my virginity.

THIRTY PIECES OF SILVER. — Any doctrine that posits the hatred of physical life will be incapable of dealing rationally with the problem of suicide. Socrates' argument in the *Phaedo*, that suicide is a form of vandalism against the gift of the gods, is hardly satisfying. Why should a pious man be grateful for his corporeality, when this is precisely what *separates him from the gods in the first place?* Christianity's problem is particularly acute. After all, if the Nazarene is the Son of God, with prophetic powers, the Christian object of worship is nothing other than — a suicide. (And here he resembles no one so much as Judas Iscariot, his *double* and *accomplice*.)

After the service the rabbi directs the mourners to the family home to begin sitting *shiva*. The rabbi is a young man, clean-shaven, with slightly reddish hair. He wears a pair of wire-rimmed spectacles, which gives him the look of a precocious scholar. As the mourning party begins to disperse, I approach to ask him what the word means. He is standing near the grave, speaking with a slightly hunched man with a long grey beard and a stern expression on his face.

What you are saying is true, I overhear the rabbi say. But remember King Saul on Mount Gilboa and the Masada martyrs. After speaking with the family, I concluded that this was a case of *Anus keSha-ul*, death under stress and compulsion, and that Zachary was entitled to forgiveness and full burial rites.

When they register my presence, they break off their conversation. The old man looks me up and down, noticing my accent when I ask my question and the absence of a skullcap on my head.

It means seven, the rabbi answers. The number of days prescribed by the Law for the mourning of a close relative. He reaches into his pocket and produces a black ribbon, which he pins to my wide lapel. This is called a *keriah*, he says. You are to rip it.

The family returns home in the black car that was waiting for them at the gates of the cemetery, whilst the others of the mourning party hail taxis on Jamaica Avenue. It seems I alone will follow on the underground. I consider asking Zach's aunt and uncle if I might share their taxi, but I can barely muster the strength to whisper, Pardon me, before he closes the yellow door behind them.

At the Hemlock Street entrance, I climb the stairs and wait for the Manhattan-bound train. From the elevated platform there is an unobstructed view of outer Brooklyn. I can see warehouses and storage spaces covered in graffiti. Chain-link fencing enclosing weedy gardens in front of squat homes from whose wooden panels the paint peels in the heat. Rows of terraced houses topped by obsolete satellite dishes that double as washing-line posts. The brick smokestacks of shuttered factories. The bell towers of immense cathedrals. Tower blocks that would not be out of place in Bedminster.

A large rat drags its slimy belly across the platform, then slips gracelessly down to the tracks to take its supper inside a discarded bag of crisps. Surviving like that, growing fat like that. With all of civilisation breathing down your back. It's no small feat. The rat scurries away as the train rattles the track and pulls into the station. How easy it would be to jump in front of it. Nothing here to stop you. No prevention barriers like the ones they were discussing installing in the tube.

The doors of the carriage slide open. I slip into an empty seat — this time I have a choice of them — and lean my temple against the cool metal pole, staring blankly ahead. An advert, framed by a light blue border. A woman's crimson-nailed thumb and finger hold a white pill. *The Choice Is Now In Your Hands*, the caption reads. Beneath it, in smaller type, the name of the company, Planned Parenthood, and addresses for its offices in each of the five boroughs.

An old black man whose long chin is dotted with tufts of white beard pauses in front of me. My peripheral vision has recorded his slow passage through the carriage, hunched over his cane, his free hand holding the brim of an upturned red cap. *Semper Fidelis* reads the inverted gold stitching on the Velcro adjustment strap, *Always Faithful*. He asks me what the matter is. I straighten up in the seat, suddenly conscious of my facial expression, which must have been a scowl, or a grimace, or some other mirror of my reflections.

Nothing. Nothing at all.

He clicks his tongue in disbelief. I seen you get on at Cypress Hills. In June in that suit? A white boy? You just come from the graveyard. Ain't no reason to deny it, brother. Balancing his cane against his hip, he pulls a packet of tissues from his pocket. Here, he says. It's for your face. I take the tissues from him and push one under my glasses, embarrassed to discover moisture there.

Cheers. His simple gift elicits the truth from me. Yes, I've just come from a funeral. My mate Zachary. Killed himself. I am suddenly overwhelmed by the urge to tell him more. To tell him my secret. Think of it as a spiritual exercise, as Dr. Inwit would say. As *parrhesia*, frankness, frankness for a change. Or as a form of self-preservation, the release of a festering tension by turning it into words and expelling it from your mouth. But it's worse than that, I continue. We had a pact, you see. A suicide pact. I raise my eyes and speak slowly to see how he reacts to what I am about to say. But I backed out at the last second.

In his expression I do not detect any disgust, or revulsion, or even judgement. Jesus wept! is his only comment. I try to return the unused tissues to him, but he insists I keep them.

You gonna be needin' those. You're in my prayers, brother. He taps his heart with the cap. Have a blessed day.

The Foederns' flat looks like a page ripped from a design magazine. Quite possibly it's been featured in a few. You enter through a private lift that opens directly onto a small receiving room, where a coat rack has been placed perpendicular to a long buffet table. Then, from the entryway, there is unbroken space to the kitchen, the dining room, and the sitting room, each of which can be partitioned by translucent honeycombed doors that slide along tracks in the floor and the ceiling. The furniture is sleek and spare. The fridge and stovetop in the kitchen would serve the needs of a small restaurant. The walls are sparsely covered with abstract paintings and the tables with small sculptures. In the sitting room, there is a wide glass coffee table, half-occupied by a stack of artist monographs, exhibition guides, and catalogues from Sotheby's and Christie's, and half-occupied by a chess-board whose pieces are all abstract shapes. At the far end, floor to ceiling windows look out onto the zigzagging fire escapes of the luxury flats over the road.

My parents' home, with its hotchpotch of furniture, its thick carpet, its decades-old couches, its collections of trinkets and family photographs, none too embarrassing to display, may be, by contrast, exceedingly common, but it does have the merit of making you feel welcome. Whereas this house is antiseptic and cold, a showroom rather than a dwelling. Beneath the renovations the Foederns have made, it's not difficult to imagine how this space would have appeared a century ago, when it would have been a factory floor, where women in high-necked dresses seated ten to a workbench would have fed strip after strip of fabric beneath the needles of their sewing machines.

Passing idly through the house, I overhear bits of conversation, chitchat mostly. Though a tad strained. A tad hushed. Given the circumstances.

...Personally? Mark Green. But whatever happens I'm glad we're finally going to see the back of Giuliani...

...went for a cool million at the auction...

...implied it wasn't an accident...

...got his kid a job as an Equity Research Analyst at Cantor Fitzgerald...

Zach's mother has retired to the master bedroom, or somewhere else out of sight. Bernard is sitting on the sofa, a woman on either side of him, each of whom is taking her turn to speak to him with concern. We briefly make eye contact and acknowledge each other with a nod, but as I approach to pass on my condolences, the two women stand and, taking him by either elbow, escort him back to the kitchen.

In the far corner of the room, Vera seems to have wept herself into what, judging from her posture, is a presentable exhaustion. Leaning against a bookshelf near the windows, she listens with half an ear to a white-haired man tell her stories about herself she would have been too young to remember. She frowns, looks aslant, and takes a sip from her cup.

...No, not the maid. The SAT tutor. The divorce is going to be *very* expensive...

...but he had everything. And so much to look forward to. I just don't understand, Joan. I don't think I'll ever understand...

...Look, when you drown your five children and claim Jesus made you do it, there's nothing to plead *but* insanity. *Non compos mentis*, as the saying goes...

...Down Under the Manhattan Bridge Overpass. Yeah, Brooklyn. No, I'm not joking. That's where the future of the market is...

Looking for somewhere to stand, where it won't be obvious that I'm the only person who knows no one here, my attention is drawn to the painting hanging over the fireplace on the wall opposite the now empty sofa. Standing before it, I adopt the pose Zach took standing before the bookshelves in the offices of *Theory*. I tilt my head up, roll my shoulders, and cross my arms behind my back, each hand resting on the wrist of the other. An awkward posture that at the same time feels quite natural: the language of the body also has its etymologies, its microhistories, its subtle genealogies.

The painting is large, almost three metres in length and two metres tall. Acrylic paint on unprimed canvas. No other frame than the wooden one on which it was stretched. The bottom of the canvas is encrusted with thick smudges of brown, green, and grey, suggesting a landscape churned by months of storm, protruding from the surface like barnacles from the hull of a ship. Above, a layer of black had been lacquered on as evenly as the rough texture of the canvas would allow. Using the nub of his brush like a pen, the painter had calligraphed wisps of cream up and down the black field. In the centre, two coagulates of black and vermillion, one horizontal and one vertical, poured straight from the paint can, mixing in places before they finally dried, emerge from the miasma. They are figurative, almost human, these two shapes. How we might appear to ourselves if all our frivolous and sentimental illusions about nature had been suddenly and violently stripped away. Next to the two figures, a sharp edge had hastily put a pair of long, diagonal slashes.

Behind my shoulder, a voice matter of factly, almost accusatorily states my name. Although I've never heard this voice before, it's immediately clear exactly to whom it belongs.

DEATH'S LOOKING GLASS.— Nothing is the silvering on the back of the glass we call Being. Without nothingness, nothing would appear to matter. Eternal life is an insult to those who live well.

I woke up naked in an empty bed with a crushing hangover. A typical late winter sky, dull and grey as an oyster shell, hung like a Rothko in the window frame. Eyes half-closed, I drew the curtains and retreated to the rippled sheets, where, for close to an hour, dehydration, nausea, and headache pitched me back and forth between waking and sleep, without allowing me to drop definitively into either. With an immense effort, I finally righted myself and groped my way round the foot of the bed in search of the clothes Claire had helped me out of only hours before.

The girls were standing near the stove. Claire had wrapped herself in a knee-length robe and Tori wore a camisole and sweatpants bearing the crest and motto of her college on the hip. They leant over their mugs, giggling about something I could not, from the ringing in my ears, quite hear. On the stove eggs and rashers were cooking. When they saw me enter, they went silent. Alarmed, I ran a hand over my face in case there was something embarrassing on it. "What?" I asked. "What is it?"

"And a good morning to you, Mr. Whiting. Claire and I were just saying. Not only do two exceptionally fit and clever women invite you up to their rooms and allow you to stay the night, but on top of that, they cook you breakfast when you wake up. You must be the luckiest lads on the planet. What have you to say for yourself?"

At that moment Zach emerged from the other bedroom, sparing me from the need to come up with a witty response. In defiance of gravity, his hair shot off his scalp in all directions, as if he had spent the evening between a pair of electrodes rather than the two halves of a pillow. He also seemed to be having a rough morning.

"For the love of God!" he bellowed. He cupped the side of his head with his hand. "A beer! A beer! Hair of the dog!" He reached his arms round Tori, kissed her like he'd been waking up next to her for years, and whispered into her ear, "Please."

"They're in the fridge," Claire said.

"Get me one as well, yeah?"

"Owen was much more gracious, I thought," Tori told her friend, who raised her eyebrows and frowned facetiously, to inform us that it remained to be seen. What I had to say for myself, finally, was that it was astonishing how Tori and Claire, who had as much to drink as Zach or I, had not only awoken before us and prepared breakfast, but were capable of banter.

Zach wasn't daunted though. He touched me familiarly on the cheek as he handed me a can of beer from the fridge. "That's because Owen has all the social graces I have come here to learn, isn't that right, dear?" He sat down at the place Tori was setting for him and took a bite of toast. He chewed, slowly at first, his brow furrowed. He examined the surface of the bread with disbelief, then horror. "I don't mean to be rude, ladies. This is a lovely breakfast and all. But I believe some algae has gotten on my toast."

The three of us broke into laughter. "It's *Marmite*, Zach."

On our way back to college, the numbers of our new acquaintances stored on the mobiles in our pockets, we said little, each absorbed in his own thoughts. Although the sky remained resolutely dour, my headache began to clear, and with its departure, small sensory details — the burnt umber plumage of the eagle painted on a circular pub sign, the shimmering streaks of red neon left on the wet road by passing motorists, the smell of lamb cooking on a vertical spit inside a kebab van, the crisp double-ding of a bicycle bell, the rich drone of the hurdy-gurdy being cranked on Cornmarket — impressed themselves on my attention with extraordinary vividness. Matching Zach stride for stride, I inhaled and exhaled deeply to watch the dense grey mist escape from my mouth, taking each visible breath for a wondrous sign of freshly kindled inner warmth.

This, I knew, was thanks to Claire. However scarcely peopled my social life had been until now, it was a teeming metropolis compared to my romantic life.

Distance was what adolescence had taught me about desire. The distance between my desires and their realisation. The distance between the person I was and the person I'd need to become in order to realise those desires. Therefore: love at a distance. I defended myself against the pain of failure by making failure inevitable, nursing undeclared attachments to the fittest and most unavailable girls in the sixth form.

A few years before, Simmsy's elder sister had kindly instructed me in the elements of kissing, but I was only able to put her lessons into practice a few times, because no one had told me what movements my mouth was meant to make to get my lips into that position. The charming and seductive form my words took as my imagination sauntered up to a solitary bird sipping an alcopop across a dark room at The Chatterton or at a party Simmsy had dragged me to vanished as soon as they threatened to become speech. The only ones I managed to pull were the ones who crossed the room themselves. In one case, I learnt later, the reason she had done so was to make her bloke jealous. In another, it was because she was so stoned that she confused me with someone else.

With Claire, that distance was finally erased. I felt a surge of gratitude for Zach as we parted ways in the Porter's Lodge.

He had promised me an experience worth remembering and he had kept his promise.

The next day, after our tute, we had a late breakfast in the Covered Market and proceeded to stop by The Bear for an early round. Independently we had both come to the conclusion that The Bear was our favourite pub. For Zach, because it was said to be the oldest in Oxford; for me, because it was within walking distance of Pembroke. (As for the college bar: it was *too close* to college for my taste. You could never have a quiet pint there without being interrupted by Rugby Drinks or Football Drinks or Crew Drinks. These were so raucous that Len, the ancient stately barman, wisely placed plastic tubs on the floor next to the benches, so an athlete shooting the boot or being pennied into oblivion wouldn't be required to leave the table should he or she suddenly need to vomit.)

So named because it had been used as a bear pit as early as the thirteenth century, the pub occupied the bottom floor of a squat white inn, tucked away in a little alley between Christ Church and the High. It was a cramped, low-ceilinged affair, with wood panelling and a collection of clipped neckties from sports clubs, universities, and military regiments from round the world. When he'd paid for our pints, I invited Zach to join me at my regular table and pointed out the buff, claret, and black diagonal stripes of my grandfather's battalion in the glass case on the wall.

From the leather satchel he produced a traveller's chess set and asked if I played. "Sort of," I said. My father had taught me all the moves and a bit of basic strategy, but I was certainly still a novice. Zach unfastened the little clip on the side of the set and removed the two kings. He hid one in each palm and extended his fists to me. I tapped the top of his right fist, which opened to reveal the white king. When the pieces were set up, I moved the king's pawn two spaces, the standard opening.

I had expected Zach's paper to contain a refutation of Socrates' four proofs for the immortality of the soul. Instead, it focused exclusively on an early section of the *Phaedo*, in which Socrates remarks to Cebes that a philosopher will be willing to die but should never take his own life. Zach found this disingenuous. Hadn't Socrates said that death was freedom from the body? What, then, did it matter if suicide was a form of vandalism? The body was a prison, not a temple. And anyhow, at the end of the dialogue, Socrates' actions spoke louder than his words. What caught my attention, though, was how vehemently he argued with Dr. Inwit about his interpretation, a marked contrast from their more collegial exchanges in the previous weeks. We traded knights. I decided to ask him about it.

"Things got a tad heated back there, wouldn't you say?"

"You mean with Dr. Inwit?" He took a sip of his stout and reflected. "I guess so."

"I thought it was rather odd. It was only a paper, mind."

"See, that's where you're wrong," he said with a smile. "It wasn't *only a paper*. I happen to believe what I was saying." He moved his bishop. "Check."

"You honestly think suicide isn't a form of weakness or cowardice?" I asked, moving my pawn up one space to defend my king. I took the cigarette he offered me. I hadn't yet figured out how to inhale properly, but I liked the way I looked holding it in my fingers and the way I imagined I looked as the smoke unfurled from my lips.

He castled on the queen's side. Surely, next turn he would move the rook in order to put pressure on my pawn. I'd have to find some way to defend against that. I moved my remaining knight back from the centre of the board to protect the piece.

"On the contrary," he said. "When done for the right reasons, there is no more courageous act. The problem," he thought, "is that we continue to regard escaping from pain as the paradigmatic rationale for suicide." He was dismissive of those who'd ended their lives to achieve respite from some excruciating, long-endured mental or physical illness. He was equally critical of those who had given in to an acute whim of momentary despair, such as when their stock portfolio or their lover had been unfaithful to them.

Zach's defence of suicide was perversely *moral*. And by no means unpersuasive. It was the best way, he said, to preserve human dignity and freedom from the *implacable annihilation* that awaited us all, the only way, in fact, *to pick the pocket of Nature*, to whom we all owed a death. He rejected the argument that it was the preservation of life (*impossible in any case*) that was our moral duty, specially when this duty was construed as a duty to the feelings of the friends and family who would survive the suicide.

"Suicide might be selfish, but it's not weak or cowardly. And in any case, selfishness isn't always a bad thing." He spoke loudly and passionately. Looking at me rather than at the board, he moved his bishop again, pinning my queen. I would have no choice but to take it. My precarious defence was already beginning to crumble. "It's pure hypocrisy! People call others selfish for not doing what *they* want them to do. They hate it when other people's selfishness gets in the way of their own. It's not at all surprising that the hypocrites who accuse suicides of being selfish also accuse them of being cowardly. Living solely for other people— you know what I call that? *Slavery*. And there's nothing more cowardly than choosing to be a slave."

To call living for other people slavery struck me as an exaggeration and I told him so, but what other word was there, he wanted to know, for the opposite of freedom? "Ever heard of Hans Abendroth?" he asked. I admitted I hadn't. "German philosopher. Twentieth-century. He wrote this book called *Null und Eins. The Zero and the One*. It's almost impossible to find in English. I myself have never seen a copy, but I came across a quote from it in an article about Lacan's Poe Seminar, and it really spoke to me. I've memorized it."

He held up a finger and recited, his dark eyes rolled reverently to the ceiling, his fringe swept to one side. " 'Every grave of every man who dies other than by his own hand should bear the same epitaph: returned to sender. But the suicide's grave should read: arrived at its destination. A man's mother may address the envelope and his father may pay for the postage, but that is no reason to allow them to dictate the letter's contents or decide how it should conclude.'" He paused and added, "Especially not sentimentality about the inviolability of life. Well? What do you think?"

"I think you've given this some thought," I said, a little uneasily. I expected him to nod solemnly, but he merely smiled and told me that it was mate in four. He told me that he would sacrifice his queen on the next move and that any rational player would respond by taking it. Then he showed me how the combination of his two rooks would lead to my inevitable defeat. "Another round?"

"Of chess?"

He held up his empty glass.

We made our way back to the bar and there the subject was dropped, but it wasn't long before he picked it up again. Zach's reflections on suicide also included a discourse on method: he thought *which* suicide you chose was also important. He didn't endorse jumping in front of trains or cars, for example, because you were *transferring your responsibility for your action to someone else*, namely the train driver or the motorist, *totally mutilating your body in the process*. Overdosing on pills he considered *a cry for help* and on drugs *hedonistic and cowardly*. Jumping off a bridge was *histrionic* and *attention-seeking*. Self-immolation was also histrionic and attention-seeking and *should be reserved for political protesters only*. Slitting your wrists in the tub had *merit from an historical and aesthetic point of view*, but it gave a person too much time to reconsider: it would not be *sufficiently instantaneous*. Likewise hanging. Filling your pockets with heavy stones and drowning yourself in the river had a *certain charm*, but *Virginia Woolf had already done it*. And sticking your head in the oven or putting a hose into your car's exhaust pipe? *Who would want to spend his last seconds in an appliance*? The same logic applied to asphyxiation with a plastic bag. And putting a gun in your mouth? That method was *serious* and *effective*, but ultimately *too messy*.

The vanity he lavished on behalf of this hypothetical corpse amused me. It was hard to take him seriously when he spoke like that. Zach had a theory about everything, but, despite what he said, he seemed wedded to few of them. Opinions were to him mere playthings and he always spoke with an ironic smirk that all but dared you to take him at his word. If you did, you would find yourself at the receiving end of the withering expression seasoned jokesters reserve for the most gullible of their marks. Which is why, in the end, it was easy to overlook his true convictions. He was not just the boy who cried wolf. He cried whole packs of them. Some he locked away in silence. Others he hid in plain sight. To understand him you had to work backwards, by subtraction. You had to decode and decipher. You had to decrypt.

THE SACRED VEIL OF ISIS.— The innermost chamber of the Temple of Isis, at Sais, in Egypt, was partitioned by a sacred veil, which it was forbidden to raise or remove. It was said that the goddess herself dwelt behind the veil, but that any mortal that looked upon her would immediately fall into the hands of Osiris, Guardian of the Underworld, who would pluck out the offender's heart and feed it to a crocodile-headed monster. To ensure that the temple priests would not themselves succumb to natural curiosity, their eyes were put out during their initiation rites. Protected by piety and fear, and the obedience of the blinded priests, the sacred veil remained undisturbed for a thousand generations. Until one day, a young Athenian nobleman visited the temple, burning with a desire to look behind the veil and see the beautiful goddess. The priests attempted to dissuade him, warning him of the dangers of his passion, but did not prevent him from entering the temple. Standing before the innermost chamber, the youth tore the sacred veil from its beam, horrified by what he discovered there: another veil. Consumed with rage, he tore down the second veil, only to find, behind it, a third. He tore and tore until he fell to his knees, weeping in despair, buried in the veils he had so foolishly desecrated. His body was later discovered, caught in the reeds along the banks of the Nile, a dagger in his chest, dead of his own hand.

You're Owen, the voice had said. You're exactly as my brother described you.

Unfortunately, I cannot say the same for her. Zach never described Vera to me. Never showed me a photo, or anything like that. I didn't even know he had a sister until our meeting with Bernard in Berlin.

As he left us, in the lobby of the Adlon, Bernard reached into his coat pocket and produced an envelope. Zach went red. Was his father really going to hand him money in front of me? Instead he told Zach, It's from your sister. Then he turned to me. It was nice meeting you, Owen. I'm sorry I didn't have more time to spend with you both. He gave me his business card and told me to phone if I ever needed anything. Then he shook my hand and firmly clasped Zach before entering the lift, neither of us knowing that he had just seen his son for the last time.

You have a sister? I asked when we were outside. A twin sister, he said. Vera. If Zach detected from the tone of my question that I thought it odd that he'd never mentioned a twin sister, he took care to hide it. As we walked back down Unter den Linden, I tried to ask about her, but he deflected all my questions with one- or two-word answers. Siblings, I remember thinking at the time, a perpetual mystery. I've never understood how they operate, the rules that are meant to apply to them. I can imagine what it would have been like to have been born in another country or during another era and perhaps even what it would have been like to have been born a woman. But as an only child, I can't fathom what it would be like to have a sibling, let alone a twin. To change the subject, I asked him about his mother. She owns an art gallery in Chelsea, he told me. And left it at that.

When we reached the Liebknechtbrücke, he opened the envelope. As he read, his face darkened. Is everything all right? I asked with concern. He handed me the letter, as though this would explain everything, but the page might as well have been covered in hieroglyphics. At first I thought his sister must have the worst handwriting in the world, but when I looked closer it became clear that the letter was written in an invented alphabet. The two communicated in *code*, for Christ's sake. Put out by this false gesture of intimacy, I held up the piece of paper. What shall I do with this? I asked. Tear it up and throw it into the river. I hesitated, wondering if he really meant it, but when his expression didn't change, I did as I was told. Good, he said, as we watched the last scrap fall onto the surface of the water. Now let's go get hammered.

I tell Vera I'm sorry for her loss— and immediately regret it.

I'm sorry for *your* loss, Owen. You were his best friend. We have all suffered a great loss. There's no reason to pretend that I'm in more pain than you are just because I'm his sister and you're in my house.

I should have known that, like Zach, she'd bridle at the slightest deference to social niceties. In the inflections of her voice, I hear his own. Like hearing, for the first time, a famous concerto played on the original harpsichord. That the similarity of their appearance was easily explained did not make it any less uncanny. Zach's face, an almost elfin collection of angles, was here softened, from the tip of the ear, down the jawline, to the smooth point of the chin. They both had bow-shaped lips, but Vera's were thicker, just as her prominent cheekbones were rounder than his. She wore her black hair — which looked like it had been recently and somewhat raggedly cut — shorter than Zach had done, but what was absolutely identical were their eyes, whose irises were so dark that they were almost indistinguishable from the pupils, and their eyebrows, which extended across their foreheads like the wings of the crows in the turbulent sky above the yellow wheatfields of Auvers.

To avoid Vera's glare, made all the more penetrating by the red corona round her strained eyes, I turn again to the painting. What's it called? I ask.

She pauses for a moment before she answers. She studies me, deciding whether to grant me a reprieve, a second chance to make a better first impression.

It's called *The Everlasting Irony in the Life of the Community*. The painter is Pavel Diminovich. He was one of those Soviet Jews the U.S. bought from Brezhnev in the 70s. Or that's what he said he was. Lots of people did that, claimed to be Jewish, just to get out of the USSR. He used to live with a couple of other artists in this loft in the building Mommy and Daddy owned on Greene Street. He paid for his rent in paintings — this one was supposed to have been inspired by the time he spent in Greece waiting for his visa to be authorized. Mommy could probably sell it for a million dollars, but she's attached to it for some reason. She thinks he's better than Cy Twombly.

I've never seen a painter cut his canvas like that before.

Oh that. Vera frowns. Her hand rises to her necklace, and, as if it were a nervous habit, she begins to fiddle with it. Diminovich didn't do that, she says. He's not Lucio Fontana or anything. When the painting was on loan to the Whitney for his retrospective, this guy, this unstable art student, vandalized it. After he was arrested, he told the judge that he thought the painting was filthy, a moral abomination, and that the only way to review it was with a box cutter. It was a huge scandal.

It was never restored?

Diminovich wouldn't let it be. He actually liked the way the cuts looked. He told the press they were *strokes of genius*. In all honesty, I think the guy who did it was on to something. Mommy should really cover *it* with brown paper. At least for today.

I wonder what it would be like to grow up with such a painting in your sitting room. Modern art is a discovery you should make for yourself — at least that's how it seems to me. It should draw you away from the assumptions with which you've been raised; it should be a revelation that the world is much larger and stranger than your hometown has led you to expect. But from *Everlasting Irony*, where could you possibly go to discover the shock of the new? To experience surprise, excitement, even wonder? Backwards. You had to go backwards. To the archaic. The anachronistic. The out of date. To the dead ends and castoffs of history. To the ruins of a medieval abbey sinking stone by stone into the marshy ground.

Is he here? I ask, gesturing with a limp finger at the other mourners.

Diminovich? He died of AIDS in the early 90s — 91, I think, or maybe 92. That was one of the first funerals I ever went to, come to think of it. The entire New York art world was there. If you want, I can show you a portrait he painted of me and Zach when we were kids. Come, you'll be doing me a favor. If I have to hear the words *since you were this high* one more time, I'll rip out what's left of my hair.

I follow her down one of the hallways that has been temporarily created by the sliding doors. On the wall opposite: framed movie posters, perhaps of the films produced by Bernard. I don't have time to examine them, though. When we reach the end of the hallway, another door spins on its axis. Zach's mother emerges, blotting her eyes with a tissue.

She looks at me and then at her daughter. What do you need, sweetie?

I was just going to our room. To show Owen the Diminovich. Now's really not the best time, dear. The tone of her voice is almost critical, as if she were reprimanding Vera for failing to uphold the most basic of social graces. She turns to me. Owen... I don't believe we've... you're a friend of...

Vera straightens and blinks twice. In a forceful whisper, she says, He was the one Zach wrote the letter to. The one from Oxford.

Mrs. Foedern connects the name to a face and the face to her son. She steadies herself and extends her hand to me, fingers first, as if I were meant to kiss it rather than shake it. With exaggerated formality, she says, I'm so sorry we had to meet under these circumstances.

As am I, Mrs. Foedern. I look at Vera and tell her mother that I'm sorry for her loss.

Unlike her daughter, Mrs. Foedern has no objection to polite condolences. She asks me to please call her Rebecca and even thanks me for coming all this way to attend the... she searches for the right word and ultimately decides on *service*. She asks me how long I'll be staying in New York, a question in which I can hear the residues of the maternal solicitousness she'll never again be able to lavish on her own son.

My flight back is in a few days. This is my first time in the States so —

First time in America! The forcefulness of her exclamation takes us, not least of all Rebecca herself, by surprise. She colours a little at having lost control of the volume and pitch of her voice. But it's only natural. She likely hasn't spoken above a whisper — or below a scream — in days.

Zach spoke a great deal about growing up here, I lie. So I thought I should go to some of the places he'd mentioned. As a kind of tribute...

Vera, who had been impatiently rocking back and forth on her heels, interrupts to ask where I'm staying. She's horrified to find out.

What! There? You can't stay there!

Why not, dear? Rebecca asks.

He just *can't*, okay? It's a backpacker hostel. East of the park, Mom. *Morningside* Park.

No really, it's quite nice. And quite reasonably —

It's a flophouse for junkies and broke tourists! You can't stay there, Owen. You just can't. You'll sleep at my apartment until you find somewhere else. A Craigslist rental. In Williamsburg if you have to. Anywhere but that place.

We are both taken aback, I think, by Vera's vehemence. Then again, perhaps it's not so surprising. Vera must have recognised that she was the intended audience of my condolences to her mother. She wanted to show me that she was not one to concede the last word to anyone else. Even if she had to get it by other means.

And where will you sleep? Rebecca asks her.

I'll sleep here. In our room. Besides, the upstairs neighbors are throwing a party on the rooftop tonight and I know I don't want to be around for that.

Are you sure?

Vera, you're very kind. But I couldn't possibly —

Refuse? Good, it's settled then. I'll text my roommate, Katie, to let her know to expect you.

I follow the whirlwind of activity Vera has become to the kitchen, where she writes the address of her flat and the directions on a Post it note.

Now go uptown and get your luggage. And make sure you check it for bugs before you bring it into the apartment. I'll see you there in the morning.

Taking my wrist, she adheres the bright yellow Post it to my palm by tracing a line across the top with her finger.

THE MAN WITHOUT QUALITIES.— My father once threatened to disown me for questioning the existence of God, whilst my former colleagues at the university, knowing the subject of my research, accused me of indulging in metaphysics. I was insufficiently materialist for the taste of the communists I once knew, though liberals suspected me of being a fellow traveller. Amongst republicans I would argue for aristocratic values, just as amongst monarchists I would praise the general will. I have been called a fascist by an aesthete and a degenerate by a fascist. Where politics is concerned, to everyone I am something else and to no one am I anything in particular. Not that this at all troubles me. Only insects are easily pinned down.

Our friendship with Tori and Claire did not pause for breath until Zach and I boarded the plane for Berlin two months later. I'm not entirely certain at what point our relationships became *relationships*, official and exclusive. Claire and I, at least, never discussed it. (To my relief: because with discussion the possibility of definitive rejection always remained.) I came along with Zach, Zach was with Tori, Tori came along with Claire, and so, by some transitive property of romantic logic, Claire was with me. Whenever I phoned, she answered; whenever I rang the doorbell, she opened the door. At some point it became less awkward *not* to wonder whether she would let me spend the night. Within a fortnight the glass on the bathroom sink in the flat on the Bevington Road contained four toothbrushes. In the chest of drawers in each room were spare sets of shirts and trousers.

At the end of term, Tori invited us to Greenwich. Her parents were attending a medical conference in Switzerland, and the empty house, a semi-detached neo-Georgian within walking distance of the Royal Observatory, was to serve as our base for a weekend in London.

On the train we discussed our plans. Tori was going to show us where she'd grown up and introduce us to her childhood friends. Claire was keen on visiting charity shops in Shoreditch. I hoped to catch a set at one of the clubs in Camden Town. That suited Zach just fine, he said, because Camden was where the party to which he'd been invited— and which we were going to crash— was to be thrown.

Despite the setback he'd experienced earlier at the Philosophy and Theology Faculty, Zach was undeterred in his quest to track down a copy of *The Zero and the One*. His next move was to contact Dr. Sybille Levine, the author of the article through which he'd come to learn of Abendroth in the first place. Uncharacteristically, he wrote her an email: *states of emergency*, he explained, *require emergency measures*. Dr. Levine, a professor of Psychoanalysis at Paris 8, replied warmly, thanking him for his interest in her work. Unfortunately, she wrote, she couldn't be of much use to him. She had only read Abendroth in the original— the translation of the aphorism in her article had been her own. What's more, her copy of *Null und Eins* had been a casualty of the harrowing bedbug infestation of the flat she had sublet with her partner in Chicago last year. "When I'm feeling superstitious," she wrote, "I'm certain the book is cursed." Since he was not far from London anyway, she recommended he attend the launch party for the new issue of *Theory* and speak with Niall Graves, the journal's editor, who might be able to help him. "But don't say I didn't warn you," her email concluded facetiously.

The four of us arrived a few minutes before midnight at the address Dr. Levine had provided. We found the place more by sound than by sight. That evening, the streets were choked with fog, visibility was low, so we headed in the direction of the discordant rumble of electronic music, which grew louder as we approached the crossroads. The offices of England's most unorthodox philosophy journal turned out to be located in the most quotidian of places, a dilapidated brown brick terrace adjacent to a veterinary college. But the aspiring vets would doubtless have been horrified to learn what went on next door after they had lain down their syringes and scalpels and gone home for the evening.

"Which button should I press?" asked Claire when we were all standing in front of the forest-green door at No. 8 Royal College Street.

"The one labeled T.A.Z.? Dunno. Just a guess," Zach said with anticipatory satisfaction as she extended her finger to the circle someone had blacked out with a marker pen. We waited a moment, but heard nothing. We looked at each other and then up at the windows, which flashed with light. Zach pressed the button a second time. "They must not be able to hear the doorbell over the music." Rather than yelling up at the window to get someone's attention, as I was on the verge of doing, he asked Tori for one of her bobby pins.

"You're taking the piss," she said, handing him the pin, brushing back the wave of hair that fell over her eye.

"Sorry dear, you're not going to get this back." He flexed the ends until it broke in two. We stared at him mutely. "What?" He shrugged. "I forgot my keys at home a lot growing up."

I took my mobile from my pocket and held it above the lock, using the orange screen as a torch. We crowded round to watch. He bent the tips of each half of the pin until they looked like miniature jemmies. Then, making an L with his left hand, he cupped the lock, holding the part of the pin he'd inserted in the top of the keyhole in place with his thumb.

With his right hand, he introduced the other half into the bottom and finessed the lock. When he heard it click, he swung his thumb anticlockwise, using the pin as a lever. We were all a bit spooked when the door seemed to recede of its own free will. All but Zach, of course, who gave a low bow and, with a flourish of his wrist, invited us up the dark staircase. "That was ace," I said. "You'll have to show me how to do that one day."

The spacious reception room, if you could call it that, looked more like the set of a science fiction film than the offices of a proper academic journal. Illuminated by multicoloured LED tendrils that dripped from the ceiling, the walls were papered with complex diagrams, mysterious hieroglyphs, technical blueprints, and anatomical drawings, which suggested some intersection between cybernetics and the occult. The floor was a snake pit of black cables slithering off in every direction, round the legs of the eclectic furniture, plugged into the mainframes of a dozen computers, whose screens glowed and flickered with charts and graphs, pornographic images, scrolling lines of binary code. A cabinet of speakers was stationed in the far corner of the room, but where one would have expected a band or a DJ, there was instead a man in a black tunic wearing two prosthetic gauntlets, somehow conducting, through the wires that were attached to them, a raving symphony of sampled beats. The dancers threaded slowly round the room, out of time with the music, carefully overstepping the intertwined limbs of the people who, sprawled on the floor, were looking at the computer screens or up at the ceiling, wiping sweat from their foreheads as they drank bottled water. Each danced alone, lost in rapt contemplation of the movement of his or her own hands, hands that traced lines through the sweet-smelling clouds of exhaled smoke, patterns invisible to us, but which no doubt appeared to them as melodious waves of laser light.

Tori looked at Zach. "So you've brought us to the spring bop at Bedlam." Zach, who was still taking in the scene, his mouth slightly open, conceded the point with a silent nod. "Let's find the warden, then, shall we?" she suggested. "He'll know where the drinks are. Looks as though we all have a bit of catching up to do."

The warden, Niall Graves, did not prove at all difficult to identify. We found him in a dimly lit back room, surrounded by a group of men and women in their mid-twenties, who, judging from the way they were dressed, may have been graduate students, street artists, computer programmers, or professional anarchists, but, judging from the way they hung on his every word, were all acolytes. Graves himself was a spent matchstick in a stained v neck t shirt and black stovepipe trousers that ended above his ankles. He was around forty years of age, already greying at the temples, with thin lips, a thin nose, and eyes the colour the sun turns when you've stared at it for too long. He stood, slightly hunched, his elbows permanently tucked into his ribs, his hands dangling in front of his slightly hollow chest, simply rotating his long fingers to his lips whenever he fancied a sip from his glass or a draw from the spliff that was being passed round the circle.

When we joined, a man in a black hoodie was asking him what lessons the left ought to take from the repression of the Seattle Uprising as it prepared for the upcoming G8 Summit in Genoa. Graves answered in a soft voice, barely audible over the swarms of sound coming from the other room, as if it pained him, physically or psychologically, to breathe.

"Right now," he said, "the single most important problem for the left to solve is the Problem of Number."

The one who looked to me like a graduate student accepted the spliff from him and asked, "How do you mean?"

"We still don't know what Number is or what its ontological status is."

Tori guffawed in disbelief. "You don't know what numbers are?"

"What Number *is*," Graves corrected. "Take, for example, the set of natural numbers, the least ontologically controversial of all sets, even when you exclude the null set from the count. Natural numbers can be defined as abstract, iterable representations of pure multiplicity," he continued. "But do they really exist? Common sense would dictate a nominalist approach to this question: numbers have the same ontological status as other empirical referents; they are mind-dependent fictions that were invented by human beings and will cease to exist when there is nothing left to count or, more likely, nothing left to do the counting. But numbers are also iterable and therefore transfinite, which means that, even at this very moment, the cardinality of the set of all natural numbers exceeds the cardinality of the set of all empirical referents in the universe. Thus, the possibility of a non-material ontology cannot be, if you'll pardon the pun, discounted. Number is not like a table, which has a referent, but nor is it like Justice, which has none whatsoever. It is some combination of both or neither. In short, a virtuality."

"Sorry, Niall," said the man in the black hoodie. "I'm afraid I don't see what this has to do with the anti-globalisation struggle."

"It has *everything* to do with it," Graves replied, coughing into his fingertips from the exertion that had been required to emphasise the word. "In fact, it will determine the tactics and their success or failure. Given what neuroscience has learnt about the mind, a nominalist approach would suggest that Number, along with all other concepts, are the material epiphenomena of a purely material substrate, namely the brain. A purely materialist ontology would conceive of the political as a play of forces between material entities over various distributions of the Material. A lateral distribution of these forces would be best achieved by revolutionary violence, that is, by a direct confrontation with the repressive apparatus of the neoliberal State, with the aim of taking it over to facilitate this redistribution. The problem with this strategy is two-fold. First, the current force differentials make it an almost impossible undertaking. Second, even when successful, revolutionary takeover preserves *ex vi termini* the repressive State apparatus. *But* if it were shown to be non-material, Number would imply the possibility of a correspondingly virtual space, and open up a strategy of revolutionary escapism, a nomadic flight *into* the cracks and fissures of material reality, of whose existence the State is not and cannot be aware."

Claire whispered into my ear, "I think the warden's as much of a nutter as the patients are." Tori, whose tolerance for bollocks was much lower than ours, had drifted away from the circle halfway through Graves' lecture, and was examining the bookshelves at the other end of the room. I took the spliff from Zach and inhaled the hot end through pursed lips.

"But virtual space. That's just a metaphor," I observed. "Material bodies can't very well flee into metaphorical space, now can they?"

"It's not just a metaphor," the computer programmer said, coming to Graves' defence. "Consider the Internet. If our research into synaptic networks confirms Niall's hypothesis, there is every reason to believe it will one day be possible to upload free consciousness into a virtual space like the Internet. Moore's law suggests that that day is not far off. All we need to do now is *speed up the future*."

"Moore's *first* law," Zach cut in. He'd been unusually quiet until now, listening considerately to what Graves had to say. But the turn the conversation was now taking was bound to displease him. "What about Moore's second law? It's not like technological progress occurs in some economic vacuum," he said. "The kind of processing power you're talking about requires levels of resource extraction and capital investment only defense departments and multinational corporations are capable of underwriting. By putting your faith in technology to solve the problem, you'd only make yourself dependent on the very institutions you're trying to use it to flee from."

A hush fell over the group. Tori rejoined us and lay a hand on Zach's shoulder. The computer programmer looked meekly at Graves to give the debate its final word. Instead, Graves squinted at Zach. "You're the lad from Oxford who's interested in Hans Abendroth, aren't you?"

Zach started. "How did you know?"

"Sybille told me you'd be coming, of course."

"I mean how did you know it was me?"

"You're the only one at my party wearing a tie." With his free hand, he pecked at it and rubbed the fabric between his fingers. "A silk tie, no less. If you give it to me, I'll tell you where the book is."

Without a moment's hesitation, Zach reached for his collar, loosened the knot, and eagerly placed the tie around Graves' neck as if he were awarding him a medal: I think he would have given him the pin number to his debit card had Graves asked for it.

"Now then. These three are your friends?" As we introduced ourselves, he took a small bag of what looked to me like Fizzers from his trousers pocket and pressed a chalky coloured tablet into each of our outstretched palms. A water bottle was passed round and we swallowed piously, without first asking what the tablets were or what they would do to us. ("It reminded me of taking Holy Communion," Claire would tell us hours later, when we were in the taxi headed back to Greenwich, preferring to huddle together beneath Zach's outspread overcoat rather than distribute ourselves more evenly throughout the cabin, perhaps because, like the dancers at the party we had just left, our hearts had emigrated into our hands, and these neither wanted nor were able to distinguish where one body ended and another began.)

"*The Zero and the One* is somewhere up there, naturally," Graves told Zach, pointing in the direction of the bookshelves with his lit cigarette. The daunting white shelves extended from floor to ceiling and from wall to wall. They must have contained several thousand volumes, more than a lifetime's worth of reading. "Alas, I can't say where exactly, because I never did get the staff to alphabetise them. But I'd estimate that you have between half an hour and forty-five minutes to find it" — he turned to me with a wan, toothless smile — " before you discover just how *metaphorical* space can become."

WORD MADE FLESH.— The relationship between thought and language is the relationship between a wound and its scar.

Again I had been directed. Again I'd followed along. Did as I was told. Passively submitted to a superior force. In this case, however, following along was in my best interests. I was grateful not to have to spend a second more on those starchy sheets on that swaying bunk in that miserable room. And I could not have done better than to have so quickly earned Vera's trust— she who was clearly a central piece of the puzzle Zach's life had made of my own. No doubt she sensed the same was true of me and that's why this trust had been extended. We were going to share intelligence. To define the absent centre that bound us both, each would help the other draw the full circumference of the circle.

Vera lives on the Lower East Side, which, according to my travel guide,

is the latest of New York's "it" neigh-bourhoods. The old countercultural flavour that has been gentrified out of Alphabet City can still be tasted here, below Houston Street, where hipsters occupy former tenements and where art collectives and experimental music clubs rub shoulders with working mazoh factories and turn-of-the-century synagogues. From bargain hunting on Orchard Street and long nights at the dive bars on Rivington to the city's best deli (Katz's) and its most surreal Chinese restaurant and Karaoke Bar (Congee Village), the L.E.S. is a must-visit for those who want to say they were there before (everyone knew) it was cool.

Near the entrance to her building an impromptu street party is in progress. Old men sit in lawn chairs drinking long-necked bottles of yellow beer, keeping cool with portable fans, blasting salsa from their car radios. Sausages and tortillas are flipped on miniature barbeques. Young men in vests and blue-and-red bandanas throw dice against the wall; women sit on the boots of well-buffered muscle cars, languidly swaying to the music, talking to each other in rapid, nasal Spanish.

In the lobby, a man is passed out, clutching a brown bag to his chest, a curve of ash that was once a lit cigarette dangling from his mouth. The parquetted floor of the lift sticks to my shoes. For five floors I hold my breath in an attempt to quarantine the rancid sweet smell in my nostrils. Clearly my senses have still to adjust to the sorts of distinctions that make this neighbourhood different from the one in which my hostel was located.

Her flatmate, Katie, welcomes me with the sort of long and soulful hug you might give to a friend you hadn't seen in years. The familiarity of her gesture catches me completely off guard, and I botch it, getting the hand I'd extended sandwiched against the bare skin of her stomach. She is wearing a bikini, with a saffron sarong tied around her waist. Sitting on the living room sofas are another girl, also in a swimsuit, and a bloke in nothing but his pants.

The A/C blew out earlier today. So we're sweating it out, Katie explains. It's not like this every day, I promise. And you in that suit! I can't believe you haven't melted!

It's quite warm, isn't it?

She gives me a bemused smile. On account of my accent, I reckon. God Save the Yanks. They can't tell whether you come from Bristol or Belgravia, whether you were born to the proletariat or the peerage, whether you were raised in council housing or a castle, simply by listening to your voice. And they probably wouldn't care, even if they could, so innocent are they to gradations of social class. To them, you're all the same strange specimen. The Brit. The foreigner whose language you happen to speak.

Katie turns to her friends. Hey guys, this is Owen, Vera's brother's friend from Oxford. That's Jake. And that's Marissa. They live in the apartment upstairs.

Jake and Marissa respond to her perky introduction with slow waves and a distended collective H-e-e-y-y-y. They inspect me for a moment, not knowing what more to say to a person who has just come from the funeral of a friend who has killed himself. Marissa looks at me with pity and Jake with slight revulsion, as though I've been infected by some invisible contagion that might rub off on him if he isn't careful.

Embarrassed by the sudden unsociable silence, Katie says, Why don't you put your stuff in Vera's room for now and make yourself comfortable. When you're done grab a beer from the fridge and join the rest of us on the roof, okay?

Cheers, I say and solemnly walk in the direction of the door Katie pointed out to me. The three of them make their way through the small window next to the kitchen sink and disappear up the fire escape.

I flick the switch: Vera's room. Original crown moulding and a ceiling fan. Cream-and-yellow-striped wallpaper. Paisley-pattern bedspread. Diaphanous violet curtains. A cork notice-board covered in photographs. Bracelets and necklaces that double as decorations hanging from the knobs screwed into the walls. Pairs of shoes stacked neatly on a rack behind the bed. A normal room, all in all. A room that acts the age of its occupant, with a feminine — that is to say *human* — element lacking from both the frigid sleekness of her parents' home and the deliberate chaos of Zach's rooms in Staircase XVI.

I hang my suit jacket over the back of her desk chair and begin to loosen my striped college tie. But I stop as soon as I notice, on the surface of the desk, next to the translucent-blue computer shaped like a virtual reality helmet, a bundle of letters tied together with a red ribbon. The envelopes, opened with a paperknife, all bear Royal Mail stamps and return addresses in familiar handwriting. I slide the topmost envelope out of the bundle, wondering which of these contains Zach's description of me, the one by which Vera claimed to recognise me, and open it, only to discover that it is written in the same invented alphabet as the letter Zach showed me in Berlin. I return it to its place and finish undressing. My trousers are creased and the inside of my collar is stained with a brown rim of sweat. From my rucksack, I grab the first t shirt I feel and make my way to join the gathering upstairs.

Before I pass through the door, I pause to look at the photographs on the noticeboard. There are several of Zach and Vera together.

There is one of them as children, walking down the strand on a cold, grey day. They are wearing shorts and sandals and windcheaters. Coming over the water a strong wind has blown their hair across their faces. Zach himself has shoulder-length hair, which makes him look like his sister's younger sister. I pull the drawing pin. The caption on the back reads *Z&V The Lido 1989*.

Another shows them in close up, in cap and gown, standing outside the gates of The Gansevoort School. Vera smiles broadly at the camera, whose flash has given her red pupils. She is wearing the same necklace—a black pearl necklace. Meanwhile, Zach, whose slightly plump face is sparsely covered with an early attempt at a beard, looks beyond the frame, bored by all the pomp and circumstance. Caption: *Z&V Graduation Day 1999*.

A third, of the two of them, sitting on manicured grass, their backs resting against the base of a bronze casting of Rodin's *Thinker*. In the background, neoclassical architecture. Zach is wearing jeans ripped at the knee. He is raising a cigarette to his smirking lips. Vera has turned to look at him, her hand on his arm in a way that suggests she has just gently slapped him for making a light joke at her expense.

Finally, a horizontal shot of them on the sofa in the living room of this very flat. The lower right corner of the frame has been obscured by Zach's arm, which has reached out to its greatest length to snap the photo. His face, in profile, looks alertly ahead. Vera is resting on his chest. Her hair is long. A few black curls have fallen over her shoulder. She is wearing a cocktail dress. And again, the pearls.

I retrieve the object from my jacket pocket, hold it up to the light from the desk lamp, and notice, for the first time, the hole, barely a pinprick, that passes through the centre. I look again at the photograph. The date stamp in the corner reads *December 30, 2000*. I pull the drawing pin. There is no caption.

On the roof is a sizeable crowd, everyone in various stages of undress. A garage rock track, its singer disparaging the intelligence of the New York Police Department, is playing on the portable stereo someone has placed on the brick ledge.

When Katie sees me come up the fire escape, she breaks off her conversation with Jake and Marissa and joins me. Good, she says. You found the beer. She takes me by the arm and leads me on a long, slow tour of the perimeter of the roof. Surprises me by asking, straight off, how Vera is doing. With Katie it seems that there is no such thing as a stranger or a secret, no thought too private to share.

I don't know if I can say. I quite literally just met her.

But you were *there*. You saw how she was.

Well, after the funeral I thought to myself that it was remarkable how well she was handling herself. She ate a little. Spoke with people. She absolutely insisted I come here, after all.

Katie lets go of my arm and places her palm over her heart, relieved. Oh, I'm so glad to hear you say that. You're absolutely right. She's an incredibly strong woman. I mean I know she's just *devastated* — and the worst is still to come. Anger and resentment and guilt and loss. Loss she'll be dealing with for the rest of her life. But if there's anyone,

anyone, who can bounce back from a thing like this, it's Vera. I'm really sorry I never got to meet Zach. Vera and I really only got to know each other when we became roommates, and by then he was already in England. He stayed here for Winter Break, but I was back home in LA. She takes a sip of her beer and holds the cold bottle to her flushed red cheek. Vera talked about him all the time, she continues. He sounded like just the most amazing person —

I interrupt her to ask if she has any siblings.

Only child, she says, warily, as if she didn't quite see how my question related to what she'd been talking about.

As am I. Vera said something to me after the funeral. She said that I shouldn't pretend that she was suffering any more than I was just because she was his sister. But I wonder if that's really true. That bond must be deeper than any friendship could ever be.

I guess Vera's an only child now too. She'll need us to show her how to cope with that... Her voice trails off, unsure if the first word that comes to mind is the one she really means. She looks away. With that loneliness...

We've made our way to the other side of the roof, hidden from the rest of the party by a water tower. Folding our arms on the roof ledge, we find ourselves eye level with a familiar series of gargoyles embedded in the cornice of the block of flats over the road. See no evil. Hear no evil. Speak no evil. I take a pull from the bottle, place it on the ledge, and turn my back on them.

And what about you, Owen? How are *you* doing?

It's a question I'd rather not answer. I know she means well, but the way she asks, with its presumption of complicity, sounds to my ears more like an invitation to gossip that an invitation to unburden my soul, which, anyway, is not something that's going to happen.

Vera told me Zach addressed his... letter... to you. And that you were the one who had to deal with the police. I can't imagine what that must be like.

My lips part. Katie's eyes are wide open, brimming with sympathy. She nods silently. With understanding. Prompting me to speak.

I feel... I feel all the same things you mentioned, I say. Anger and resentment and guilt. Confusion as well. Everything he ever said about suicide keeps coming back to me, like warning signs I failed to notice or take seriously enough. I blame myself. I do. For not seeing the signs. For not acting when I could. It's taking a toll on me. I'm having trouble keeping food down. When I sleep, I have nightmares. I'm knackered. Exhausted.

Suddenly I begin to feel dizzy, on the verge of blacking out. I place my palm to my forehead to stabilise myself. It's time for this conversation to come to an end. I've already said enough as it is, even though everything I've said has been half-truths.

In fact, would you mind terribly if I went downstairs again? I think I ought to lie down.

My God, *yes*. You must be so tired! With the flight and the time difference and the funeral and— this is your first time in New York, isn't it? New York is enough to run anybody into the ground. Not to mention all those other things.

Thank you, Katie. You've been very kind.

In Vera's room I disassemble all the pillows on the bed, trying to remember the arrangement so I can replace them in the morning. It's too hot to sleep beneath the sheets. Somehow I feel I'm fouling up the quilt just by lying on it. For half an hour, I watch the red lights on Vera's alarm clock change. Adding five. Sweating. Trying to tip my clammy fatigue into unconsciousness with boredom. Just after three o'clock, I hear noises in the living room. The sounds of laughter. The click of bottles falling in the rubbish bin. The slamming of the door. Katie's voice saying, Goodbye, No problem at all, Call me, I'm free all next week.

Then, silence. I sweat. I watch the clock. The door to the room cracks open. I come to my senses and sit up. Is it morning already? No. It's only four. Somehow I feel I shouldn't be here. In Vera's bed.

It's me, Vera says. It's okay. It's just me.

I'm so sorry — I didn't mean to — I thought you were staying —

Really, Owen, it's fine.

I can go to the sofa — so you can have your bed to —

I begin to stand, but before I can, she puts her fingers on my shoulders. It's alright. Stay. Please stay. I want you to.

In the darkness, I hear two heels drop, and then a zip. The rustle of fabric. A dull snap. A shadow, whose form is illuminated only by the faint glow of the clock, crawls into the bed and rests a cheek on my chest. I can feel her breast heavy on my stomach. She wraps an arm around me, curled up. Her knees touching my thighs. Touch. More than the other senses, more than even speech, it's touch that connects us to other people. When you go without it for long enough, you feel like you no longer have a body, that you are floating through the world, immaterial as a ghost, a conduit for sense impressions, with no weight or gravity or solidness, little more than a block of ice that has become aware of its own numbness. After I threw the pistol into the river, right after, muddy bloody suit and all, I went straight to Claire, not only because I needed an alibi, but because I needed to be touched. To prove to myself that I still existed.

Curled up against my body, Vera begins to shake and sob. I just couldn't, Owen. I just couldn't stay there. I tried to be strong, I tried to be, but I just couldn't I couldn't. Her breathing grows louder and faster until from the back of her throat, she coughs a shriek. She makes a fist and begins to pound my chest, asking with each contact, Why?

Shhh... Shhh... As she beats it out of her system, trembling, each blow more emphatic but less forceful than the last, I curl her close to me. Stroking her hair. Her arm. In one of the sweeps, my fingers pass over the skin of her bicep. Vera, shhhh. It's all right, Vera. I feel two ridges. Perfectly straight.

Embossed into her skin. It's all right. Just to be certain, I pass my palm over them again, inconspicuously as possible, so she doesn't notice that I've noticed what I've noticed. Two scars. It's all right. Two perfectly straight scars — but on her left arm.

I'd noticed an identical pattern, in the same location, on Zach's right arm, the night we hired that prostitute in Berlin.

IDOLATRY.— Idolatry is above all a matter of space: the idolatrous object is the one that is both infinitely close and infinitely far away.

In Berlin, the days seemed to turn themselves inside out. We sang the sun, but only in its flight, rising to greet the pink-grey dusk and retiring red-eyed when it came out again to light the way for men and women in business attire, also red-eyed, with whom we exchanged mutually uncomprehending stares on the tram every morning. *Like two species of vampire sizing each other up*, Zach quipped.

We heard the last calls of Club der Vision.re and White Trash Fast Food and Caf. Zapata and Tresor and half a dozen others whose names are now nothing more to me than a blur of umlauts and neuter articles and hard consonants. We put Zach's theories on dancing to the test, with great success, practicing our indifference to ridicule to the sound of techno and house (things I wouldn't have been caught dead doing back home), usually under the inspiration of the little psychoactive Fizzers Niall Graves introduced us to, which could be had for a fiver under table after table in club after club to be chased with pilsner and vodka and energy drinks.

If we'd extended ourselves too far the previous evening, we would spend our recuperation wandering through the strange flat on Sch.nhauser Allee that Bernard rented for our stay. We would peek under white sheets to examine the absent owner's furniture, or we'd pluck an unmarked video at random from the hundreds that had been stacked in the drawing room and watch whatever it contained. (I remember: Fassbinder's adaptation of *Despair, Looney Tunes* dubbed in German, a grainy recording of the 1990 World Cup Championship Match.) Or we dictated poetry to one another, which we typed up on the black machine I discovered hidden beneath some cleaning supplies in the pantry, posting the results to the addresses of various literary magazines in London.

Certain lines of those poems return to me now, ghostly tremors in my fingertips and faint images in my brain. I remember how they felt to type as much as how they were laid out on the page or how they resonated in my ear. They return to me in lines and stanzas, in snatches and fragments, like the damaged papyri on which the fragmented wisdom of Heraclitus or Sappho is preserved today.

"Eadem, Sed Aliter" is the only one I remember in full. Zach came up with the subject, I think. I decided on the title. We wrote it together, trading places at the typewriter. He would dictate two lines, then I the two following. The sonnet, I daresay, gives a good indication of our general mood:

Even at our most modern moment,
Blinded by migraines, rotting with syphilis,
Vomiting, trembling, raving, delirious,
Bludgeoned by nightmares, dependent

Upon a betrayer's kindness— even then, weak
Of hand, he lifted our pen to sign "Dionysus"
Beneath his letters to posterity. Alas,
It seems there is no escaping the Greeks.

Now more than a century since, modernity
Chews quietly on the asphodel;
The dynamite has exploded, but still the spell
Remains unbroken. Our history

Is tail-swallowing Ourobouros, whose billion
Scales are fashioned from the bodies of men.

Circumstance may have been the actual reason Zach and I spent our holiday there (his father was going to be there; his father was going to foot the bill), but Zach was travelling on business of his own. What business? None of the city's famous museums or important historical sites made it onto our itinerary. We spent a month there without ever seeing the inside of the Pergamon or the Staatsoper or the Reichstag. We paid no respectful pilgrimage to Sachsenhausen, nor did we walk by Lindenstraße to see how the construction of Daniel Libeskind's Jewish Museum was coming along. We didn't even see the stretch of famous graffiti on the Berlin Wall, though it was only a short tram ride from our flat. Had we not gone to visit Bernard at the Adlon we would have been the only tourists in history to visit the capital of Germany without seeing the Brandenburg Gate.

No, for Zach, the only true point of interest in the whole bloody town was to be found at 13 Richard-Wagner-Straße, where the offices of Nothung Verlag, Hans Abendroth's publisher, were located.

From the Translator's Introduction to *The Zero and the One*, Zach would have learnt that his new idol was born to an affluent family of civil servants and booksellers in Frankfurt in 1909. His uncle Hermann was a famous conductor, heading orchestras in both England and the USSR, though he later joined the Nazi Party and conducted *Die Meistersinger* at the Bayreuth Festival in 1944. Against the wishes of his parents, who hoped he would go into law, Hans studied classical philology at the University of Freiburg and wrote his *Habilitationsschrift* ("*Allegorien der Seele vom* Phaidon *zur* Hymne der Perle") under the supervision of Martin Heidegger. In 1935, he relocated to Berlin, where he worked as a researcher at the Prussian Academy of Sciences, as a part of the team tasked with translating the Akhmim Codex, a fifth-century Gnostic manuscript, from Coptic into German. He taught at the University of Berlin until 1949, retiring shortly thereafter to begin work on *Null und Eins*, his magnum opus, which would be published, to little notice, a few years later. It was thanks to Lacan's interest in the book and to a deft translation by Pierre Klossowski that *Null und Eins* became a touchstone for a generation of French philosophers and psychoanalysts. By then, however, Abendroth himself published only sporadically and never appeared in public. As of the publication date of the English edition, 1972, he was said to be living in a state of reclusion somewhere in Charlottenburg, West Berlin.

The week before our departure Zach had spent furiously gathering as much supplementary information about Abendroth as he could, not that there was much to be found. The house that had published his copy had long since gone out of business and the translator, Bettina Müller, was killed in a car crash in 1981. No one at Nothung Verlag returned Zach's emails requesting, "as research assistants of the internationally renowned philosopher, Dr. Marcus Inwit, of Magdalen College, Oxford," an interview "to be printed in the upcoming issue of *Theory*," which Niall Graves was surely as little aware as Dr. Inwit was of being used as a reference. When we arrived in Berlin, we passed an entire afternoon at the Staatsbibliothek looking for some news of his existence. We found none. But the absence of an obituary gave Zach hope that, though he would be quite old, Abendroth was still alive and capable of being called on. What Zach hoped to do once he found him — given the rudimentary state of his German and the philosopher's reclusiveness — no one could say. I think he supposed, as all Americans do, that Abendroth would be happy to converse with him in English.

As there was no doorbell at 13 Richard-Wagner-Straße and Berlin's door locks didn't seem to yield as willingly to bobby pins as London's, we waited for almost an hour for someone to come in or out of the building. We were finally able to enter on the black-and-yellow tails of a postman, whose red and round face, as he watched us sneak past, was frozen in that comical mixture of suspicion (*this is not meant to be happening!*) and disbelief (*hang on, is this really happening?*) one rarely witnesses outside silent cinema. We quickly made our way up to the third floor and knocked on the door next to the bronze plaque with the name and address of the publishing house. The door was opened slightly by a brittle old woman, the receptionist I assumed, and we sped through before it could be shut on us again.

The offices of Nothung Verlag were hardly larger than the flat where we were staying. There was no computer on the front desk, only a large olive-coloured electric typewriter loaded with what looked to be a half-finished letter. There were the standard floor to ceiling bookshelves, but even I could see that some of the titles had been gathering dust there for years. No wonder they hadn't returned Zach's email. They probably weren't even aware he'd sent it.

Zach enthusiastically reached out to shake the delicate, unproffered hand of the elderly gentleman who had emerged from his office, the one on the right, to see what the bother was. "*Kann ich Ihnen helfen?*" he asked Zach with frigid politeness.

"Can... I... you... help — yes, you can help me, Sir," Zach answered, making no attempt to have the conver-sation in German. This did nothing to elevate the frown that was then plummeting into the old man's jowls. "Allow me to introduce myself. I am Zachary Foedern and this... this is my esteemed colleague Owen Whiting. We are here from Oxford on behalf of the journal *Theory*. We sent you email corre-spondence regarding the work of Hans Abendroth, which, I don't know if you are aware of this, Herr..."

"Wilhelm von Nothung."

"Uh yes, I don't know if you're aware of this, Herr von Nothung, but there has been a wide resurgence of interest in Herr Abendroth's work among select circles in Britain... and America too, and we... my colleague and I... were wondering if we could meet with him, with Herr Abendroth, in order to interview him, as I wrote in my email, for the... the uh, *Theory*."

Von Nothung waited for a long time before responding to make sure Zach's avalanche of falsehoods had indeed finished falling. He spoke slowly, in perfect, if somewhat prim, English. "Ah yes. Mr. Foedern. I recall your email. Please accept my apologies, but your interview is quite simply out of the question. I hope you have not come all this way to hear me tell you this in person."

"No, Herr von Nothung— and please, call me Zach — we have come all this way to hear you tell us that it *will* be possible and to help us arrange the interview and perhaps even to translate for us, since your English is so good. We understand, and respect, yes respect, the fact that Herr Abendroth is a... doesn't like to see many people... but if you were to tell him how many people — philosophers — of the new generation — are interested in his work, I'm sure he'd reconsider."

"Mr. Foedern. How shall I say this? Aside from the fact that you appear to be no more than twenty years of age and aside from the fact that you speak no German and aside from the fact that your connexion with *Theory* is tenuous enough for you to be unaware how deeply Niall Graves and I despise each other — the reason an interview is impossible is that Herr *Doktor* Hans Abendroth has just two days ago passed away. I am, in fact, preparing his obituary now. I wish, however, to thank you for your interest in his work. It is possible that I shall include a line about how, after so many years of unwarranted obscurity, *Null und Eins* is being rediscovered by — how did you put it? — *the philosophers of the new generation*." And with that von Nothung showed us the door.

Zach looked almost as cross as when he'd read the letter from his sister a few days earlier. Both times, his face clouded with sullenness. His pout twisted into a scowl as his silence condensed into outright anger. This time, at least, I had enough information to understand the cause of the sullenness: he'd narrowly missed the opportunity to meet a person with whom he felt a strong kinship, a person whose ideas had given him hours of intense pleasure, in whose aphorisms he must have found elegant formulations of his own inchoate thoughts, whose book was an achievement he believed he alone had recognised.

What confused me, however, was the anger. At what? That Abendroth was dead? Zach seemed to take it personally, as if this death, though it was the death of a person whose existence he was unaware of only a few months before, was some sort of betrayal. He seemed to regard this physical fact of death as evidence that the universe was maliciously bent on foiling his plans and defying his will. As on the first occasion, we solved the problem the only way we knew how: through a systematic derangement of the senses.

SAILING OFF THE EDGE OF THE EARTH.— The fantastical etchings of galleons sailing off the edge of the flat earth and toppling headlong into the void are more accurate representations our of lived experience than the spherical empirical truth in which we happen to live. Columbus' discovery of the Americas is surely a watershed moment in the History of the Forgetting of Being.

A breeze passes through the open window, blowing the thin curtains back into the room, encouraging one to hope that the hot spell has finally broken. My rucksack, there in the corner. My suit jacket, hanging on the chair. The top of the envelope peeks out of the book that is still in the jacket pocket where I left it. On the pillow next to mine is a baby-blue envelope with my initials on it. The note inside is written on personalised stationery. Across the top, the letters of her name rise slightly from the cardstock. I run my fingers over them.

VERA FOEDERN

O—

Thank you for your kindness last night. You were a dear to be of comfort to me when I needed it. I wanted to wake you up and tell you this, but you looked like you needed your sleep. Going uptown today. Appointment with my therapist. Then I'll be at school, getting ready for next semester, doing my best to pretend that life goes on. Maybe if I fake it, it'll start to happen. Sounds like something Z would say, come to think of

it. Talked to Mommy this morning. She says you should come to dinner tonight. Nothing fancy. Just Chinese takeout. 6:30?
— V

I read it twice over. Very slowly. In the script I notice a difference between brother and sister. His letters were compactly cloistered. Then they exploded (in the case of *l*'s or *h*'s) well above or sank (in the case of *p*'s or *y*'s) well below his otherwise miraculously straight lines. Hers, on the other hand, have a feature I've never seen before in anyone else's handwriting: sizeable lacunae between the letters that require more than one stroke — splitting, for example, the lowercase *d* in *dear* into a *c* and an *l* and the lowercase *h* in *Chinese* into an *l* and a backwards *r*. The *V* of her signature is composed of two obliques that barely manage to meet at the point. The lines float across the cardstock like fish in a small aquarium.

The living room is empty. The light in Katie's room is out. I have the place to myself. Collecting my clothes for the day, I head to the shower. On the shower curtain, a map of the world. I point to an unmarked spot due west of London, beneath the chin of the boar's head of Wales, and trace an invisible line across the clear plastic Atlantic, landing on the dot that reads New York. This far. I've come *this* far.

Under the hot stream. Eyes closed. Water cascading off my nose and lips and chin. The taste of Claire's mouth. My prick stirs. Signs of life. Finally. I put my hand to it. Claire's small nipples in my teeth. Her soft calves wrapped around my waist. The way she breathes *oh God oh God* before she comes. My hand shuttles back and forth. The weight of Vera's breast on my chest last night. Didn't get a stiff one then, thank Christ. And if I had? What if I had tried to slip off her knickers? Would she have let me? Let me lift her hips. Let me peel them off. Roll between her thighs? Shuttling back and forth, faster. Letting me inside, wet like saliva, my tongue running the length of her neck, my fingers pushing between her teeth into her mouth. Shuttling back and forth. Saying my name. Slowly. My name.

I return to Vera's room wearing new skin, all the filth and sweat rubbed out. Wearing only a towel, I sit at her computer. Claire must have already written. A small circle with the mouse. A click on the icon of the web browser on the screen. In place of a homepage, what appears is Vera's inbox. The sight of the email addresses and subject headings causes the same stab of embarrassment one feels when one opens the door to an unlocked public toilet and discovers it's occupied. My first instinct is to log her out (as one would immediately apologise and shut the toilet door again). But as I bring the cursor arrow to the upper right hand of the page, two considerations prevent me from clicking x. First: logging off now would only inform Vera that I'd used her computer and seen the contents of her inbox. Second: here before me must be some of the information I was looking for two days ago when I tried to guess the password to Zach's email account. Surely he'd written something to *her* in the days leading up to his death. Something he hadn't told me. Just as he hadn't told me he would be including a pearl in his letter. I dip my hand into the pocket of the jacket that is hanging on the back of the chair. Still there.

With my right hand, I scroll down, vowing not to look at anything except what was on the first page. But in a collection of emails, read and unread, dating back three months, there are none from her brother. I type his name into the search box at the top of the page. The only emails in which it appears are those from their parents and short messages informing people of the date and time of the funeral. The most recent exchange between them was sometime in late December. Surely something more than Zach's aversion to email would have to be responsible for such a long drought. I rifle again through the letters on the desk. The last is also postmarked in December. The letter Bernard delivered to Zach in Berlin had upset him — that much was clear. This might explain why there were no emails after April, but not why there were none between December and April. Unless she's erased them all from her account.

In another window, I check my own inbox, and finding nothing there from Claire, I log out. Unless I somehow manage to crack their sibling code, what I'm looking for, whatever it is, I won't find without Vera's help. Meantime, it's late. I should get on with my day.

Half six at the Foederns'. Gives me five hours to kill. What to do? In New York City? With five hours? Anything. But not everything. One week in New York is beginning to strike me as totally inadequate. Oxford, around for a millennium, can be mastered in a month. New York, not half as old, would take a lifetime. The situation of the tourist in New York is not unalike that of the ass in Buridan's fable. Placed between two equidistant bales of hay, the donkey dies of indecision and hunger. The moral: not to act is an action nonetheless. One must choose, even if that choice is arbitrary. Even if you have to leave it to chance. As Dr. Inwit did when he flipped the coin to see who would read first.

I start flipping through the pages of my travel guide at random.

Page 91: Museum Mile — Metropolitan Museum of Art, Guggenheim, Whitney Museum, Jewish Museum

Page 64: West Village — Macdougal Street, Washington Square Park, NYU

Page 109: Harlem and Morningside Heights — 125th Street, Apollo Theater, Columbia University, Cathedral of St. John the Divine

Page 37: Twin Towers — Windows on the World restaurant, Top of the World observation deck. Says here that on a clear day you can see the curvature of the earth. The legendary photograph of Philippe Petit on his tightrope. *Take train to: Cortlandt Street, Fulton Street, Chambers Street, Park Place, World Trade Center.* No direct lines from Delancey station, though. Five hours to kill. How long would it take to walk?

From one hundred and ten storeys up, the vault of the heavens loses some of its grandeur as a metaphor. It now appears no farther than the vaulted ceilings of actual cathedrals. The scatter of white clouds is now no more remote than the capitals that separate the columns from the ribs. The clouds lack the serenity and indifference they seem to possess when you view them from the ground. They appear just as confused as we are. Less unfettered than unmoored, they have no better idea of where to go or how to get there than we do.

The Stoics, I read in one of Dr. Inwit's books, used to recommend imagining how the world would appear from the perspective of the heavens. From that vantage, they thought, all human problems and anxieties would be seen as they really are. Minimal. Unimportant. Easily forgotten. Needlessly suf-fered. Dr. Inwit calls this spiritual exercise *The View From Nowhere*. Aside from the windows of an aeroplane, this must be as close to a literal view from nowhere as a person can get. Ironic, then, that it should be found directly above Manhattan, New York, USA. The very heart of somewhere.

Buffeted by the wind, I walk to the edge of the deck. I thread my fingers through the netting, the suicide prevention netting, and look down. At the roofs and buildings. At their aerials, spires, water towers. At all the ant pedestrians and all the vehicular beetles. At their frantic scurrying in all directions on the street below.

There is a flaw in the exercise, I think. Something neglected in its design. When I look down I do experience my problems as the Stoics said I would. But when I look out I'm only reminded of them. When I look out I see: the curvature of the earth. A faint, almost clear arc in the field of blue. Like a scar from a knife that long ago sliced open the tissue of the firmament.

At an Internet caf. on Water Street, I buy a half hour, find myself a terminal in the corner to see if Claire has written to me yet.

FROM: clairecaldwell@st-annes.ox.ac.uk
TO: owenwhiting@pmb.ox.ac.uk
SUBJECT: Re: "Arrived Safe and Sound"

I can't tell you how relieved I was to see your name in my inbox this morning. I was so worried that something had happened to you. I went through all the possibilities. It's fine that you hadn't anything to say. I completely understand. It's getting harder and harder to find words for what is happening to us these days. All you needed to tell me was what you told me, that you were all right and that you loved me.

And to that I respond: I love you. But I can't pretend I'm fine or that things are fine. Things are worse. I'm no longer in Greenwich. The only way to put this is to simply tell you what's happened. Tori has been hospitalised. I found her in the tub this morning with all her clothes on, unconscious, next to an empty bottle of her mother's sleeping pills. We rushed her to the emergency room to have her stomach pumped. She survived, thank God, but now she's been relocated to Bethlehem Hospital where she's under observation. I considered not telling you this, but it would be better that you know, rather than discovering it when you get back.

I don't know when she'll be let out, but I plan to visit her as soon as I'm allowed. It probably won't be until you're back home. If you are feeling up to it we can go together. It won't be easy, but we need to stand by each other and support one another. God, that seems like ages from now, even though it's only a few days away. It seems anything can happen between now and then. I'm praying — yes, literally praying — that nothing does. What I wouldn't do for a week of nothing happening. Keep writing to me, short notes if you must, just so I know not to worry about you. (Not that I won't anyway.)

All my love,
C

The letters on the screen begin to blur. Alone. I've left Claire there alone. To deal with the mess I've made. With the repercussions of my actions. Of my failures to act. I picture Tori's body in the white tub. Her limp arm dangling over the side. The empty orange bottle. Claire screaming when she opens the door.

A scream. Long, loud, and violent. Sound waves rippling across the Atlantic. Into my ears. Did Zach's body make ripples when it slid down the bank, into the river? If so, I didn't see them. By that point, I was already fleeing the scene, trying to cross Port Meadow as fast as I could to get to the safety of Claire's door. But they are becoming visible now. Now I can see them everywhere. Zach's death is a virus. A contagion. His madness is infecting everything he touched. Moving outward. One ripple at a time.

**MALE FRIENDSHIP.— The shortest distance be-
tween the hearts of two men is the body of a woman.**

Many hours and several bars later, we were stumbling through
the middle of Mitte when Zach asked me if I'd ever been
with a whore. At first, I wasn't sure I'd heard him rightly.
"You know. A prostitute, a hooker, a sex worker, a painted
lady, a streetwalker, a working girl, a woman of the night."
    Within a few steps I saw the reason for his abrupt shift in
subject. With his perfect vision — he called it his *fighter pilot
vision* — he could see distant things clearly, things that, behind
my glasses, I only perceived as indistinct smudges. Up ahead,
dotting Oranienburger Straße, staggered at a distance of a few
metres each, were women. Standing. Waiting. Serving.
    "Me neither," he continued when I said nothing. "And
I don't think I want to die without knowing what it's like
to pay for sex. Maybe it's thrilling, Maybe it's depressing.
Maybe it's just totally unremarkable. But it would be too bad
never to find out. I'm just drunk enough to want to. What do
you think?"
    "I think you're taking the piss." To show him I meant it, I
laughed a little. A forced laugh, awkward and uneasy.
    "I assure you I'm not. Are you in?"
    From the way he looked at me I could tell his question
was purely rhetorical. The first objection that came to mind
was: what would Claire think? — and Tori? But no sooner
had it come than it was followed by what would be his
obvious rebuttal. To have a thought about it, they'd have to

123

know about it, and so they'd think nothing, since we would never tell them. Zach was always asking me if I was in for something, if I was up for something, if I was down for something. And I was always indecisive, always dragging my feet, before I eventually went along with his plans. Considering how generous he always was with me and how he went out of his way to include me in everything he did, it was bound to try his patience at some point. After all, if it weren't for him, I'd never have met Claire in the first place; I'd be back in my rooms in Oxford, alone, reading.

"How does it work?" I asked.

"No idea!" he confessed. "We ask one of them what's on the menu? Ha!" He spoke quickly and animatedly, incapable of hiding his excitement that I'd agreed to do this with him. "Tell you what. Run down to that club on the bottom floor of Tacheles and get us a pair of condoms from the machine in the bathroom. Just in case she doesn't provide them herself. While you're doing that I'll find out how much it costs. Any special requests?"

"No. I trust your taste."

At the club I bought the two condoms and stopped for a fortifier at the bar. I wasn't going to do what I was about to do without another drink. If Zach wondered why I'd taken so long, I'd tell him that there was a queue. A metal band was playing the club. The guitarist and the bass player had their Marshall stacks turned up too loud for the tiny room, so I had to shout *"Ein Jameson's, bitte!"* three times before I was understood.

The glass appeared and I drank the gold liquid in a single swallow, slamming it down on the counter. I sneered at myself for making such a contrived gesture. I felt then, as I'd felt so often since I met Zach, that I was reenacting a scene, stepping into a fantasy of life rather than actually living. Granted, for me this represented a marginal increase in spontaneity, but it was still one degree removed from spontaneity proper. I had tried to live *through* books — Zach was showing me what it would be like to live *in* one. That was where he got that look from, that calm, unflappable expression he wore even when his face also bore the marks of some other emotion, like enthusiasm or melancholy. It was the expression of a seasoned spectator for whom nothing, not even the radically novel, is unforeseeable or unexpected. I saw him genuinely surprised only once — exactly once. Quite possibly it was the first time as well. The first and last time.

Zach was waiting for me. He pointed over the road, at a figure leaning against a streetlamp that illuminated the ornate Moorish fa.ade of an imposing, onion-domed building.

"See that girl over there. That's Nadya — or so she says. That's our girl. Speaks pretty decent English actually. I've already negotiated the program with her. Turns out you pay by the time and not by the act. Double for two of course. And not unreasonable rates. I mean, I *assume* we're being overcharged. But to pay anything else? That would *actually* be criminal."

Nadya wore the same uniform as the other prostitutes on Oranienburger Straße: knee-high platform boots, miniskirt, long faux-fur-collared coat, black plastic corset, hip pack. She had a round face and dark, expressionless eyes. Her black hair was set back in a bun. Her broad shoulders, large breasts, and solid legs suggested peasant stock to me. She must have come to Berlin from some mudsunk village in Eastern Europe. Romania. Ukraine. Poland, perhaps. I've never been a good judge of age, but I reckoned Nadya to have been anywhere from five to fifteen years older than we were. Whatever the number really was, it was obvious from her eyes that she was no longer young, and probably never had had the chance to be.

We followed her up a few fluorescent-lit flights in a concrete block of flats located so close to the course the Wall had once taken that it could have only been the former lodgings of the most loyal functionaries and servile bureaucrats of the GDR. Now it was a brothel, with many cunning passages, many contrived corridors. On the jaundiced walls above the metal banisters were portrait-sized discolorations and angry-looking slogans in black spray paint. My stomach was roiling with booze and nerves and the increasing certainty that what we were about to do was wrong.

In the room, Nadya hung up her coat and turned on an old lamp that revealed a quiltless, pillow-free bed. In one corner were two wooden chairs and a table, with a clean ashtray, a jug of water, and a small stack of plastic cups. In the other, a coal stove. The place reminded me of a Travelodge. Its shabbiness didn't seem to dampen Zach's spirits, though. Quite the contrary. This slumming was blatantly turning him on. Whilst Nadya counted the money he had given her in the wardrobe toilet, he took hold of the two chairs and positioned them side by side facing the bed.

"Well," I said, wondering what he was doing with the chairs. "Shall I wait outside, then?"

He looked at me, genuinely perplexed. "What do you mean?"

"You'd like *me* to go first? I'd rather not go—"

"No, we're going to do this at the same time."

"What! At the same time! You didn't tell me that we—"

"Must have slipped my mind," he said crossly. He didn't approve of my sudden vacillation, which he must have taken as a sign that I was bottling out. "Look. I don't just want to fuck some whore. It's not even *about* fucking the whore. It's about fucking the whore *together*. It's about us. Doing this. Together. Don't you understand?" His eyes flitted back and forth, searching my face for some sign that, yes, I understood. "Besides, it's what I've paid for. If you don't like it, you can renegotiate the terms with her yourself."

At that moment Nadya returned. Zach and I exchanged a tense glance. When I said nothing and remained in the room, he patted the edge of the bed, signalling that she should come and sit. "Will you do me a favor?" he said to her, pointing to the top of his head. "Let your hair down." She pulled the

126

hairgrips out of the bun and shook her head back and forth, letting the dark curls fall to her bare shoulders. When we were seated in the chairs in front of her, he put his hands together like a penitent in prayer, slowly opening his fingers to indicate that this was what she was to do with her legs.

"Very good," he told her. "Now the panties. Slowly."

"Panteez?"

"Yes, off." He put his hands to his belt and pantomimed knickers. "Slowwwwly." When she pulled the red-and-black twist of fabric to the top of her boots he said *Stop!* and made upside-down quotation marks with the fingers of his right hand. She started to play with herself. "Now both hands. That's right. Both hands."

He lit a cigarette and examined her with a cold expression. After a few drags, he stamped it out in the ashtray. He stood up and began to unbutton his shirt. I followed, refraining as best as I could from looking at his unclothed body. Nadya stopped masturbating and slid her knickers fully off, careful not to let them catch on her tall heels. On her knees, she unbuckled our belts, using one hand for his and one hand for mine. It was then, as she began sucking Zach off, that I looked at him. He was concentrating on her mouth, oblivious to me. In the garish light of the room, his immaculate torso — defined without being muscular, slim without being gaunt — gave off a delicate, blue-tinged glow. Unlike mine, his body was perfectly hairless, save for the dark tufts beneath his arms, and the one in which Nadya's nose was now buried. The long lashes of his half-open eyes began to flicker; his lips separated slightly. He lifted his hand to his face, running his fingers through his fringe. As he did, I noticed the two thick lines, paler than his pale skin, crossing his bicep. I blinked. I had been staring. Zach's jaw was clenched. He exhaled sharply through his nose and tapped the back of her head to let her know that it was time to switch.

My trousers had collected around my ankles. Whilst I fumbled with the condom, Nadya took them off, the way a mother would undress a child. She lay me on the bed with a gentle authority, straddled me, and began to move back and forth. Her breasts, which pendulated closer and closer to my face, gave off the faint smell of powder and milk. Zach grabbed the cheeks of her arse, spread them, gobbed, and thrusted. Nadya didn't even look back at him. She stared indifferently at the blank wall above my head. Zach's eyes were fully closed, his mind elsewhere, evidently recreating some private fantasy. Mine were still fixed on his arm. The three of us rocked in an awkward rhythm for what seemed like an eternity, though it couldn't have been more than a few seconds before I came and slipped out. My cheeks were warm and, in all likelihood, red.

We reshuffled. I got up, stripped the condom off, threw it into the bin, and began to dress again, with no comment from Zach, who had taken my place on the mattress. I sat in one of the chairs and smoked the remainder of Zach's crooked cigarette waiting with mounting unease for them to finish up.

They were now looking straight into each other's eyes, with what seemed to me like intense mutual contempt. Their bodies were at that moment disgusting to me. Two sordid pumping pistons of meat. How, I wondered, could anyone find this activity meaningful, let alone beautiful? Nadya started to scream and moan, not out of any pleasure Zach was causing her, but in the histrionic manner that would be called for by the director of a skin flick. He found the noises she was making absurd, hilariously so, but his sardonic burst of laughter was brought to a sudden halt when she slapped him hard across the face. I shot up from my chair. Zach looked stunned for a second. Then he began to laugh again, louder and crueller than before.

She rose from the bed and informed us that our time was up. I felt a surge of compassion for her, followed shortly thereafter by a stab of concern for what would happen if she reached for her mobile and rang her pimp. I lunged toward the bed and grabbed Zach by the arm. He shot me a dazed and hostile look, as if he had no idea who I was or why I was touching him. Then his eyes widened and a grin crawled across his face.

No longer naked, Nadya was searching her hip pack. The mobile appeared, just as I feared. Whilst she touched the buttons with her curved red thumbnail, I threw Zach's clothes on his lap and shouted, "We need to bugger off. Now. Now! Do you understand me?"

I had to push him out the door and down the stairs, holding him so he wouldn't trip as he pulled on his trousers and buckled his belt. As soon as we were outside, my hand flew up, catching the attention of a beige taxi. Zach slumped into the passenger seat and leant his head against the window. His shirt was still open and one of the points of his collar jutted up to his cheek. Oblivious to the danger he had put us in, he looked inordinately pleased with himself. I gave the driver the address of our flat and looked through the black window. Nadya was conferring with a blur whose basic features — white male, shaved head, yellow teeth, leather jacket, brass knuckles — I could only imagine. What I saw clearly enough was that she was pointing in our direction. "*Fahren Sie schnell, bitte!*" I shouted at the front seat, making use of one of the few German phrases I knew. The driver accelerated through the light and we turned the corner. I took another look through the back window and heard Zach, who must have been watching me in the rearview mirror, say, "Jesus, Owen. Relax. No one's following us."

GENIUS.— Genius is the ability to know when to take a metaphor literally and when to take the literal metaphorically.

At the Foederns', Bernard gives my hand the same vigorous pump with which he'd taken his leave of me, first in Berlin, then in Oxford a week ago. I'd spoken with him the day I brought the note to Richard at the Porter's Lodge. And when the inquest was complete and the death had been officially ruled a suicide, I helped him clean out Zach's rooms.

Barring the typewriter and the box of cartridges, which remained in the custody of the police, the room was just as he'd left it: an utter shambles. His bed was unmade. Three ashtrays, filled to the brim, made the room reek of stale smoke. Suits and shirts were left in piles on the floor, some ripped, some stained with wine or ink. His wood-handled umbrella was open and overturned in a corner. A chess problem was halted in progress on the travel set on his desk. The rubbish bin overflowed with sweet wrappers, dried-out tea bags, aluminium cans, crumpled up papers, empty pens, used condoms, and the blue packets of the brand of French cigarettes he'd taught me to fancy. There were books stacked everywhere but on the beige metal shelves where they belonged. Instead, on them were several back issues of *Theory* and every *Big Issue* published since his arrival in September. Dotting the walls were the brown-and-red smudges of the flies and mosquitoes he had whacked with the magazines; they had been left there for months like severed heads impaled on the spikes of some mad prince's castle walls to serve as a warning to future invaders not to fly through his window.

From the disorderliness of the room, it would have been easy to make inferences about the extreme mental agitation of the occupant. But this would have been a case of *ex post facto* reasoning. In truth, the room was always that filthy. I thought of the scout Zach dismissed and hoped Richard wouldn't report her for any dereliction of duty.

The temptations of retrospection were nonetheless difficult not to yield to. Every object Bernard and I buried in the two black suitcases he had bought earlier that morning was saturated with prefiguration. Specially the books. *The Sorrows of Young Werther* and *The Blind Owl. Anna Karenina* and *The Possessed. Madame Bovary* and *Mrs. Dalloway. The Sound and the Fury.* Works by Seneca and Petronius. By Kleist and Thomas Bernhard. By Chikamatsu and Mishima. The collected poems of Crane, Plath, and Berryman. The essays of Montaigne, Hume, and Schopenhauer. *The Myth of Sisyphus* and *The Space of Literature*. His tattered copy of *The Zero and the One* and the copy of the *Phaedo* that was missing its title page. Research, I couldn't help but think. It was all research. For his father's sake, I'm glad he didn't trifle with Durkheim, whose famous study of suicide has its subject printed in big letters on the spine.

Distraught, Bernard offered them all to me, the books and the clothes, anything I wished, but I declined, saying it was best to wait until more time had passed in case there was something here he — or Mrs. Foedern or Vera — would regret parting with later. When he absolutely insisted I take something, I immediately went for *The Zero and the One*. I wanted to search it for clues he might have scribbled in the margins or for insights hidden in the passages he had underlined.

Now that I am standing in his kitchen, Bernard is offering me something else: a tumbler containing two fingers of scotch.

He motions for me to join him on the sofa. I take a coaster from the stack on the coffee table with the chess set and put the glass on it. To make conversation, I ask if it was he who taught Zach how to play.

When he was very young, he answers. But only the basics. Pretty soon I had to send him over to the Manhattan Chess Club where he would be with players of his own caliber. It was getting a little embarrassing, being beaten by a nine-year-old.

Yes, I say, with good humour. We also stopped playing after a few games when it became clear I'd never win.

His teacher told me he could see as many as ten moves ahead.

Ten moves ahead: in chess, a way to win; in life, a way to lose. Not yet into the midgame of his life, Zach had scanned the pieces, toppled his king to the board, and extended a hand to the cold phalanges of his opponent. Checkmated by Death. As it was with him, so too will it be with us. What prevented me from following him, then? Is it that I don't confuse metaphors for life with life itself? Or that I just can't see ten moves ahead? Zach thought there was more dignity in conceding defeat than there was in playing out the moves that would lead to the inevitable outcome, the only possible outcome. What if what I lacked was not his vision, but his courage?

Rebecca and Vera have just come up in the lift. I shake Rebecca's hand and go to do the same with Vera, but like Katie before her, she bypasses my hand and kisses me on the cheek. She wears jeans and a t shirt, both black; in place of the mourning ribbon, she has kept on the string of pearls.

Paper plates are distributed round the dining room table. The cartons of noodles, dumplings, vegetables, and rice are passed from hand to hand, followed by soft drinks. We each rip off a paper towel from the roll. The Foederns unsheathe their chopsticks, rubbing them together to clear away splinters, whereas I transfer the food to my plate with the fork Vera brought me from the kitchen, as she wondered aloud how a person could have got so far in life without having mastered the use of chopsticks.

The disposable dishware and the red and grey aluminium cans look out of place on the design-store placemats and coasters Rebecca has lain out on the thick glass tabletop. Not that any of us proves particularly keen on eating. The three pairs of chopsticks and the lone fork only make it from plate to mouth at long intervals. The plates are going to soak through with sauce before any of us contemplates a second helping. Next to me, Vera is merely pushing the noodles round her plate. Her cheekbones look swollen, her grey-tinted skin drawn. Her lips are pale and dry. Like me, she probably hasn't finished a meal in a week.

The conversation wanders and all too deliberately avoids mention of the person whose chair I can't help but feel I'm sitting in. At first, there is only idle talk. Rebecca halfheartedly volunteers an observation about the weather (improving, in her opinion) before appraising us of goings-on at her gallery (the opening of a group show of new painters was less than a month away) where she'd stopped in for an hour, on her way to the Chinese restaurant.

Then it is Bernard's turn. Today he rang Moscow to tender his resignation to someone he calls Ilya, the director, I gather, of the film he was producing, the one whose name he was so careful not to mention in Berlin. It's impossible not to notice the change in him. How his eyes, once tensed like a cat on the point of pouncing, are now as stupefied as its unsuspecting prey; how his speech, once delivered in quick bursts, now trails off at the end of sentences, as if he saw no point in going on to the next one. Even the shape of his face seems to have lost definition now that he is no longer troubling to contain the growth of ashen stubble on his cheeks and chin and neck.

I colour when Rebecca asks Vera about her session with her psychiatrist. But Vera answers without hesitation. What

Dr. Stein and I discussed today was the difference between mourning and melancholia, she tells the table. Mourning is a perfectly normal and healthy response to loss. But it can easily turn into melancholia, a pathological introjection of guilt and anger. Unlike mourning, melancholia has long-term effects on mental health, and that's why Dr. Stein thinks it's important for me to actively work through my grief in our sessions together.

Her response couldn't have been more different than mine when I was sent to counselling. With the NHS psychiatrist, I was taciturn and uncooperative, treating our session as an interrogation to survive rather than as an opportunity to heal. When I phoned my parents to tell them that my friend had been killed in an accident (that's the word I used, *accident*) and that I'd be spending nearly all the money I'd saved that year to fly to the funeral in New York, I certainly did not mention that the college had all but forced me to see a therapist. Just imagining my father's expression were I to say, *My mate killed himself and I've been to see a shrink, makes me cringe.*

It's difficult to picture Bernard on the couch, going on about his feelings. Though as he listens approvingly to his daughter, it seems possible that they all have therapists. Perhaps in the Foedern family, therapy was the sort of thing one simply did— on the weekend, after tennis. Everyone was seeing a therapist, it seemed. Vera and me. And now Tori as well.

Did Zach? Can't imagine him approving of it, given the bent of his personal philosophy. I know he saw something romantic, even heroic, in mental illness. He regarded psychiatry as a *coercive attempt to homogenize unique ways of thinking and being.* Above all, he frowned on the new reliance on pharmaceuticals, for their use implied that the mind was just an *organic machine* that could be *predictably manipulated* with the proper chemical inputs. But if he disapproved of psychiatry, mightn't it have come from experience?

I lay down my fork on what will remain an uneaten bed of noodles and take the fortune cookie Rebecca passes me. I crack it open, leaving the peach-coloured shards on the paper plate. We each take a turn reading our fortune aloud.

Thorough preparation makes its own luck, Rebecca begins.

Then Bernard: *The only thing we know for sure about future developments is that they will develop.*

A great mystery will be revealed to you, says Vera.

I read: *Faithless is he who quits when the road darkens.*

Afterwards, there is a moment of silence. But it's not long before it's my turn to talk. It's not long before the question I've been expecting, the question I was invited to answer, is finally asked. Dropping her mostly full paper plate into the bin in the kitchen, Rebecca says, as though the thought has just occurred to her: Tell me, Owen, how did you meet our son?

I didn't tell them everything, obviously. Not about my feelings of loneliness during the term before I met him. Nor about the black eye he got at The Cowley Arms. Victoria or Claire. His experiments in petty theft. How much we drank or the drugs we did. The whore we fucked. I didn't tell them, it goes without saying, about our pact. My aim was to cast Zach in a flattering light rather than to illuminate his character. And parental pride, I think, was satisfied by my account. Bernard and Rebecca visibly swelled at the idealised portrait that resulted when I brushed over certain truths, left others vague, and subtracted yet others in their entirety from the composition.

Only Vera sensed my omissions and was not content to let them remain. Unlike Rebecca, who interrupted me from time to time with anecdotes that drew continuities between the boy I described and the one she raised, Vera listened to my stories with raised eyebrows. After I recited Zach's speech about voting, for example, she said *she happened to know* he filled out an absentee ballot and *voted for Gore* and was as *outraged* and *disgusted* by the result of the election as everybody else was. I could tell she was waiting until we were on our own so she could question me further. So she could hear the parts of the story I wasn't willing to speak of in front of her parents.

On our way out the door, Rebecca brings her a small envelope, containing, I gather from their hushed conversation, tickets to some kind of performance. Daddy and I aren't in the mood to go tomorrow night, she tells her daughter, but it's the last performance of the season and it would be a shame to let the tickets go to waste. Besides, it couldn't hurt. Maybe it will help you two take your mind off things.

But I'm not in the mood to go either! Vera protests.

Rebecca turns to me. Do you like the opera, Owen?

Vera casts a sharp glance in my direction. Once again I've found myself the arbiter in a disagreement between her and her mother. Once again, I'm not sure with whom it would be more polite to side. Where my loyalties are meant to lie.

I don't know. I've never been to the opera, I answer her, as tentatively as possible. Mum often listened to Radio 3, so in my house there was always a Bach cantata or a Beethoven symphony decorously competing with whichever Sex Pistols or Disorder track was blasting from my stereo upstairs. But I could count the performances of classical music I'd seen on one hand. They were all at the Sheldonian, all during Michaelmas Term, when I could think of nothing better to do after a day of studying than to find new ways to improve myself. Honestly, it would be a treat to see what the opera was like.

Would you like to go? Vera asks.

I shrug, doing my best to feign indifference. Why not?

We say our goodbyes and step into the lift. On our way down I ask Vera which opera we'll be seeing tomorrow evening.

You know, I didn't even think to ask, she says, opening the envelope. Ahhh. Now I understand.

Understand what?

Why they didn't want to go. She flips one of the tickets between her thumb and forefinger so I can read what is printed on the other side: Richard Wagner, *Die Walküre*.

I nod silently.

Vera directs our taxi to an address on Rivington Street and sits in silence until it comes time for us to pay the fare. None of the tenderness from her note this morning is apparent in her expression or her posture, but it's unclear whether her change in mood is to do with me, whether it's about something I said at dinner, the opera tickets, or something else entirely. When she wants me to know she'll tell me. Until then, I'll have to wait. Unless she never wants to tell me, I think, my lips tightening.

I follow her down a set of stairs, through an unmarked door covered in band stickers, into a cellar bar. The bearded barman doesn't acknowledge us as we enter. In the back, two tall men in skinny jeans and t shirts, cues in hand, are examining the distribution of billiard balls on a green table illuminated by a sickly lamp that hangs from the low ceiling. The only other customer is an old man, who stacks silver cans of beer on the corner table where he sits, walling himself in.

As soon as we are seated with our drinks, she asks: Why did he do it, Owen?

I'm taken aback. I expected the question, but neither so soon nor so directly posed. It certainly shows in the way I mumble my way through my answer, my lips moving like a glass that has been knocked over, and which all watch, paralysed, as it totters in slow motion, unsure if it will right itself or fall and break.

Maybe it was just... just as he said in his note —

I haven't read his note. Daddy wouldn't let me see it. All I know is that he wrote it on some *typewriter*.

Well... in it... in his note... he said that... suicide... was a principled act of defiance... against the natural imperative of self-preservation. A defence of the freedom of the will against our servitude to causality. An inability to ignore the fact that, percentage-wise, the difference between dying at twenty-one and dying at one hundred is nil when measured against the billions of years that passed before his life began and the billions of years that would pass when it was over.

She straightens visibly, her shoulders pinned back, as she leans away from the table. She seems offended to discover what was written in his note. Offended, but at the same time relieved.

And you believe that? You think that's why he killed himself?

I mean, if it were me. I swallowed hard. If *I* were going to write a suicide note, I wouldn't trifle with things I didn't actually believe.

But it's nonsense! No one kills himself for abstract principles like that. Not even my brother. Principles are things to live for, not reasons to die. And *why not* at one hundred rather than twenty-one? By his own lights what difference would it make? I just don't understand. How do you sit down and write out all the reasons that there is no reason to live? On a typewriter for God's sake! I mean, did he write a rough draft and edit it for spelling and grammar too?

Vera looks at me expectantly, waiting for me to answer. In fact, he did write a rough draft. Or rather, we wrote it together. Taking turns at the typewriter. Just as we had done when we wrote the sonnet in Berlin. And he *did* edit it. For spelling at least. There were to be no extraneous English *u*'s in his note to me, nor any American *zeds* in my note to him. Vera's intuition is chilling. I take a cigarette from the open packet on the table and give her the answer I rehearsed last night with Katie. I try to remember whether it was he or I who actually added to the note the argument I just recited to Vera. Me, I think. Though in all fairness I was only regurgitating *his* ideas.

He talked of suicide quite often, I tell her. In the very same terms he wrote in his letter, but I always thought he was only being theoretical. I even admired him for it. For his willingness to consider anything. But I never thought, I never thought he was being serious.

To entertain an idea without endorsing it. The mark of an educated man. Thus spake the Stagirite. What about entertaining *and* endorsing? Bravery or folly? Can one know except in retrospect? Discuss. You have ninety minutes. Vera leans forward abruptly, her elbows on the table, her hands thrown in the air in a gesture of exasperated incredulity. *I know!* she exclaims. The whole thing was just so *theatrical*, wasn't it? Such a *production*. Shooting himself in the chest like that. In white tie, with a flower in the buttonhole of his tuxedo. Dressed for a wedding. A wedding! Near some rocks in the forest. It doesn't make any sense. If it wasn't my brother, the person I love more than anyone else in the world, if I was just reading about the story in a newspaper, I'd have called the whole thing mannered. Baroque even. I might have laughed, awful as that sounds.

I frown. Her reaction to the rationale for and the so called theatrics of her brother's death is not what I expected. That she was furious with him went without saying. Fury must be a gross understatement for what she feels. Perhaps she was even resentful that his suicide note, which should have gone to her or her parents, had been addressed to me. She didn't know he'd left one of her pearls in the envelope after all. I thought she might nevertheless show *some* sympathy for what he was trying to do and the way he had done it. Instead she was openly dismissive of both. If twins, as is sometimes said, are connected by an invisible string, it was becoming clear to me that, whilst he lived, the connexion between Zach and Vera was like a balloon string: Zach's end was tied to the rising rubber oval, whereas Vera's was in the little fist whose firm grip was the only thing preventing the balloon from floating off into the clouds where it would inevitably pop.

I swirl the melting ice round the bottom of my glass. Why do *you* think he did it, then?

139

I think he did it because he was disappointed in love, she tells me, sliding the pearls along the necklace.

I raise my eyes. Level my gaze at her. There is no irony in the tone of her voice. Nor does her expression underline the statement in any way, in order to emphasise its significance. She is not giving me what Russian novelists call a *meaningful look*. Everything about what she says and the way she says it suggests that she is making a candid statement about what she genuinely believes. But that? Could she possibly believe *that*?

Vera, with all due respect... I know you understand your brother far better than I do. You think I admire him uncritically, and even idolise him too much — no, it's fine, you needn't deny it — but what you have just said cannot possibly be true. Whenever he spoke to me about suicide, he always said it had to be *disinterested* — not motivated by any emotion whatsoever. Not by despair. Or fear. Or the desire to escape from suffering — physical *or* emotional. And when he gave an example of emotional suffering, it was always *having a broken heart*. It's probably a good idea not to treat his suicide note as holy writ, but what he wrote there can't be discounted either. And the only time the word *love* appears is to anticipate one of the reasons people will *misunderstand* his death. Besides, in the time I knew him at least, he wasn't at all disappointed in love. Sure, things weren't always perfect between him and Tori. But on the whole they were going very well, right up to the day of his —

What? she hisses. He never told me about any *Tori*.

I'm as shocked to learn that Vera doesn't know who Tori is as she is to find out about her. If Zach had told her about me, wouldn't he also have mentioned her? I think of Vera's inbox. The letters on her desk. There had been none from Zach since *December*. Was it possible that he'd spoken to her of me before we'd ever met?

Victoria Harwood, I say, my voice faltering. Vera is glaring at me, waiting expectantly for me to clarify what I had said.

She and Zach. Went on a few. Were in a. Were seeing each other. A bit.

Listen. Vera collects herself and begins to stand up. I've just noticed our drinks are empty. You're going to get the next round. And when I come back you can tell me all about Zach and this, this *girl*. Okay? Okay. I'll have the same thing as last time.

Leaning on their cues, the billiard players pause to watch her as she passes. The door to the toilet closes behind her and they turn back to their game. I don't even ask her to remind me what she had last time. Haven't got to. She drinks Plymouth martinis: dirty, dry, and stirred.

ET IN ARCADIA EGO.— It's a terrible thing, at any age, to be able to point to some period of your past and say, *Those were the best days of my life*. For it means that when you divide what is to come by what has already been, the remainder will be the same decimal repeating repeating repeating to infinity. Happy are those who realise this in the final seconds before the completion of a long life. Happier still are those to whom it never occurs. But how few can say this of themselves! For everyone else, those who realise it too soon, whether they are in the first act of their lives or the final one, there are only different methods of tending to one's wounds. Some dedicate what remains of their lives to regaining the lost time. Others consecrate themselves as shrines to its memory. Still others draw a line over the repeating decimal and put themselves to sleep. Happiness, when ill timed, can maim a life just as thoroughly as sorrow.

Only later, replaying the incident again and again in my memory, did I understand that the white lines on his arms were *scars* — and that they were too straight to have got there by accident. But I never plucked up the courage to ask him about them. Though our eyes would sometimes meet and share what seemed to me a silent complicity, furtive looks that could have only alluded to a single source, Zach and I would never again speak of that night.

The day after our return to Oxford was a clement aberration in the cruellest month: twenty-one degrees, a crisp blue sky, sunbeams visible through the clouds, a warm soft breeze, and not a single sign of precipitation on the horizon. No one could say how long this glorious preview of May's coming attractions would play before the rainy April regular feature overtook the screen of sky, so we decided to make the most of it and spend our day out of doors.

Tori filled a picnic basket, Claire bought Pimm's and champagne, and together we made our way down to the Magdalen Bridge Boathouse to show our American friend a classic Oxford afternoon. After I gave an (expurgated) account of our holiday in Berlin, we heard stories of what the girls had got up to in London. From the sound of things, they'd had a perfectly fine time without us. They spent it mostly in the company of Tori's friends, drinking and dancing just as we had. Claire persuaded Tori to accompany her to a performance of Sarah Kane's *Blasted* at the Royal Court Theatre. In exchange, she spent a few hours with her friend making phone calls and delivering leaflets for Labour. That day, Tori had pinned a white-and-red button that read THE WORK GOES ON to the summer dress she was wearing, the one she bought in Shoreditch on the day we went to the launch party.

All Oxford had come out to enjoy the fine weather. Cyclists sped by on their way to Port Meadow or the University Parks. Outside every restaurant people were queuing up, not minding having to wait before they were seated. The students who were not enjoying the day sunning on the quads of their colleges poured out of the arched wooden doorways, headed for any pub with a back garden. We strolled down the bustling High, hurrying only to pass the Porter's Lodge at Magdalen, so Zach and I wouldn't accidentally run into Dr. Inwit, who might have wondered why we were hiring punts rather than completing our revisions.

It took Zach and me a few minutes to learn how to properly navigate the boats. There were a number of comical false starts. I wedged our punt in the arches of Magdalen Bridge and Zach bumped the bow of another and almost went toppling into the water. But little by little we became accustomed to using the spruce poles as rudders and allowing them to simply slide through our hands as we touched off against the shallow riverbed.

Before long, we were making our way. Zach and Tori's punt took the lead as we floated by the Botanic Garden and down the eastern edge of Christ Church Meadow. Ours followed leisurely behind. At the bend where the Cherwell becomes the Isis, Tori pointed to a pair of willows shading the bank. "There," she said. "That looks like the perfect spot, doesn't it?" I moved my pole to the left of the till and let the bow drift until it touched ground. Zach and I pulled the punts ashore to prevent them from drifting. Then, like the belle .poque gentlemen we were pretending to be, we bent our wrists to offer our palms to assist the ladies up the bank.

From the picnic basket, Tori took a wool blanket to spread on the slope. Claire handed the two bottles of champagne to Zach and me. "Let's see if we can fire the corks across the river," he said, crumpling the gold foil into a ball and unscrewing the wire cage. The sound of popping was followed by a rush of fizz. Zach's cork almost made it to the other side. Mine made a graceful arc before it plopped in the river. We poured the champagne into the line of flutes Claire set up next to the blanket. She topped them off with a splash of Pimm's and garnished the cocktail with slices of cucumber and sprigs of mint.

We raised our glasses:

"Cheers!" "To love!" "To youth!" "To beauty!"

A second glass was poured and with it came a second round of toasts:

"To Claire!" "To Zach!" "To Tori!" "To Owen!"

It was midafternoon and it seemed like it would be forever. For a long time, no one spoke. I lay back, resting in Claire's lap, pleasantly drunk, and felt the champagne evaporating through the pores of my skin, as all the pink-gold bubbles I'd consumed returned to their homes in the sun. I heard: the sound of oars on the river, the flutter of birds, a breeze through the drooping willow leaves, the click of the wheel on Zach's lighter, his indrawn breath. But these were only soft exceptions that drew my attention to the gauzy density of the surrounding silence. I opened my eyes. Claire was looking at the large white tuft above our heads.

"What do you see?" she asked us.

Tori craned back her neck to look at the cloud. "I see a ship. With two masts. See? There's the hull and there's the keel and those are the billowing sails."

"A corsair's frigate prowling the Barbary Coast," Zach embroidered. He languorously tapped my arm with the back of his hand. "What about you?"

The cloud was beginning to change shape. The billowing sails Tori had identified were merging together and what was once the keel had slowly broken away to form a cloudlet of its own. The result was a large, oval-shaped mass that flared out at the top and culminated in a nub. To me, it looked like a custodian helmet. The cloud was God's bobby on the celestial beat, making its rounds, spying on us sinners here below.

When we reached Folly Bridge, it was the girls' turn to take up the spruce poles and steer us back to the boathouse. Leaning back against the cushion, I looked over at the other punt. In private, Claire and I gave a good deal of thought to the question of Zach and Tori. Sometimes it felt as though we pondered their relationship more than our own, which merited as little study as a Year 6 maths worksheet. But perhaps that was only how it seemed to us, I thought, letting my fingers skim the surface of the water. Perhaps, late at night, in the other bedroom of the flat, similar conversations were being had, with Claire and me as their subject.

To have a relationship with Zach, I told Claire, you either had to be content to yield him the spotlight — or be capable of stealing the show. Tori fell into the latter category. She attracted him by never being overly impressed by him, I hypothesised, by never confusing his theatricality for reality, and knowing, without ever having to be told, which of his statements to take seriously, which to let pass without comment, and which to lovingly ridicule. In public at least, their affection expressed itself as skirmishes of wit and verbal jousting, a merry war very different from the earnest more-things-in-heaven-and-earth conversations that resulted when he and I were the principal characters on stage.

Not that they hadn't any disagreements. Like Gregory Glass, Tori clearly did not share Zach's nostalgia for putatively superior bygone eras, or his contempt for the compromises entailed in political action. She believed that not only was the better the enemy of the good, but that providing the good, defined as concrete improvements to people's economic well-being, was the legitimate aim of a life's work. (She hoped, in fact, to enter the civil service one day.) Unlike Gregory, though, she didn't take Zach's disagreement personally. She deflected his criticisms with insouciant humour rather than attempting to volley them back with *ad hominem* rhetoric. "Where'd she learn to do that?" I once wondered aloud. Claire told me I'd understand as soon as I met her parents, next to whom Tori was apparently solemnity personified.

Claire agreed with my general assessment, but naturally, as Tori's friend, she took the view from over her shoulder. Therefore it was Zach's thick skin that impressed her. "Before we met," Claire told me, "Tori was seeing a DPhil student called Sam Finchley. Normally she wouldn't go in for such a dour, reedy bloke," but Sam was the first opportunity to present himself after her previous long-term relationship came to the conclusion of its protracted collapse. Sam, alas, was quick to wither under what he perceived to be Tori's scorn. "I don't think either of them," Claire said, "could stand being in a relationship with a woman who was cleverer than they were."

That things were not perfect between them, however, was only made apparent to me a few weeks later, by the slamming of a door.

I was sitting at the kitchen table, book open, pencil in hand, trying to understand the difference between free and bound variables before my eleven o'clock logic lecture. With Zach and I no longer in the same tutorial, and Prelims looming for me in six weeks, Trinity Term had dispersed our group somewhat. Since our return from holiday, Claire had taken my place as our most diligent student. Always an early riser, she was already off at her tute, where she'd be presenting her analysis of a lesser-known work by the Gawain Poet. Tori had a free day. And Zach, who began the term by declaring that there was no point in going to lectures any more, was, I wrongly assumed, sleeping in.

My attention wandered. A serious discussion, I could hear, was taking place in the other room. The volume of their voices steadily increased from studied whisper to heated debate to shouting match. I put my pencil down, now fully intent on deciphering the indistinct words being spoken behind the door. Only their emotional register revealed itself clearly to me. Zach was cross. Tori, upset.

When the door opened suddenly I quickly lowered my eyes back to the book. This didn't fool Zach, who remarked, "You know, when you're listening in on someone's private conversation, the best thing to do is look up, not down. Because a person naturally looks up when he hears a door open. The fact that you're looking down at your book can only mean that you were eavesdropping, the very thing you were trying to hide by looking at your book. Sometimes I think I've taught you nothing." And then, as he left the flat, he slammed the door behind him.

My first instinct was to run after him. But Tori must have heard him speaking to me, and it wouldn't do for her to come into the kitchen needing someone to talk to and find herself alone in the flat, abandoned. I gently knocked on her bedroom door — that one Zach had cruelly left wide open. I stepped into her room, but before I could ask if everything was all right, she pointed a finger in the direction of the dining room and shrieked, "Out! Out! Out!"

I collected my books and ran out the door, following the path Zach would have likely taken back to college. I caught up with him on St. Giles', just as he was entering a pub. Short of breath, I asked, "What the bloody hell was that about?"

"She wants to go to something called Commems with me," he said petulantly.

I was relieved. As I ran to catch him, the thought crossed my mind their row had been caused by Zach's confession, in a moment of guilt and weakness, of what we'd done in Berlin.

"It sounds like a ridiculous way to spend an evening," he continued. "It costs nearly a hundred pounds a pop. It's Carnival themed for crying out loud!"

"Brazilian?"

"Venetian."

I looked at him with incomprehension. The Commemoration Ball was an Oxford tradition in which you drank and danced until sunrise dressed in white tie and wore, in this case I presume, commedia dell'arte masks. Ridiculous or not, it sounded like the very sort of evening on which Zach would normally be quite keen. As for the expense: I'd never known him to complain of it before. He'd been sponsoring my travel and my books and my drinks for several months now. What was another few hundred quid to go with Tori to a ball?

"You're going to lecture then?" I asked.

"I'm going into this pub here and I'm going to drink until I'm in a better mood. Then I'll see what I want to do about Tori."

Later, after the two reconciled, Claire told me the other side of the story. Their row, as he said, was about Commems, but as so often happens, from such small beginnings it had quickly expanded into more emotionally volatile territory. And this Zach had completely left out of his account.

As I had, Tori found his reasons suspect. She pressed him on them. The hidden cause was his imminent return back home at the end of the term. When Tori enquired into the future he envisioned for their relationship — would they remain together, do long distance, reunite in a year when both graduated? — he responded angrily. He hadn't given it the least bit of thought. Thinking about the future, he'd argued, only ruined his ability to enjoy their relationship in the present. After all, they'd only been together three months. How was he supposed to plan for a year from now?

Zach returned that evening to the Bevington Road to apologise. He had a bouquet of clover and thistle he'd picked himself in Port Meadow in his extended hand and Chaplinesque penitence all over his face. Tori stood in the doorway with her arms crossed and declared, through a defiant frown she was having trouble maintaining, that she could not be appeased by such a mawkish gesture.

Then he produced the two tickets.

Claire thought that this was a concession that amounted to victory for Tori. The tickets were an expression — an implicit one, granted — of his desire to remain with her after he left for New York. I thought otherwise, but kept my opinion to myself. It seemed to me that Zach had slyly concealed his postponement of the subsequent question by returning Tori's focus to the original point of contention. Looking back on it now, I can't help but think he ultimately decided to buy the tickets because, already, he knew he would not be attending that ball.

TRANSCENDENT VICES.— **If Darwin is correct, what ultimately distinguishes human beings from other organisms is not reason, language, religion, or tool-making, but chastity, sodomy, castration, and suicide.**

Rivington Street has gone from deserted to dense in the hour since we disappeared into the bar. Now we must navigate the cracked and crowded pavement back to her flat, a task Vera entrusts entirely to me. She leans her head on my shoulder and threads her arms through mine. Make a left at the corner, she says. I extend my hand to her waist and pull her hip to me. I lean my cheek on the crown of her black hair, and we take the unsteady steps together, with our four feet, back to her flat. We wade through a queue at a cashpoint. Step around a guitarist sitting on his amplifier, looking at his watch, waiting for the rest of the band to come. Walk past a couple obliviously snogging against a wall, on which a stencil of a large rat holding a paint roller has been spray-painted. Vera's steps echo irregularly on the pavement, sounding clearly above the loud music spilling out of the bars. Above the loud rows being conducted on the fire escapes above our heads. Above the car horns and the police sirens. Stanton, she says. Make a right.

At the door, she gives me her handbag to search for the keys. This makes me uncomfortable, but I do it anyway. A memory: Mum slapping the back of my five-year-old hand, saying, *Never go through a woman's handbag*, prying a sweet from my grasp. A rule I've adhered to unquestioningly, almost superstitiously, ever since. My fingers graze a paper notebook. A purse. Tubes of lipstick. A compact. Tampons. Loose change. The sharp edge of a jewel case. A CD player. A string of headphones. Then, finally, the metal ring with the keys on it.

Silver square key for the outside. Diamond-shaped bronze key for upstairs, Vera tells me, her eyes half-closed.

The lights in the flat are off. I make to turn to the sofa, wordlessly volunteering to sleep there. In case things have changed since last night. In case last night was an aberration. But she catches me by the tips of my fingers and leads me to the bedroom. Feebly, I begin to protest, I'm not sure this is a good — but she covers my mouth with her own.

We struggle to get out of our clothes. Ripping and pulling as much as we unbutton and unzip. I step out of my trousers and peel my socks off with my toes. Rather than yielding to my attempt to lay her on the bed, she holds me at arm's length, palm open on my bare chest. She turns round and crawls across the bed on her hands and knees. Where the bed meets the wall, she places her cheek to the sheets, intertwining her hands at the base of her neck. Like a schoolgirl taking cover during an air raid. Offering herself to me impersonally. Almost with resignation. The way Nadya offered herself to Zach. Not how I imagined it. But is it ever how you imagined it? I try to enter her, but she stops me, saying, Not there. Please. Don't ask me to explain. There's some lube in the dresser drawer. Yes. Now, slowly. Slowly.

I rest my chest on her back and clutch her breasts to stabilise myself as she begins to move her hips. Slick with sweat, my hands slip down her chest, my fingers meshed into the cogs of her ribcage. She grabs me by the scruff of the neck. Digs her nails in. Pushes herself against my pelvis. She breathes in sharply through her teeth, the sound a child makes when she skins her knee. A sharp cry ejects itself from her throat. Hard to say whether these sounds are indications

151

of pleasure or of pain. Whether they mean I should keep going or I should stop. She whispers unintelligibly into the sheets. As though she were praying into them. When she lets go of my neck, I straighten, holding on to her by the hips. The groove of her lower back is glistening with sweat. Hers. Mine. She is using me, I think, using me as an instrument of her suffering. Besides the afflicted cries and the mad whispering all I hear is the sound of the necklace, clicking like clockwork against her chest.

You know, she starts to say, when we are lying on our backs, catching our breath. You haven't...

I suddenly feel quite sober. Judging from the way her words slip from the corner of her mouth, I think I may be the only one. The portentousness of the pause that follows is unnerving. I slink out of bed to find the packet of cigarettes in my pocket. Some confession is coming, of that I'm sure. Words I've longed to hear. Words I'm afraid to hear. To prepare myself for them, I curl into the windowsill, letting the smoke from my lips plume into the humid night air.

You haven't said anything about the lines on my arm. And don't tell me you didn't notice them. I felt you running your hands over them last night.

Yes. I noticed them. Zach had them as well. On the same place. But on his other arm.

Did he tell you how they got there?

I shake my head. Is this something I really must know? Something I'm ready to know? Is it time for that?

I inhale deeply. Tell me.

Last summer, before Zach left for Oxford, was a terrible time for us both, she begins. And for me in particular. It's difficult to explain, but Zach and I are one person, not two. Very few people know what this is like. Even if they can understand it intellectually, they can't imagine what it feels like. You see, before this year, we'd only ever really been apart once before. One summer. When we were thirteen. Me in the city, Zach up at a summer camp near our aunt and uncle in New Hampshire. We wrote each other letters all summer, pages and pages in this secret code we invented, pages and pages about how unhappy we were to be apart. I told him to come home. And the only way he'd be allowed to come home, he figured, was to get kicked out for misbehaving. Mommy and Daddy began getting calls from the counselors about how Zach wouldn't participate in any of the activities. Including meals. Then, a few days later, they called to say that he'd punched another camper in the face while he was sleeping. That was the final straw. They were forced to send him home. Now, the thought that we'd be separated for a whole year caused us a great deal of anxiety. There were times when Zach said he didn't want to go, but Mommy and Daddy insisted. We weren't going to be able to go through our whole lives attached at the hip, after all. Dr. Stein thought it was a good idea too. Still, my anxiety started to get out of control. So she prescribed me medication for it. For Zach too. But he never took it. On principle. We've both been diagnosed with depersonalization disorders. Maybe this was a misdiagnosis, or maybe the dosage was too low, but for me, the medication never seemed to work. Have you ever had a dissociative episode? It's crippling. You feel like your mind is detached from your body. You feel like your thoughts have suddenly acquired bodies of their own, faces of their own, hands of their own. And they've all got these thought-hammers and thought-files and want nothing more to do than to break out of your skull. In a state like that — and it seems to last forever — it's impossible to summon up the will to do anything at all. The secret to overcoming this, Zach believed, was not medication, it was to remind your thoughts that they were only thoughts. And the only way to do *that* was through pain. Actual, physical pain. So when an attack would come on, he'd go to the freezer and get an ice cube and hold it until it melted and his hand went numb. We tried that every day for weeks, until we got used to it. We stopped feeling the pain and the ice no longer achieved its purpose. So we had to try... other things. The night before his departure, I was in the kitchen at our parents' house. My hands were wet and cold from the ice. I took one of the knives from the drawer and rolled up my sleeve, but I couldn't bring myself to do it, to cut myself. I brought the knife to Zach and asked him to do it for me. He didn't say anything, he didn't ask me what the hell I was doing, he understood immediately. Without a word, he took the blade and swiftly ran it across my arm. There was no blood at first. Just a white line. A slit. We watched as it opened, hypnotized. It felt like it was breathing. Like the gill of a fish. Then the blood started oozing out, thick and dark as oil. It barely hurt at first, it only stung a little, but the stinging was enough to bring me back to reality. You won't believe this, but getting cut was almost... pleasurable. I'd forgotten to bring a towel with me to clean up. Zach took off his shirt and wrapped it around the cut. Then he handed me the knife and said — no, whispered: *Now me. Do it to me.* I remember giving him a confused look. He wasn't feeling any anxiety at that moment. It was something else. A desire to share in my experience. To be marked by me, as he had marked me. He hadn't protested when I asked him, he hadn't judged me, so I felt guilty at the thought of refusing him. I took the knife. And ran the blade across his arm.

She stops for a long moment and says nothing more, reflecting, I imagine, on the enormity of her confession, which she must have made for the first time. But she looks relieved to have spoken. Will I ever feel such relief? Her moist, bloodshot eyes move back and forth. Begging me to comment. To say something. To say perhaps — *You're off your head the both of you.* Or else to say — *I understand, I completely understand.*

Instead, approaching the bed, I observe, or rather my mouth insinuates without quite receiving clearance from my brain, that her anxiety must have got so much worse this past week.

It's become unbearable, she admits. I've been alternating between fits of weeping and catatonic numbness. Dr. Stein's already increased my dosage. But the feeling just isn't going away...

In the fading echo of her words I think I hear a plea she cannot vocalise. I sit down next to her. Her eyes grow large. The question forming in her brain is pushing them out toward me. I reach for her arm, which yields to my grasp. Gently, I stroke the white lines, asking, with my thumb, whether I have understood her correctly. At the point of contact, our skin vibrates with an unspeakable, almost shameful desire.

Vera, I venture with a whisper. Do you need me to —

Yes. I need you to. There's one in the drawer to the left of the sink.

Without dressing, I walk slowly through the unlit living room into the kitchen and open the drawer to the left of the sink where she and Katie keep their cutlery.

MIDWIFE OR ABORTIONIST?— When Socrates calls the philosopher the midwife of truth in the *Theaetetus*, he does not seem to be aware of the full implications of his metaphor. Precisely because truth requires a midwife to be brought into the world, it is never enough for a judgement to actually be true for it to be taken as such. Only at his trial would Socrates realise, too late, that the message is invariably compromised by the messenger.

I was the first to arrive at the Queen's Lane Coffee House for our study session. There were two empty tables in the back corner. I pulled them together and covered the surface of the second with my books and notes, so it would appear taken, its owner having just stepped out to use the toilet or the telephone. I sat facing the windows that looked out onto the High. Whilst I waited for the others, I looked over the menu, though I already knew what I would order, because I ordered the same thing every time we went there. It was pointless to begin revising, because waiting made it difficult to concentrate: lifting my head every few moments to see if they were the ones coming through the door would be too distracting. The menu was only to keep myself — and the table — looking occupied.

I sensed a presence near the chair opposite mine and put the menu down, expecting to see a waitress. Instead it was Gregory Glass. He sat down, and before I could coldly inform him it was being saved for someone else, he said, "Don't worry. I won't be long."

The waitress, under the impression that this was the person I'd been waiting for, swooped down on us, pulled a pen from the tangled bun of her hair, flipped open a notepad with the brusqueness of a Fleet Street reporter, and said, "Something to drink then?" I ordered my tea and told her I'd be ordering food when the rest of *my* friends arrived. Much to my irritation, Gregory ordered a cup of coffee.

He waffled on about his tutors that term and about some of the people at Pembroke he considered, wrongly, our mutual acquaintances. I wondered what he could possibly be driving at. We had barely spoken a hundred words to each other the whole year and the time for casually sharing my table to engage in friendly chitchat had long since passed. I wished he would say what he had come to say, or leave me alone. It was imperative that he not be there when the others arrived.

"You and Zach Foedern are pretty tight, aren't you?"

Of course. He'd come to talk to me about Zach. Zach was the only thing Gregory and I had in common. He was the former friend and I the current one. What else could it have been? In answer to his question, I said nothing. I didn't even nod my head. In fact, it wasn't a proper question, since we both knew what the answer was. Rather it was one of those statements in an interrogative tone Gregory was so fond of making. It was a throat clearing, a way to announce the topic of conversation. I looked straight ahead, hoping to be as discouraging as possible. Whatever Gregory was so keen on telling me about Zach was certainly not something I was interested in hearing.

"You know he and I know each other from Columbia."

How would Zach deal with such an imposition? Probably he'd say something elegant, cutting. His words ambiguous, his meaning unmistakable. The waitress arrived. She placed Gregory's coffee in front of me and my cup of tea in front of him. Awkwardly, we swopped saucers. As he nattered on I looked out the window until something he said caught my attention.

"What did you just say?"

"About his sister? You know he has a twin sister, right?"

"Of course," I replied. I resented the implication that he knew something important about Zach that I didn't. "Vera."

"Ever met her? Strange girl. Beautiful. But definitely strange. Maybe even a little unwell if you know what I'm saying."

I said nothing.

"She lived in my suite freshman year. In a double. With another girl named — well, her name's not important. Zach had a single in a dorm across campus, but he was always over. The TV in the common area was basically theirs. They were always watching movies on it, always these foreign arty movies. And if you wanted to use the TV to watch a baseball game or a *Seinfeld* rerun, or if you asked them to turn it down, because you couldn't concentrate on your problem sets with all the shouting in Japanese or French or German or whatever, you'd get sneered at and ignored. Anyway. At some point during the middle of the first semester, Zach convinced Vera's roommate to switch rooms with him, something that just isn't done. In fact, I'm pretty sure coed dorms are against the rules, even if the people living in them are siblings. Rumor has it they bribed the RA and Vera's old roommate not to report it. Point is they were inseparable. I never saw the two of them apart. Never. Not in the library. Not in the dining hall. Not at parties. Not in the bars. Not even when they were walking between classes."

"And?"

"*And* I just thought it was kinda weird that Zach showed up by himself this year. I tried asking him about it, subtly of course, indirectly you know, but—"

"Listen, Gregory." My patience with this one-sided conversation had finally worn out. "What is it you're trying to tell me?"

"What I'm trying to tell you is: keep your eyes open."

My eyes *were* open, but they were not looking at him.

Through the window, I could see Claire and Tori locking up their bicycles. Thankfully, Zach wasn't with them. I raised my hand when they entered. Gregory looked over his shoulder to see whom I was signalling. He turned back and gave me the kind of pitying look priests give to those who are deaf to their warnings about the infinite torments of hell. For their benefit, he said, as he stood, "Nice talking to you, Owen." Then he picked up his saucer and found himself a seat at an open table.

"Who was that?" Claire asked. I moved my rucksack to the floor so she could have the seat it had been saving. It occurred to me that, save for Zach, Claire had never seen me interact with any other students from Pembroke.

"Some bloke from college. We were in the same economics lecture Michaelmas Term."

Tori sat down. "Zach's not here yet?"

"I thought he'd be coming with you," I said. "Not that he has much to study for, mind. Should I text him?"

"Don't bother." She set up her study materials at the table. "You know he never responds to them."

An hour later, he made his entrance in his habitual manner, in a flurry of manic speech. "I've just had the most incredible experience!" he exclaimed. "I probably won't be able to do it justice, because I'm almost certain it's beyond the limits of language. In fact, as soon as I became aware that I was *having an experience*, it stopped." The other customers looked up to see who was guilty of disrupting the volume level of the caf.. Disapproving glances were shot in our direction. At the periphery of my vision, I saw Gregory note Zach's presence and adjust his chair, leaning imperceptibly toward us.

"Well. What was it?" I asked.

"On my way here I was walking across Pembroke Square and as I was walking I heard the heels of my shoes echo on the cobblestones." We waited for him to go on, but he didn't. That was the end of his story.

"You're stoned, aren't you?" Tori said.

"Not at all. Why would you say that?"

"You heard the echo. Of your heels. On the cobblestones. That's your incredible experience, love? That's all?"

"What do you mean, *that's all*!" he shouted, to a chorus of hushes from the other customers. He continued in a vehement whisper. "It was incredible. The border that normally separates us from the external world disappeared and I felt no difference between me and the cobblestones and the walls of the college and the parked cars and the sky. I was perceiving, of that I'm certain. But without subjectivity, without self."

"As if you were 'one with everything,'" said Tori, air quoting the phrase with her fingers.

"I suppose so, my dear, though it sounds trivial when you put it that way. Maybe this is what people mean when they talk about the *unio mystica*. But since we know there is no God I think it would be more accurate to say that it was like I was nothing at all or that somehow I, Zachary, or my ego or personal identity or whatever you want to call it was suddenly subtracted from the world. Like 'I'" — and here he responded with air quotes of his own — " was experiencing 'my own' death. All in all it lasted only a moment, but 'to me' that moment seemed to go on for a long time. A very long time."

"How did it feel?" Claire asked, with genuine curiosity. As she was the only one of us who had been raised in a religious household — her father was a Methodist minister — Claire was disposed to take seriously statements that bordered on expressions of faith and spirituality, even when they happened to come from the mouth of an avowed atheist like Zach.

"Blissful. Truly blissful," he told her. "A pleasure such as I've only ever felt once before in my entire life."

Tori looked at me, not knowing how to respond. I shrugged my shoulders.

"Had to be there, I guess." Zach sounded disappointed. Whatever he had been expecting us to say, it was clear we weren't saying it. Seeing that everyone was more interested in working, he rummaged around in his satchel and took out a pen, a notebook, and a German grammar. The state he described reminded me of how I felt walking back from Claire's that first afternoon, and of how I felt when I'd swallowed the tablet at the *Theory* party. But between my distracting conversation with Gregory and my anxiety about having for too long postponed my revisions, it had been difficult to pay much attention to his story.

I looked in Gregory's direction. He was looking out the window at the passersby on Queen's Lane. *Conspicuously* looking, it seemed to me, as I had been conspicuously looking at my book when Zach burst through the door after his row with Tori. I was certain he'd been listening in on every word Zach said. Wonder what *he* made of it.

THE ORIGINS OF CLOTHING.— The origins of clothing should be sought in man's desire to forget that his skin is already a kind of uniform. Masks, disguises, costumes — these are worn above all to conceal something from the *wearer*, who wishes to appear as someone or something else, in order to convince *himself* that his body is not what it really is: a mask, a disguise, a costume worn by Nature. Just so, we are never more deceived than when we speak of the *nakedness* of truth. Truth is something tailored, something we have sewn together, stitched up, embroidered, woven, hemmed, and cut. It is something that has to be put on — one leg at a time.

No note this morning. I search under the pillow. Nothing. I throw off the sheets in case it had fallen. Check the surface of her desk. Of her chest of drawers. Nothing.

Was hoping for a note. Had been counting on one, in fact. To give me some indication of how she was feeling. To explain what is happening to us. Between us. Or at least to tell me where I should meet her. Here? Her parents' flat? Outside the opera house? I half suspect we'll meet tonight and pretend that nothing happened. But something *has* happened.

The only message for me this morning is from Claire. In my inbox. And it I'd rather not read. It's not just that I worry about what I'll discover there. What awful new news she'll have of Tori. How can I write her back words of comfort now? After last night. Our relationship has managed to survive my silence about what happened with Nadya. But I don't know how it can survive my silence about Zach. Or Vera.

Though I have less than forty-eight hours left in New York, I'm not at all keen on leaving the flat. I try to think on all the things I might never see if I don't summon up the will to put on clothes and walk out the door. The Empire State Building. Times Square. The Museum of Modern Art. Fifth Avenue. The Brooklyn Bridge. A slide show of a holiday that may never be. Tonight there will be the opera: maybe that's enough sightseeing for one day. One can't see everything anyway. Even if it would never be included in a travel guide, to me, Vera's room is just as much of a sight as the view from atop the World Trade Center.

If I board that aeroplane tomorrow night, I know I'll regret it for as long as I live. Falling in love is like that, I'm coming to understand. Falling in love — with a place, with a person — is like being infected by an incurable disease. A virus of permanent longing, which cannot be treated, even by large doses of time. One must learn how to accept this, I reckon. Or learn how not to fall in love at all.

In the kitchen, Katie is adding a banana to her bowl of yoghurt and granola. She is dressed for the gym. A sweatband separates her golden hair from her high forehead. The blade moves with professional swiftness and precision between her forefinger and her thumb. The fleshy yellow-white circles that fall into the bowl are perfectly thin and even. I can't help wondering if she's using the same knife Vera washed clean before we fell asleep last night. On the sleeve of my white t shirt is a reddish-brown stain. I cover it with my palm. A private thought bends my lips with pride: I have a scar on my bicep, just like the Foedern twins.

Good morning, Owen. I was just making myself breakfast. Can I interest you in something to eat?

I'm not hungry, but I tell her I'll have what she's having. Just to watch her slice her way through another piece of fruit.

Katie is a student of biology. This year she will be applying for Master's programmes in Public Health. When she finishes, she hopes to go on to get her medical degree and pursue a career as an epidemiologist. For the World Health Organization or the Centers for Disease Control and Prevention. Her research specialty: infectious diseases. Real diseases, not metaphorical ones. Of the sexually transmitted variety.

What for? I ask.

What do you mean, *what for*? She is sincerely perplexed; perhaps it has never occurred to her to wonder. To save lives, obviously. To make a difference. A real, tangible difference. People in the Third World lack access to adequate health clinics, affordable supplies of medicine, and up to date information that will help them take steps to improve their sexual health and prevent the spread of HIV.

She hands me a bowl of yoghurt and a spoon. We haven't found a cure, she acknowledges, but with antiretroviral drug cocktails we've at least found a way to make it easier for people to live with the disease. Every person who dies of AIDS in the Third World is dying a preventable death.

I wonder what Zach would have made of his sister's friend. Wouldn't have approved, is my guess. He always treated do gooders and optimists not as stupid, exactly, but as hopelessly naïve. Blissfully ignorant or unwilling to face up to the facts of life. Specially the fact that we're all going to die.

But they're all going to die anyway, I tell her. On Katie's face a frown begins to form. Slowly and with effort, as if her muscles were performing a strenuous stretch made particularly difficult by lack of practice.

Have you ever seen someone die of AIDS? It isn't a pretty picture.

So that's what life's about? The absence of suffering?

Fine. Why do you study philosophy? Or whatever it is.

She's right. It's much easier to ask questions than to

answer them. After a long pause, I say: Who knows really? Maybe to find an answer to just that question: what's life about, what is it *for*. Although it doesn't seem likely, does it? We've been studying the problem for almost three thousand years and haven't figured anything out. To pass the time, then? One has to do *something* whilst one waits to die.

Katie takes her bowl to the sink. She pours some thick green washing up liquid in the bowl and begins to scrub it clean. I join her there with mine.

You know what I call that? she says, taking my bowl from me. I call that despair. And despair is a luxury. A First World problem. I spent last summer in a farming village in Botswana. The men would work from dawn till dusk in the mines and every morning they got up and did it again. There was no indoor plumbing, no running water, no electricity. Dire poverty. Illiteracy. People barely living past their fifties. Conditions you or I would call *not worth living in*. And yet no one there gives up or gets depressed or —

Kills themselves? I interrupt. What a joke. Am I really going to be lectured to about luxury by a person whose father probably makes one hundred times as much money as mine does? You're right, Katie. That's what everyone says. Only the *affluent* have the resources and leisure time to worry whether life is worth living.

She drops the bowl and the dishcloth into the sink and throws her arms around my neck. Into my ear she whispers, Listen to me, Owen. Life *is* worth living. It just is. There's no reason why. You just have to believe me, okay?

She lets her hands slide to my shoulders and looks deeply into my eyes. Her sincerity and compassion are moving. What if what she's saying is true? What if the solution to the problem of life is the vanishing of the question? She seems to have understood this better than Zach and I had done. By never needing to consider it. The disease of doubt: some people just aren't born with it. The rest of us may very well be incurable, no matter how many books we read. Throw away the ladder once you've climbed it? Easier said than done. Some people get to the top rung. Look out. Jump.

Vera returns to the flat at five. She passes through the door, still lost in the thoughts she has brought with her from the outside; the corners of her eyes have sunk to the angle of capsizing boats. I am sitting more or less where Katie left me, on the sofa, reading. I place the letter between the pages of the book, slip it into my pocket, and rise to greet her. But Vera takes one look in my direction and says she won't be seen in public with me. Not in *that* suit.

At first I think she objects because this is the same suit I wore to the funeral, but it soon becomes clear that what she objects to is the suit itself. Its poor quality. Its unfashionable cut. Its double-digit price tag. We've not got the time — and, anyway, I haven't the money — to buy a new suit and a clean shirt. In a vanquished voice, I tell Vera I'll understand if she'd prefer to go to the opera with someone else. She dismisses this idea with a curt laugh. No, she meant nothing of the sort. I would simply wear one of Zach's suits instead.

I doubt they would fit me. Zach... is... so much taller than I am.

You look to be the same height to me. How tall are you?

One metre seventy-five.

In English, please.

I look to the ceiling, make the calculations, and answer, Approximately five feet, nine inches.

As I thought. Exactly the same height.

She, of course, is dressed exquisitely. A sleeveless dress in gunmetal blue. High-heeled sandals whose leather straps intricately cross the tops of her feet. A silk shawl draped delicately over her shoulders. For the first time, I notice, she's wearing makeup, her lips an elegant pair of crimson strokes. I couldn't believe such a beautiful girl had allowed me to sleep with her. And not just any girl — Zach's sister. It hadn't been making love, exactly, it was tense and fraught,

166

and not exactly what one would call *good*. Still, it was a fact. And I had the scar, the physical proof. Just like my connexion with Zach, my connexion with Vera will last as long as I live. As for the sex: the first time is bound to be awkward, isn't it? Tonight will be better, of that I'm certain.

Bernard and Rebecca are not home when we arrive. Neither person nor propriety now stands between me and Zach and Vera's old room. Our room: that's how she referred to it. In it, Diminovich's painting hangs over their beds like a cross on the wall of a monk's cell. Why she called it a double portrait, though, I can't say. The canvas is split into two horizontal planes: one black, one white. Where the planes meet, the paint, thickly applied, had been mixed by the regular application of the edge of a palette knife or some other straight surface. The resulting pattern looks like the diagram of the pulsar on the cover of the first Joy Division album.

But I barely have time to study it. Having forgotten that only the day before yesterday she was hell-bent on showing it to me, Vera directs me instead to the wardrobe and slides opened the mirrored door. Our image disappears. In its place are Zach's suits, eerily shrouded in dry-cleaner's plastic. The whole collection, minus one. Vera watches me run a finger across the row of sleeves like a student searching a row of books for the shelf mark on the spine of a specific title. She stops me when I touch what looks to be the dress suit he wore to our first tutorial together. I pull the hanger off the wooden rail, drape the suit over one of the beds, and, with a single tear, unseam the plastic from the nave to the chaps.

I've always thought that... this shirt... and this tie... go really well with that suit, she tells me, handing them to me.

She leaves the room to let me try it on. I think of the other suit, the dinner jacket he was wearing when he died, which would have had a fray in the fabric, no larger than a centimetre in diameter, dead centre, where my palm is now placed. I close my eyes and imagine myself covering up that hole with the tip of my finger, believing, for a moment, that by this small act I could reverse time, undo the cause, heal the wound, and bring my friend back to life. That with a bit of magical thinking I could make things otherwise than they are. Which they never can be.

I slide the trousers to my waist and button the two buttons. To my surprise, they do not immediately fall back down my legs. Nor do I find myself crushing hem under heel. My thumb fits between the back of the button and the elastic band of my pants, but that's not a distance too large to be erased by a tucked in shirt and a belt notched to the farthest hole. The cream shirt is a tad snug in the chest and in the biceps. The stiff collar comes together across my throat and, though it's somewhat of a stretch, I can breathe without any difficulty. The tie she picked out for me is silk, with small white dots on a dark blue field. Too skinny for a proper Windsor: I'll have to four in hand it. According to a superstition of my father's, which proves, to my chagrin, to be correct, this means I'll only manage to tie it properly on the third attempt.

Owen! You're worse than a girl! Vera shouts from the other room. What's taking so long?

Where does Zach keep his cufflinks? I call back.

Check the desk drawer: they should be in a small jewel case! comes the response from outside.

In the box, there is an assortment of shirt studs, collar stays, and cufflinks. It's my first time wearing a French-cuffed shirt, and it takes me a minute or two to twist each link into place. Now the final test. The jacket. With its thin lapels, its two buttons, and a label on the inside pocket marked, as I suspected, with a Jermyn Street address.

There's an urgent rapping on the door. We're running out of time here!

What should I do with my suit?

Just leave it here! We'll come back and pick it up tomorrow.

The book with the letter inside is peeking out of the pocket of my suit. I hesitate for a moment and then fish out the pearl and the book. Better, I think, to keep them close, on my own person, than to leave them here where they might be discovered. As I hastily transfer the two items from one pocket to the other, where, it occurs to me, they will feel right at home, the letter slips out and falls to the floor. Cursing, I pick it up and stuff it back into the book at random: there's no time now to find the place it had been keeping. But before I do, something on the page catches my eye. There, three lines from the top, is the very aphorism I'd been searching for. In the margin, Zach had written no commentary, only the following fateful words: *Discuss w/ O.*

THE MEANING OF LIFE.— Anyone for whom "the meaning of life" is a meaningful problem should be considered an extremely dangerous person. Either because he believes he knows the solution to the problem, or because he believes there isn't one.

When Zach texted, I was sitting in the JCR with a few other students watching David Dimbleby present the BBC's coverage of the general election. The room was mostly empty. The biggest story that evening was not the election result — from the exit polls, it appeared Labour would win in a landslide, conserving the same number of seats in Parliament they had won four years before, returning Tony Blair to Number 10, making him the first Labour PM to serve two consecutive terms — but the voter turnout, which was projected to fall to the lowest levels in almost a century. Translating Zach's electoral theories across the Atlantic, I myself had contributed to this statistic, though Claire and Tori had not, the former out of a sense of duty and the latter because she wholeheartedly agreed with Labour's manifesto. My father had certainly voted as well, casting a futile ballot at the polling station at the primary school on South Street. No doubt at that very moment he was also watching telly, lager in hand, cursing through his teeth.

Usually Zach and I made plans to see each other the old-fashioned way, by pidging each other short notes. That he had texted meant he had something urgent to tell me. *Are you at Tori and Claire's?* read the dark letters on the orange screen. It never failed to amuse me that he bothered to use proper punctuation and grammar in his texts, specially as he never activated his mobile's T9 function. As with the emails necessity sometimes forced him to write, he considered the ownership of a mobile phone an unholy compromise with the twenty-first century (his parents, he explained, *made him buy one* when he came to Oxford). The abbreviations, initialisms, and omissions that made textese an efficient means of communication were, to him, signs of *widespread leveling down*. I texted back to say I was at the JCR. *Good*, came the reply. *Drop by the Macmillan Building when you're done.*

Named for the former Prime Minister and University Chancellor, the Mac, as everyone but Zach called it, was the most modern building at Pembroke. The unsightly structure was located just around the corner from Staircase XVI, wisely tucked away from general contemplation. I made my way there, walking along the path round the grass of Chapel Quad, where, despite the impending examinations, a drunken game of croquet was in progress. An errantly malletted ball struck my shoe as I passed, which provoked a chorus of infantile laughter amongst the players. I kept walking, making no effort to return the ball to them. One of them shouted something I didn't hear at first, which was then distorted when taken up by the whole group. "Lapdog! Lapdog!" was how it sounded to me. Was that what they were saying? Could they possibly have been saying that?

Zach was sitting alone in the common room on the first floor watching a film, drinking champagne straight from the bottle. He drank regularly now. Since Berlin his fingers were rarely far from a pint or a martini or a glass of whisky. I took a seat next to him. "Want some?" he asked. "My sister had it shipped to me all the way from New York." He passed me the bottle. I took a sip, winced briefly, and examined the white label. Bollinger. Special Cuvée Brut. 1980. I know very little about wine, but it looked quite dear. He was drinking it lukewarm.

"What's the occasion?"

Without taking his eyes off the telly, he mumbled — to the room as much as to me — " It's our birthday." It struck me as odd that I didn't know this already, and that he didn't know when my birthday was. On the screen, Peter O'Toole lay prostrate before a tomb in the crypt of a cathedral, surrounded by monks in black robes who were taking turns flagellating him.

"That makes you — what — twenty-one, doesn't it?" I was trying to sound excited, wondering what had put him in such a foul mood. "That's a big birthday for you Yanks, isn't it? Let's ring Tori and Claire. They'll meet us at Freud's and I'll buy your drinks for a change. Your first legal martini. It would be a real honour."

"Thanks. But I'd rather not. I absolutely hate birthdays. Ours especially. Besides, as you've probably guessed, there's something I want to talk to you about."

He stood up. O'Toole, now wearing a crown and a cloak, was telling a group of armour-clad barons that justice would seek out the murderers of Thomas Becket.

"You're not going to finish watching, then?" I asked.

"No need. It's almost over anyway." He touched the remote and the screen went black. I followed him out of the Mac, back to Staircase XVI. The bottle of champagne Vera had sent him was left half-full on the wooden table.

I sat down, as I usually did when I visited Zach, on the bed, the only empty surface in his rooms. I expected him to clear off the books piled on the chair and join me. Instead, he motioned me over to the desk. He opened the voluminous drawer meant to hold file folders and pointed into the depths, where I saw two pistols and a box of cartridges. He took one out, cradling it like a newborn cat in his upturned palms, and presented it to me. I'd never held a firearm before.

"It's heavy," I observed, not knowing what else to say. At that moment, the object struck me as an absurd prop, a prop he'd requisitioned from the warehouse of his imagination for the film of his life. I threaded my finger around the trigger and thrust out my arm, aiming it with one eye closed at one of the mosquito stains on the wall, pretending I was in the title sequence of a Bond film. Step into the circle. Turn and fire. Blood drips down the screen. Theme song: you only live twice, live and let die, the world is not enough. Though I'd seen it done innumerable times in the cinema, holding the pistol and aiming the barrel and touching the trigger still didn't feel at all natural.

"Be careful," he said. "It's loaded."

I looked at him incredulously. For once, he didn't curl his lip or raise his eyebrow. My arm dropped to my side. I brought the pistol before my chest, supporting it in my palms with the same fearful reverence as he had. When he took it back from me, I unconsciously wiped my hands on the sides of my trousers, as if I'd just been handling something filthy. I remarked on the age of the pistol and asked him if it still worked.

"Of course it does!" He looked offended. "I've even tested it!" Then, after a sharp breath, he summoned the courage to tell me what he was planning to use it for. He spoke slowly. Deliberately. Fixing me with a stare. "Owen," he said, "I've decided to end my life."

What he had told me at The Bear after our tutorial on the *Phaedo* returned to me in a flash. *That's where you're wrong*, he had said. *It wasn't only a paper*. Could it have been true? What if, for the boy of a thousand theories, this was the one he took seriously enough to put into practice? I looked at the pistol in his hands and then back at him. My eyes begged him to break character. I longed to see the withering smile appear on his face, but his features remained stiff, intensely studying my reaction to what he had just said, compelling me to respond, though again I had no idea what to say. Finally, in a faltering voice, I asked him what he thought happened when we died, hoping by my question to return our discussion to the plane of the purely theoretical. We had talked a great deal about preparations for death. But never about what happened after.

"Nothing at all," he responded, as I knew he would.

"Doesn't that thought frighten you?"

"Why should it? Death will remove the fear of death along with everything else."

"What I mean is: won't you miss being conscious and perceiving the world and experiencing new things?"

"To do so would require me to imaginatively project myself into a state I will never experience. But imagining the abyss doesn't terrify me. Unlike most people, not a day goes by when I don't think of death. Most people try to run away from death, and that's why they live such meaningless lives. To embrace death freely is to prove that life *actually matters*. Life will never mean as much, experience will never feel so full, if you are fully conscious when you die. And the only way to do that is to *plan* your death. What I want to do is to exchange ten thousand experiences that don't matter for one that really does. Since the moment I decided to die, I've felt the most extreme freedom. I've been released from manners and politeness and morality — which are all just euphemisms for the fear of death. Now that they've become limited, each and every moment has correspondingly increased in intensity. The last one is going to be the most intense of all. I just know it. In fact, I've never been more certain of anything in my life."

"But what if you're wrong? Don't you worry that, daft as they sound, all the things people have said about the afterlife are actually true?"

Zach placed the pistol on the table and walked over to the tower of books he'd stacked on the floor. It wasn't necessary to ask which book he was preparing to quote from.

Swishing page after page between his forefinger and thumb, he bent the book three-quarters in. Holding it in one hand, he read, "'The early Church did not put an end to the cult of martyrs to promote an essentially worldly...' No, it's a little further, the passage I'm looking for. '...promises a fundamental stability... That's why, in Dostoevsky's novel...' Ah yes, here." He held up his finger and spoke deliberately for emphasis: "'That's why in Dostoevsky's novel *The Possessed*, Kirillov isn't entirely mistaken about the outcome of his suicide. When he kills himself, he will indeed kill God, as he believes. Suicide violates the most fundamental of Christian moral principles precisely because it permanently disrupts the very stability of identity God's existence is intended to guarantee. In killing himself Kirillov *becomes God*, that is, something that does not exist.'"

He looked at me insistently, waiting for me to understand the passage, to feel the logic of the argument wash over me with the same force of revelation he had obviously experienced when he read it. Perhaps what Abendroth had written made more sense if you knew the novel, but all I had read of Dostoevsky was *Notes from Underground* and *The Double*. I asked Zach what he thought it meant.

"It means that — in answer to your question — we shouldn't fear God's punishment, because he who kills himself shows that God does not exist. For the suicide there is precisely no one to fear. But it's not God we should be worrying about, it's *Nature*." He continued reading. "'The Divine was invented by the primitive imagination as a weapon against death, but when this fact is forgotten, the weapon is turned back against its inventor. When the Death of God is finally announced, those who have killed him do not realise that something will inevitably take His place. Nor do they suspect the obvious usurper: Nature. Rather than vanishing along with God, the problem of suicide actually intensifies. It goes from being a mortal sin to an unnatural act. Thus, in order for Kirillov to be truly successful, he would have to perform a miracle: *he would have to kill himself twice*.'"

Zach closed the book, placed it on the table, and grabbed the pistol. "What we have to fear, Owen, is not some future state no one has ever seen, but what we already see around us, everywhere around us, right now. It is all of this," he said, gesturing around the room with the pistol, before placing it back in the drawer, "that the *unnatural* act of suicide strikes against."

The drawer slid shut and we both looked at it for a moment, in silence. I felt overwhelmed by a sense of unreality. I had the unsettling impression that were I to have opened the drawer again, it would be empty. Zach's words were contaminating the things he described. Suddenly, the objects in the room, including me, seemed to lack all substance. Everything had been hollowed out, drained of significance, menacing in its meaninglessness. Without taking my eyes off the shape that until that moment I would have had no qualms about calling the handle of a drawer, I asked of the now invisible pistols, "Why two of them, then?" half expecting he'd have no idea what I was referring to.

"Because I was hoping you'd come with me." He said it without hesitation, almost casually, as if he were inviting me to the pub for the evening, rather than to nothingness for all eternity.

With an abrupt twist of my neck, my eyes met his. A whisper evaporated from my stunned, open mouth: "Why me?"

Zach grabbed my shoulders and looked me straight in the eyes. "I didn't consider anyone else *but* you. From the beginning, the very beginning, I had a feeling about you, a feeling that's proven to be correct."

"And what was that?"

"That you were lonely — and not just lonely: alone, deeply alone." I tried to look away, to hide my shame at the truth of his words, but he shook me so I would not break his gaze. "If I was able to see this it was because I felt the same way about myself. You laugh? You think that because I was always surrounded by people, talking to them and going out drinking with them, that I was any less alone than you were, sitting by yourself at Hall or at The Bear? No, the only difference between us is that, unlike you, *I knew why* I was lonely. And also why you were lonely. You want to know the reason? *It's because we're special*, Owen. That's why. Being special means being singular and being singular means being lonely, even if, like me, you have to surround yourself with meaningless chatter in order to drown out the voice in your head that reminds you how alone you really are. But the amazing thing is that we found each other. That's the rarest thing in the world, don't you think, two singularities finding each other like that? I wasn't wrong about you. You were the only one capable of understanding me, understanding me like one brother understands another. To understand someone, to truly understand them, requires more than intelligence, which you demonstrated right away, it also requires empathy, the willingness to understand. That is what is so rare. And to have that, to have empathy, you must have had the same experiences as I did. To understand the question that most people are too stupid or too afraid to even pose, you must have had certain experiences that would enable you to understand the need for that question to be asked, why it needs to be wrestled with, why there is nothing more important than finding the answer. And that question is —"

"Why is life worth living."

He let go of my shoulders, now that he believed I was capable of standing on my own two feet.

"*Exactly*. If you can ask that question, if you are even capable of posing it at all, it must be because all of the traditional answers — service to God or falling in love or having children or achieving peace on earth or even experiencing as much physical pleasure as possible — fail to satisfy you. They must fail to alleviate the suspicion, the miserable suspicion that all *those* answers come at the cost of submission — submission to a religion or a political ideology or even the natural order. And that a person who answers like that, who submits themselves like that, has already given away their freedom. For people who submit, death is nothing

177

more than a redundancy, because their lives are not worth living. How to be free and alive at the same time? I've come to the conclusion that it's not possible. And between freedom and life, I choose freedom. And I want to *share* my choice with the only other free person I've ever met. Share my freest act with him — with *you*. Because only another free person would be able to understand what I'm talking about."

As he spoke, a rush went through my body. The objects in the room, which his earlier words had emptied of significance, were now resurrected, one by one. They overflowed with the purpose he had stripped from them only minutes before. Everything now seemed radiant and clear. Everything stood in its proper place, where it had to be, a mathematical proof made out of objects rather than necessary truths. All that had to happen was that two people understood each other as perfectly as we did. Zach and I were the deduction. The Q.E.D. Later, I'd go through my habitual pattern of indecision and self-doubt, second-guessing his motivations and mine, but at that moment I was prepared to do anything he asked of me.

"So, Owen, what I want to know is: are you in?"

I'll never forget the look on his face when I gave him my answer. The change in his expression was nearly imperceptible, but I couldn't help but detect a glimmer of triumph emanating from the corners of his lips and from the deepest recesses of his dark eyes. He looked as though he expected me to respond as I had and at the same time couldn't believe his good fortune that I had done so. Everything was going according to plan; he wouldn't compromise his end goal by gloating over a merely intermediary success.

He told me how, on the day he and Tori got into their row, he'd entered the pub, where he reread the passage he had just quoted me. Afterwards, he took a long walk up the river to Port Meadow, where he'd stumbled on the ruins of Godstow Abbey. That old nunnery, he said, was the perfect backdrop for the scene he'd envisioned. The scene that, in a week's time, we were going to enact.

"Let's begin then, shall we?"

"Begin what?" I asked.

"We're going to compose our note." Yes. Of course. There would be a note. What would a suicide be without a note, a philosophical flourish before curtain's close, and no need to absent felicity for a while in the telling of our tale.

The typewriter, whose taupe hatchback case Zach proceeded to place on the table, was nicked from the flat in Berlin. It materialised in our pile of luggage the day we returned to England. If I kept silent about its unexpected presence there, I suppose it's because, by then, I had learnt better than to remark on such things. When he returned to his flat, the typewriter's rightful owner probably wouldn't notice it had gone missing from the miscellany he stored in his pantry. Even had he done so, I doubt he would have missed it much. But these were rationalisations, my rationalisations. Zach simply came, saw, purloined.

He opened the case. It was a beautiful machine. A portable Rheinmetall-Borsig KsT from the 30s. The company logo in gold on the glossy black metal. Four rows of circular white keys in QWERTZ layout, with keys for all the umlauted vowels, and one for the Reichsmark sign. Zach loaded a piece of paper, turned the knob, and released the carriage. A bell sounded.

"Same idea as Berlin," he said. "When we've finished our draft, I'll type up two copies, one for you and one for me. Everything will be the same, except the names, obviously, and the spelling. Now, have a seat." I ran my thumbs over my knuckles, cracking them one after the other. "What do you think for the salutation?" he asked. "'My Dear Owen comma,' or just 'Owen comma,' or maybe 'O dash'?"

"'O dash,'" I ventured. "'My Dear Owen' sounds treacly to me. Even if you were to cut out the 'My' it would still be a bit casual for the subject, wouldn't it? Just 'Owen' on the other hand is too businesslike. The way a father would open a letter to his son scolding him for his overspending. You're not going to fancy signing it 'Zachary,' after all, are you?"

"Right," he agreed. "Let's go with the first initial." I watched the ribbon rise and fall three times as I typed a black oval and two short dashes on the white paper. "The first line... should announce the purpose." He paused to have a think on how this should read.

"'By the time you read this I'll be dead,'" he suggested.

"Good. But not exactly true, is it?"

Zach returned my knowing grin. "No, I guess not. Not literally at least. But that doesn't really bother me. It's not the literal truth we're after here." I typed the sentence and waited for him to continue. "I think the next few lines should be about why we've chosen each other to be the recipients of these letters."

"Go on," I said, my fingers at the ready. I watched them climb up and down the alphabet like a spider on its web as I typed the words he dictated to me:

By the time you read this I'll be dead. I write to you because by my death I would like something to be understood. Of all the people I have ever met, you are the most likely to be sympathetic to my reasons and thus best able to explain them to those, blinded by love or prejudice, who will not grasp what it is I have done. I apologise for what will no doubt be a burdensome task, but I am not asking for your — or anyone else's — forgiveness. The first thing that must be understood is that I am going to do nothing that calls for forgiveness. And anyway, by the time you read this, there will be no one left to forgive.

I read the sentences back to him. He read along with me over my shoulder, circling a word here or there with his pen. I could smell the champagne on his breath. He capped the pen and placed it behind his ear. "Paragraph break." I flung the carriage with animation: time to switch places. As I stood up from his chair I couldn't suppress a recollection of the thin parting through the black hair on the crown of Nadya's head,

180

her mouth bobbing between Zach's unbuckled belt and mine. "What we need now is a statement about our motives," he said. "Think you can do that?"

I touched my fingertips to my forehead to help me conjure the words.

"It is important... to make perfectly clear that..."

I began to pace. With the lit cigarette in my mouth, I must have looked like a miniature locomotive speeding back and forth on a very short track. I spoke quickly as well, enjoying the way my words found their echo in the clacking of the typewriter and encouraged by the exclamations of approval that surged from Zach whenever he heard one of his own thoughts return to him with a majesty alienated only by the timbre of my voice and the small inexactitudes of my paraphrase.

"To make it perfectly clear that my death has not been motivated... by any pain dash... physical comma emotional comma or psychological dash... that I have undergone in this life comma or at least comma as these things are conventionally understood full stop."

"'Conventionally'! Great! Keep going."

"Relative to the sufferings I know to be the lot of the vast majority of humanity comma I have lived a life of privilege comma comfort comma and contentment full stop. I have every reason to believe my life would have continued roughly in this way in the future full stop."

"Hold on a sec!" Zach shouted as he rushed to keep up with me. "... roughly... this... way... in... the... future. Okay. Got it."

"Nor has anything I've ever experienced comma no setback or frustration of my desires comma been strong enough to... damage? This contentment? I'm not sure if that's the best way to put it."

"Why don't we try something stronger. Like poison: to *poison* this contentment."

"All right... *to poison this contentment* full stop." My cigarette was now a cylinder of grey ash. I found it a resting

181

place in the crowded ashtray and lit another. "I feel it necessary to state this clearly because it is of the utmost importance to me that my final action is not regarded as a self-interested or cowardly comma —"

"Good!"

"— some sort of inability to face the particular sufferings of my life full stop. Rather it is the opposite comma a disinterested action —"

"*Good!*"

"— one that goes directly against my self-interest comma a sacrifice of myself in the name of something higher than myself full stop paragraph break."

The bell sounded and the carriage moved. Zach said, "It's brilliant, Owen!"

"Read it back! Read it back!"

The note was to continue for three more paragraphs. Two more relays between sitting and standing. Between talking and typing. At each break, there was a noticeable increase of speed in our lips and fingers. Our speech became more fluid, our prose more florid, as each paragraph wildly dared the next to do more, to say more. When I typed the final "Zed," ripped the paper from the platen, and began reading the final paragraph back to him, I was short of breath. I reached for the packet of cigarettes on the desk next to the typewriter. There was only one left. I lit it and smoked slowly with my eyes closed as I listened to him type the second letter. My copy. The one that would be found in his pidge after our deaths. When he finished, he brought it to me and handed me his pen, tapping the empty space between the valediction and my first initial, where I signed my name.

READING THE WORLD.— When medieval theologians compared nature to a book, it is likely they had scientific treatises in mind. While that may be a suitable metaphor for the prose of minerals, vegetables, and animals, when the chapter that introduces humanity is finally written, it becomes clear that we are dealing with an altogether different genre. Human patterns bend into segments — story*lines*, dramatic *arcs* — that can be plotted on a plane whose axes are Time and Desire. As these segments are recorded and passed on by the billions, events, limited in number, begin to repeat themselves, and the plane *crystallises with allusions*. The difference between being in the world and reading the world breaks down and woe to the man who does not recognise which story he is living in!

The taxi leaves us next to a small triangular park consisting of a few trees, a wedge of grass, a few benches, a clock imprisoned in an irregularly shaped iron polygon, and a large statue of Dante Alighieri. The neon sign of the Hotel Empire shines red light onto the shoulders of the bronze Florentine, imbuing him with a suitably underworldly aura. We cross the road and enter the opera house just as the ushers begin to circulate through the lobby, tapping handheld xylophones with mallets to inform those who have just arrived or who are still loitering there, finishing their conversations or their drinks, that it's time for everyone to find their seats.

Vera swiftly leads me up the red-carpeted stairs to the mezzanine, where we overtake scores of elderly men and women who proceed slowly on canes, on Zimmer frames, on the elbows of their tottering spouses or their obliging grandchildren. Aside from these last, and from a few girls with round Slavic faces wearing lurid pastel dresses and skyscraper heels, Vera and I look to be the youngest members of the audience.

Holding me by the hand and moving with urgency, she blazes by the outstretched programmes offered to us at the door. We step over court shoes and loafers, whispering apologies to those who are momentarily forced, some with considerable difficulty, to stand as we pass. We find our seats — dead centre, five rows back — just as the starburst chandeliers ascend to the gold-scalloped ceiling. The house lights dim. I quickly crane my head, first over my right, then over my left shoulder: for four floors not a single empty seat is visible. The stage lights reflect off pairs of opera glasses and catch the crystal pieces of those miniature chandeliers that hang from the earlobes of every third or fourth member of the audience.

The conductor takes his place in the pit and lifts his baton to ready the orchestra. When he brings it down again, it's as if he's maliciously swiped a hornet's nest. The cellos vibrate like angry wings, a sound I do not so much hear as feel in my spine, whose vertebrae unlock just in time for the bows of the double basses to saw back and forth against my exposed nerves. The monumental curtain opens on a flood of fog and mist, blown downstage by a gale whipped up by the violins. The floodlights pulsate blue and white, suggesting flashes of lightning, whose jagged bolts descend to the stage floor in the notes played by the brasses and fade into the thunderous roll of kettledrums.

A figure appears in the mist. Dressed like a medieval woodsman in a loose-fitting tunic, with leather gauntlets and soft boots laced up to the knee, he staggers forward, battered by the storm. He falls. Then rights himself with great effort, clutching his side, a wounded man using his last reserves of strength to flee some as yet invisible terror. As he struggles to make his way downstage, the floor begins to rise, revealing on its underside the joints and rafters of a wooden ceiling. From an opening in the stage, the gnarled and blasted trunk of a once-proud oak extends through the L shaped hole in the ceiling. The woodsman climbs through the hole, collapsing at the base of the tree. Extending one exhausted arm after the other, he drags himself toward the embers of a fire that gives off a glow the same colour as the words that appear, translated into English, on the black rectangular screen embedded into the back of the seat in front of me. *Whoever's hearth this may be*, he sings, *here must I rest*. The orchestra goes silent so we may hear the first lines of the soprano, who is dressed in mourning. Awakened by the sound of the stranger's voice, she has courageously entered to investigate.

Halfway up the tree trunk, something, something metallic, glints in the light of the fire. I slide my glasses to my nose, trying to see what it might be. Though I have by now grown accustomed to watching foreign films with subtitles, I find the need to change my sightline disorienting and uncomfortable. By the time I realise the metal object is a sword that someone has plunged into the tree, I have missed the soprano's next lines. I touch a button to the left of the screen and the red text of the libretto disappears. Better, I think, just to watch and listen. Better not to bother about the words for now, but simply allow the gestures and the voices, the costumes and the instruments to tell me what I need to know of the plot.

An hour or so later, I am startled from the daydream into which I'd fallen by the abrasive sound of rapturous applause. On stage, the curtain is slowly closing on the woman and the woodsman, who are embracing, he between her spread thighs, she pulling his face to her breasts with white fingers visible through the weave of his long, unkempt hair. Her neck is thrown back in ecstasy, her own hair spilled on the stage like a puddle of strawberry blonde blood. Lying beside them is the naked blade of the sword that, in the course of the act, he must have drawn from its oaken sheath.

I put my hands together, since that's what everyone else is doing. Everyone but Vera, that is. Vera's left hand is tugging at her necklace, the forefinger of her right curves into her mouth. She is biting her knuckle. Her eyes are red and wet. My lips part to ask if she's all right, but already she is standing, her back turned to me, halfway to the aisle.

How foolish it was to turn off the subtitles after all. I consider asking one of the ushers for a programme so I can read the synopsis of the first act, to see what she found so disturbing in it, but by the time we are through the auditorium doors she has already broken away from the crowd, in a furious rush to the exit, and it is too late.

Whilst the curtain is opening on the second act of the opera, we find ourselves seated instead at a booth at a diner down the road, mutely sipping from grey plastic glasses of ice water. The waiter takes our orders and we surrender the long, laminated menus to him.

Without them, there is nothing we can use to hide our faces from each other. I look away, my gaze falling, at first, on the backs of the old men seated on the high round stools, who slump over the counter, thick sandwiches in their frail hands, and then on the small screen above the cashier's till, which is playing the evening news. A bespectacled grey-bearded journalist is interviewing a man in army fatigues with five stars on his collar and a black beret on his bullet-shaped head. Beneath BREAKING NEWS the name strap says, CENTCOM: MIDEAST FORCES UPGRADED TO THREATCON DELTA. The interview concludes. The journalist thanks the general, turns back to the camera. *Up next*, the closed captioning reads. *The state of Texas may seek the death penalty in the case of the Houston mother accused of killing her children. We'll be joined by her lawyer and the reporter who's been covering the crime. And this week the Supreme Court ruled on two hot-button issues: affirmative action and political fund-raising. We'll have live analysis from our senior Washington correspondent. When we return.*

I have an idea, Vera says finally. Let's pretend we've just met. That we've been fixed up on a blind date.

How does that work? I ask. My only other blind date was the outing organised for me by Zach. In a way, though, isn't that what this is as well?

I don't know. I guess we ask each other questions? Find out about each other to see if we're... companionable?

Shall I go first?

If you like.

Would you have consented to go on a date with me if I wasn't a friend of your brother's?

Owen, *please*. Just give it a try.

The waiter returns with our orders. He places a hamburger and a pint in front of me, a glass of white wine and a bowl of fruit in front of Vera.

All right, then. Where were we? Your name is Vera Foedern. We are on a blind date. All right. With a parodistically eager and friendly tone of voice I tell her it's a pleasure to meet her. Then I ask her the first banal question that comes to mind.

I'm a New Yorker, she answers. Born and bred. I grew up downtown, in Tribeca.

You've lived your whole life here, have you? Are there other places you'd consider living?

Berlin? LA maybe? New York is the only place I can envision living long term, though. After New York, where is there, as the saying goes. Still, I'm not sure if I'd want to raise my kids here. Kids who were raised in New York do everything at such a young age. They become jaded. World-weary. They learn pretty quickly that there's nothing new under the sun. And that makes it hard for them to feel excited about anything. Or impressed by anything. Even if a New

187

Yorker was impressed by something, there's no way she'd be caught dead admitting it.

You still live with your parents then?

No, but not too far from them either. I see them pretty often, but I have my own life. Here, if you live a mile from someone, that's far enough away that you have to make a conscious effort to see them.

What do they do? For a living, your parents.

My father used to be in real estate and now he's a film producer. My mother runs a gallery. Contemporary art. Chelsea.

I can tell she's become irritated that what was meant to be a conversation has turned into something more like an interview. Pointedly, I ask if she has any siblings. Rather than giving me the nasty look the question deserves, she pauses to consider it for a moment. A yes or no question to which either answer would be false. With downcast eyes, she shakes her head.

An only child, then. Just like me. Do you believe what they say about only children? That they're spoilt?

I haven't given it much thought. I suppose they are — we are — but then, people like us are all spoiled, whether we have siblings or not.

Like us?

You know. Rich parents, nannies, prep schools, SAT tutors, Ivy League schools, trust funds, six-figure salaries straight out of college, wedding announcements in the *Times*, that sort of thing.

I see.

I'm sure it's basically the same idea in England.

Basically. But I wouldn't know, really. My father works at the Somerdale Factory.

Vera looks at me, as if for the first time. Your father works in a *factory*?

For Cadbury's. They make those chocolate-covered cream eggs for Easter, I tell her, making a C shape with my forefinger and thumb to indicate the approximate size of the sweet.

Surely they sell them here. At any rate, he's the assistant foreman in charge of wrappers. My mum's a court reporter. Neither of them went to uni, so that makes me the first in my family.

She says, genuinely: They must be very proud of you.

Must be, I mumble. The direction our conversation has taken makes me uncomfortable. Suddenly I've become an exotic creature. One that needs to be studied anew. One perhaps deserving of her pity. I try to redirect it: And you? You are?

A student. Vera senses that she's touched a sore spot and looks hurt by my unwillingness to be more forthcoming. A junior at Columbia. An Art History and Visual Arts double major, she says, reciting facts off her CV in a bored, dull voice. Next year I'll be writing my senior thesis, entitled, "Performing Pain: Representations of the Body in Chris Burden's *Shoot* and Marina Abramović's *Rhythm 0*" — listen, you know what, you're right, this is pretty tiresome.

Perhaps I'm asking the wrong questions. What's the meaning of life?

She snorts derisively and rolls her eyes. You're really asking whether I think life has any meaning? You're strange, do you know that?

I can't think of a more important question. Recently someone told me that the purpose of human life was to reduce as much suffering as possible so that people could achieve personal fulfillment and happiness.

Whoever said that was being naïve. Humans are just random collections of atoms that evolved to operate under the illusion that they control their destinies and thus, with a *little hard work* and a *positive attitude*, can achieve equally illusory things like *fulfillment* and *happiness*. I used to think that love, being in love, the perfect communion with another person, was the meaning of life. But I was wrong. Now I know that life doesn't have any meaning at all.

I give off a defeated sigh. The bright yellow, pale green, and peach wedges of fruit in the clear bowl in front of Vera have remained untouched, drowning in their own juices. I make one final effort at conversation. Why don't you tell me something you've never told anyone before?

I just did, she says.

The waiter returns to take our plates. Vera orders another glass of white wine and, since I've done so poorly, it is agreed that she ought to take the lead. She shares her brother's curiosity, but her natural tendency, I can't help but notice, is to earnestness rather than irony. She had been made visibly uncomfortable when she told me something I already knew, or when she felt the need to refrain from saying too much, or when she said something we both knew was untrue for the sake of the pretence we were trying to keep up, the pretence that our conversation hadn't been arranged by her brother's death.

For my part, not long after I began, I overcame my initial resistance and allowed myself to get carried away. I spoke with the unleashed enthusiasm of a person who has returned home from many years abroad, back to a place where my language was understood, my customs shared, my name known — even though in each case the opposite was true. Each of her follow up questions, each murmur of understanding, each sympathetic nod said to me, I recognise you. You exist. You are not merely a dream of yourself.

Even with Zach and Claire I'd never been so forthright. With Zach, my place in our conversations was more sparring partner than confidant, a meeting of two minds I'd interpreted as a meeting of two hearts. As for Claire: she and I were satellites, only visible to each other because we were reflecting someone else's sunlight. With Claire, I never felt the same thrill of direct exposure, of total nakedness, that I do now, finally summoning up the courage to tell Vera what my life was like before I went up to Oxford.

By the time the bill arrives, it feels as though a corner has been turned. She accepts my offer to pay, unlike at the bar last night, where she insisted on paying for her own drinks. It is a pleasure to pay, even though (specially because?) three tenners are all that is left in my wallet. Thirty dollars to last me between now and the time I board the aeroplane tomorrow night. I feel, not for the first time today, the imminence of my departure. What would happen if I were to miss my flight? What if I simply failed to show up at the airport? I could disappear. Drop out. Wipe my slate clean. Start anew. Here in America. That's what it was made for, wasn't it?

On the trip back to the Lower East Side, a sequence of fantasies passes through my imagination as swiftly as our train passes through the stations of its route.

Me: waking up next to Vera, kissing her tenderly, cooking her breakfast, sending her off to the library to do research on her thesis.

Me: helping to move paintings at Rebecca's gallery.

Me: accompanying Bernard to the set.

Me: writing Zach's story on the typewriter, raising more of him from the dead with each keystroke.

Me: one of the Foederns, an only child no more.

But as I begin to follow her through the door into her room, she stops me.

Listen, Owen, she says. Maybe it would be better if you slept on the couch tonight.

She waits for me to tell her that I understand, that I completely understand, and when I say nothing, because I am speechless, she says good night and kisses me on the cheek. The door closes softly in my face. I hear the lock turn inside and stare at the door, dumbfounded, until finally I resign myself to spending the night here. Where I spent the whole afternoon. Waiting. For her.

**FREEDOM TO, FREEDOM FROM, FREEDOM FOR.—
The use people make of their freedom is the best
argument against allowing them to have any.**

That week, I retreated to my rooms, pleading revisions as my
excuse. Zach gave me a sceptical glance, but said nothing.
Not only so as not to contradict me in front of Tori and Claire,
but probably also because he simply didn't believe me. He
told me he would collect me from the Exam Schools (he did
not add: on our way to Godstow Abbey), but it hardly seemed
possible that a person would choose to spend his last days on
earth studying for a test.

Yet that is exactly what I did. I had my reasons, though I
wasn't about to share them with him.

I needed to take my mind off what we'd discussed, first
of all. Rather than spending the week brooding and second-
guessing and wondering if he really meant to go through
with it, or if this was merely another of his elaborate jokes,
I'd distract myself with intense concentration. The second
involved one of those small points of personal honour
that sometimes confound the behaviour of even the most
rational people. If I *was* going to die, I thought, I certainly
wasn't going to do it without scoring the Distinction my
tutors predicted I would. The last, I'm sorry to say, resulted
from a certain lack of imagination on my part. Rather than
making each moment more precious, as Zach had said, the
thought of impending death had the effect of equalising

them all. One way to pass the time was as good as any other, it seemed to me. Why not just sit for Prelims as was expected of me?

For months, my rooms had been nothing more than the place where I changed clothes and stored books on my way between tutorials and the Bevington Road. The curtains were open, letting in the afternoon light through the thick glass windowpanes. They had been tied back in loose knots and hung neatly on either side of the desk, on which my scout had stacked the books that needed to be returned to the library. (On top was the copy of *Against Nature* I'd finished in February, and which was by now long overdue.) The creases of my sheets were sharp. The undented pillow was placed on a folded blanket at the foot of the bed. My scout had even cleaned my teacups and left them upside down next to the kettle she had thoughtfully unplugged. I ran the tips of my fingers along my desk, the bedside table, the surface of the shelves, the spines of the books. I rubbed them together. Not a speck of dust anywhere. The place had been cleansed of me.

During the day, I worked myself to exhaustion, rereading every essay I had written since October. I pored over hundreds of pages of notes I'd taken at lectures and answered the sample exam questions posted on the PPE website. When it seemed like I might exhaust my study materials, I began to read aloud the passages from the *Dialogues* I would likely be called on to discuss during that portion of the exam, repeating Socrates' words until I could recite them by heart. I left college only to visit the kebab van in Pembroke Square, and only when my empty stomach could no longer be ignored.

But distraction was only taking me so far. In the college library, returning the overdue books, I ventured, for the first time that year, over to the room containing the history stacks. On one of the shelves labelled "England," I found a *History of Oxfordshire from the Stone Age to the Second World War*, pulled down the red cloth volume devoted to Wolvercote, and read the entry on Godstow twice over, attempting — and failing — to understand why Zach had thought a nunnery, of all places, would be the *perfect backdrop* for the *scene* he'd envisioned.

Later, as I waited in the queue to order my supper, I wondered what he was doing at that very moment. How he was spending the gift of *extreme freedom* the thought of his impending death had given him. Which manners and social niceties he was then flouting. Whereas I had clearly opted for asceticism, Zach, I guessed, would probably have chosen decadence. I bit into my kebab and imagined him sitting opposite Tori at the restaurant of the Randolph Hotel, circling burgundy liquid around the bottom of a crystal glass, dipping his nose inside, then frowning mischievously as he removed it from his lips and ordered a nonplussed waiter to return to the cellar to find him yet another bottle of wine.

As soon as I fell asleep I found myself at the mercy of my unconscious. More than once I relived our hour with Nadya. From the moment Zach saw the prostitutes on Oranienburger Straße to the moment I pushed him into the back seat of the taxi, the dream was as vivid as an experience and as realistic as a memory. I shouted the address of the house where we were staying just as I had then. But in the dream, the driver turned round and said, to my horror, "You meant to say Ruby Street, didn't you?" It was my father. "Time to come home now, Owen." Zach laughed his cold, cruel laugh and my eyes flew open. Outside my window, the sky was turning pink and orange.

Later that afternoon, I phoned Claire in a state of near panic, unable to stand the thought of spending another night alone. During the past few months, my body had grown accustomed to sharing a bed with her. The cycles of our shifting positions — her head in the hollow where my chest met my left shoulder, her arm around my waist; my stomach snug against the small of her back, my hand clamped to her breast; my cheek on her shoulder, my leg, bent at the knee, extended across her torso — I now associated with the rhythm of sleep itself. Without her there, my narrow bed seemed infinitely vast. Each time my limbs, performing their regular motions without their regular partners, brushed up unexpectedly against empty space, it felt as though I had missed a step and was on the verge of falling headlong down a flight of stairs.

Claire met me at the Porter's Lodge, where Richard registered overnight visitors, a takeaway bag hanging from one wrist, the handle of her brolly hanging from the other, and a familiar expression — caring, yet concerned — on her face.

Other than the two teacups, I kept no crockery in my rooms, so we scooped the curry she'd brought straight from the polystyrene boxes with plastic forks, sitting opposite each other on the floor. She told me how she'd spent her week, but when she began to describe the most recent row between Zach and Tori, I stopped her. "Let's talk about something else." I ripped a piece of naan in two and handed her the other half. "If you wouldn't mind." So we talked about us instead, about our future together, beginning with the summer holiday, in that tone of voice in which the concreteness of a plan soon becomes indistinguishable from the exaggerations of a fantasy. We spoke of spending it abroad, of getting a small flat together in a large city on the continent, somewhere that could be reached otherwise than by aeroplane. Amsterdam, Paris, Barcelona, Venice, Prague: as we reeled off their names, the thought that I'd only ever know them through films and photographs, novels and postcards, mediated entirely by the experience of others, struck me as immeasurably sad.

On the morning of the exam, I put my gown over my jacket with the solemnity of a soldier whose furlough has finally, and all too quickly, come to an end. Claire helped me with the bowtie, twisting the white cotton halves into perfect loops as she had done for her father, she explained, on so many Sunday mornings. As I made my way to the door, she stopped me.

"Before you go," she said, "I have a present for you." She unfastened the clasps of her handbag and took out a white carnation, which she slid into the buttonhole of my lapel. "There." She rested her hand on my chest and raised her lips to mine. "Now, take no prisoners."

The walk from my door to the Porter's Lodge was fewer than fifty steps long, and I walked each one slowly, whispering to myself, *Don't look, don't look, for God's sake Owen, Do Not Look*. The wooden shelves of the pigeonholes were now to my right. I could sense them hovering at the border of my field of vision. *Don't look*, I repeated, as I did just that, and saw the very thing I hoped I would not see.

The long white envelope in Zach's pidge.

The long white envelope in mine.

THE METAPHOR OF THE SUN.— Insofar as truth has been correctly identified with the sun, it is *not* because the sun *enlightens*, but because a man can approach neither and survive. The desire to solve riddles, to dismantle paradoxes, to discover new continents of fact and the hidden treasures of buried secrets, to know, in short, what one does not know, may be heroic, but it's also suicidal. The idea that the danger of knowing consists in being blinded by the light of the truth is, in fact, rather quaint; the real experience would undoubtedly have more in common with *instantaneous immolation*.

What is *this*? Owen, *what the fuck is this*?

Vera's voice. Pinched, threatening. Air flowing between clenched teeth. A whirlwind of outrage. Confusion. Horror.

She wakes me up by waving something in my face. Without my glasses, it looks like a white blur. But there is only one thing she could be holding.

One moment, let me find my glasses, I tell her, trying to keep calm. I reach toward the chair. Must delay. Vera is dressed. The envelope she is holding, the envelope with Zach's name on it, Zach's name in my handwriting, has been opened.

Most of all, I am conscious of wearing nothing but pants. How absurd, at a time like this, when one is in danger, to think, first and foremost, of what one is wearing. But I feel my unclothed state puts me at a disadvantage. No longer wearing trousers and no longer in possession of the letter, which she must have already read, I feel doubly naked. I grab the nearest clothing to hand, Zach's suit, from the back of the chair where I'd hung it up last night. As if it were the most ordinary object in the world, I tell Vera, Appears to be a letter. I step into the black trousers. Thread the belt. Hold out my hand. May I see it?

Vera is not fooled by my pretence of ignorance. You can see it just fine from where you are, she hisses. No, don't move. Don't you fucking take another step. Stay right where you are *and tell me what this is.*

I put on the shirt. Then the jacket, leaving the unlinked cuffs hanging awkwardly from the sleeves. I draw out a cigarette from the packet and light one. Vera is audibly breathing. Her nostrils expand and contract like accordion bellows. Exasperated by the evasive deliberateness of my movements and combustible with suspicion, it would take only the truth for her to explode into fury. I calmly ask her a question I already know the answer to. Must delay.

In the book in your jacket pocket! she shrieks. And how did she come to be looking through my pockets? Her voice modulates as she attempts to explain. I was just... just going to take Zach's suit... to the dry cleaner. I took out the book and the letter just... just fell out.

So she could lie as well. Just like me. The things we always fail to consider. The ones that lie right before our eyes. How easy it is to take for granted the truthfulness and decency of others when we display so little of it ourselves. What other falsehoods, I wonder, has she told me in response to my falsehoods? Clearly she'd seen the letter in the jacket and pulled it out herself. It was a question, as my tutors had taught me, of procedural justice: the admissibility of evidence wrongfully obtained against what that evidence reveals. Vera's voice had cracked. Cracked with the knowledge of not standing on entirely firm ethical ground.

Give me back the letter, Vera. It doesn't belong to you.

Don't take one more step. She holds up her mobile phone with her other hand. I swear to God, if you take one more step, I'll call the police. She punches three digits into the phone, holding her finger over the send button as if it were the trigger of a pistol.

And what will you tell them? That you've opened up someone else's post? That's a criminal offence if I'm not mistaken.

What I'll *tell* them, she snarls, is that two nights ago you *raped* me and now you're holding me hostage in my room.

I reach into Zach's pocket, the pocket, unhappily for us both, she hadn't looked into. Does this belong to you by any chance? I ask.

Puzzled by what she perceives as a non sequitur, she squints to see what I'm rolling between my thumb and my forefinger. When she understands what it is, her eyes expand. They begin to fill with moisture, poised to overflow. Shock. The shock of recognition.

She gasps. Where did you get that?

It was included with the letter Zach posted to me. Perhaps you can explain why he did that.

Give it back to me! she cries, lunging toward my hand. I close my fist tightly round the pearl and wing my arm away from her, putting a menacing shoulder forward to discourage her from trying again. She loses control of the mobile phone, which falls to the ground halfway between us. She looks at it, trying to decide whether or not to collect it. Whether to focus her energy on retrieving it or the pearl. She thrusts out her empty palm, just as I had done only moments before. Give it to me! You have no right!

Right has nothing to do with it! I shout, edging my words with the threat of violence. I have something you want. You have something I want. Let's swop — and forget this ever happened, okay?

Swop. Our tokens of sorrow and grief. The plugs we use

to keep the hulls of our hearts from flooding. Besides the memories, besides the scars, these objects are all that remains of the person we've lost. Her pearl. My letter. A struggle between us. Over who's to get Zach. In the end.

I have a better idea, she says, the tone of her voice calmer, more conciliatory. Why don't you explain what this means. And I'll tell you what that is. Then we'll decide what we want to do.

Fine, I say. I hear the sound of movement in Katie's room. Our shouting must have woken her up. But would you mind having this conversation in your room? I tilt my head in the direction of Katie's door. I'm not exactly keen on others hearing what I have to say. Perhaps you feel the same.

What I have to say. A tale of two letters. The story she wished to hear all along, but hadn't known it until now. Vera snatches up the mobile and opens the door to her room. The letter and the phone are pressed protectively to her chest. She never once takes her wary eyes off me. I sit on the windowsill, but she remains standing. Her back is against the door. Within reach of the bronze knob. And escape.

It's a suicide note, I explain. This she has understood, but she doesn't interrupt me now. Now she's confident that, finally, the truth will out.

With one important difference, it is identical to the one I turned over to the two police detectives who carried out the investigation into Zach's death and who, with my permission, gave it to your father.

From her expression I can tell she is making the connexions, beginning to understand.

There was a pact. A suicide pact. Zach and I were supposed to die together. What happened was this: when I walked through the doorway of the Exam Schools, shortly after half six on June 15th, Zach was already there, smoking a cigarette, waiting for me.

THE MORAL AND THE TRAGIC.— In practice, everyday morality rarely ever rises to the level of the tragic. Most moral decisions are as simple as basic arithmetic; just so, failures are not matters of knowledge but of social training. Where genuine moral problems are encountered — that is, what are called tragic dilemmas — it is the nature of the dilemma that none of the possible responses ultimately suffices. Any decision, therefore, made in response to a tragic dilemma, will still be, to some more or less pardonable extent, immoral, and any moral agent, when faced with such a dilemma, no matter how much he deliberates, according to whichever ethical system he favours, will not fail to be responsible for this immorality. Nor, if he is truly a man of conscience, will he fail to be permanently damaged by the outcome of his response, whatever it may be.

When I walked through the doorway of the Exam Schools, shortly after half six on June 15th, Zach was already there, smoking a cigarette, waiting for me. I didn't see him at first. On the pavement, a crowd of students had gathered, giddy with excitement, many already drunk. They were waiting for their friends to emerge from the imposing wooden doors — so they could trash them.

Trashing was an end of the-year Oxford tradition. After

one of your mates finished his exams, you were supposed to congratulate him for his hard work by covering him in a mix of celebratory substances, the standard ingredients of which were confetti, Silly String, glitter, and shaving foam, although those who were a bit higher up the social ladder would add a spray of champagne, and those who belonged to the secret societies and private clubs, and whose finances were thus inversely proportional to their scruples, had been known to inundate their friends with buckets of mud, raw eggs, and even pig's blood, which could be had from the butcher in the Covered Market, before dragging them off to the back room of a posh restaurant or club, where they were rumoured to kindle cigars on rolled up hundred-pound notes and lay waste to crockery and furniture in states that challenged the biological limits of inebriation. Because townies and tourists frequently found themselves as the collateral damage of these indiscriminate bombing raids, and the sordid antics of the clubs and societies sometimes made headlines in the tabloids, the university tried to put a stop to the practice with fines, paradoxically ensuring that it would be a tradition only the rich, who were in any case the worst offenders, could afford to maintain. But university officials were not the only ones who frowned on trashing. Many students, Claire and Tori among them, also found it insufferable, which is why, I suppose, they hadn't minded when Zach volunteered to collect me from Prelims, whilst they prepared the flat for an entirely more civilised celebration later in the evening.

He was standing toward the back of the scrum, one shining patent leather shoe on the kerb and one in the road, the only person there with a serious look on his face. As a visiting student, he wasn't required to sit exams, but he was dressed subfusc anyway, down to the white carnation in the buttonhole of his lapel. His jacket fit him poorly for once, I thought, before I saw the two large bulges in his pockets and understood the reason for it. When he saw me come through the doors — there was an anticipatory swell of cheering from the crowd which died down as soon as all realised I was not the friend they were waiting for — he let his cigarette fall, stamped it out, and lit another. We greeted each other without a word and began to walk, the soles of our shoes echoing on the pavement.

Although it was summer, a weather system that had been conceived in the North Atlantic a few days earlier had finally begun to drag its belly over the Thames Valley as it pawed its way toward the continent. The sky was prematurely, unseasonably dark, and the High appeared to be an inverted world, one whose steeples, spires, and towers had not so much sprung up from the horizon as dripped like drops of slate and limestone wax down wicks dangling from somewhere deep within the low-lying clouds. The unstable air, warm and damp and windy, seethed with electricity. Any minute now rain would begin to fall, and I immediately regretted not having asked to borrow Claire's brolly this morning. Zach, it seemed, had forgotten his at the Bevington Road; actually, as I was later to discover, he had deliberately left it behind in his rooms.

I found myself falling a pace or two behind him as the two mechanical centurions beneath the clock on the Carfax Tower hammered at their brass bells, and he turned, without looking back to see if I was following him, into Cornmarket. Zach's stride was always brisk (unless it was I who was walking more slowly than usual, reluctance clutching me by the ankles, dread blowing hard against my face and chest), but this time there was something unusual in it. This time he was all business, his attention single-minded, fixed. He remained quiet, his brows tensed, as if he were pondering something that required every last watt his concentration could spare. It occurred to me that he might be nervous, a feeling that, in turn, communicated itself to me.

Now and again I lost sight of him. Cornmarket had suddenly become an ant colony of black caps and gowns, in various states of cleanness and dryness, madly to ing and fro-ing between the doors of the colleges, the Exam Schools, and the pubs. I caught up with him again only as the swarm of students began to thin out on Magdalen Street and we stood, our backs to the stone needle of the Martyrs' Memorial, as we waited in silence for the light to turn green. Rather than turning up St. Giles', in order to approach Godstow from Jericho, where we might accidentally run into Tori or Claire taking a last-minute trip to the shops to buy something for the party, Zach continued down Beaumont Street, past the Randolph Hotel and the Ashmolean Museum. We would make our way through the small, less foot-trafficked roads behind the gargantuan neoclassical offices of the university press, until we reached the canal. There we would take the towpath north and walk into Port Meadow.

The canal was largely empty. The few people we saw were occupied, securing their houseboats in anticipation of the coming storm. No one seemed to pay us any mind, or find it at all odd that two students, in academic dress, were taking a stroll up the river on a rainy night rather than celebrating in one of the city's hundred pubs. Oxford students were famous, after all, for getting up to strange things this time of year. They would have no doubt assumed that he and I were taking the long way to The Perch or The Trout for a pint or ten. Even had they noticed the bulges in Zach's jacket pockets — which they almost certainly had not, considering how dark and foggy it had become — they would have never guessed what they were.

It felt like Zach was leading me back in time. To our right, the husk of the old Eagle Ironworks, a soot-stained redbrick foundry, which had in its prime furnished England with everything from manhole cover and decorative gates to ploughing engines and munitions. It had survived the era of coke and steam and ore, but just barely. The local papers regularly featured articles warning that its new American owners were planning to shutter the factory, clear the site, and develop the wharf into a block of flats.

Farther on, we crossed a stone footbridge and came at

last to the entrance of Port Meadow, a pasture stretching from Jericho to Wolvercote. Port Meadow remained to this day common land, where cattle and horses were allowed by law to graze freely, as they had done under feudalism. Beneath these patches of mud and thistle, which caked the leather of our shoes and caught in the hems of our trousers, archaeologists had unearthed a Neolithic burial site, shards of Roman pottery, Cavalier fortifications from the Civil War, and the scattered rubbish of soldiers closer to us in time, my grandfather among them, who encamped here following the evacuation from Dunkirk.

Save for the cows, which had taken to their knees, and a gaggle of geese, which glared and honked at us as we passed, we were now completely alone. I looked over my shoulder. Beyond the darkening line of poplars on the edge of the meadow I could no longer see the dreaming spires of the High, where we had come from centuries ago, or so it felt. The only visible structure was the campanile of St. Barnabas Church, on Hart Street, behind the university press, and it was slowly disappearing behind a slow-moving wall of fog.

I stopped: "This has gone far enough, hasn't it?" It was the first time either of us had spoken, and the words stuck in my throat, as if they were also lumbering through a muddy field. Zach misheard me, or deliberately misconstrued what I'd said. He pointed off in the distance, beyond the bend in the river. "No. We still have a little farther to go," he said and continued walking. I hesitated for a moment, not sure whether I ought to follow him. The first drops of rain were falling on my forehead. The poplars began to sway in the intensifying wind. I wiped my glasses dry with the untucked tail of my shirt and took a final look in the direction of the city, wishing I were still there, standing on the steps of the Exam Schools, part of a past that still belonged to me. Zach was now a dozen paces ahead of me; soon I wouldn't be able to see where he had gone and I'd find myself alone in the large, empty meadow. Reluctantly, I quickened my steps to catch up with him.

Godstow Abbey, I had read, was built to house nuns of the Benedictine Order and to educate the daughters of the local gentry. Now it lay in ruins. All that remained of it were the south walls of the chapel, a ragged triangle with empty tracery and two long rectangles with tufts of moss and grass peeking out of the gaps in the uneven stonework. At their base, the walls were slowly being swallowed up by the marshy ground, which sloped downward toward the river. Here called the Isis, the Thames is no more than a stream five metres from bank to bank, so narrow that it's almost impossible to believe that this little twist of dark green water becomes the river that flows beneath London Bridge and out to the North Sea.

Zach contemplated the ruins critically for a moment, with the look of a man adjusting his hair in a mirror. According to legend, the place where we were standing was haunted ground. I wondered if he knew it. The mistress of Henry II was poisoned by his jealous queen and buried here. Throughout the Middle Ages, the abbey was a popular shrine and pilgrimage site, until it was destroyed during the dissolution of the monasteries. After the Civil War it was abandoned to the picks of local quarrymen and the pens of minor Romantics, who found in its picturesque setting and melancholy history inspiration for heroic couplets on the subject of illicit love.

When he was satisfied, Zach sat cross-legged on the top of the slope, his back to the river. His shoes and his trousers were covered in mud. What a shame, I couldn't help but think, to ruin such a smart suit. He motioned for me to sit opposite him, my back to the abbey walls. "It's time," he said, fixing me with a stare. Then he reached into his pockets. He entwined our arms as if we were a wedding couple drinking a glass of champagne before the cutting of the cake. But in our hands he had not placed two flutes, but two pistols, now pointed chest level. I could feel his breath on my face.

When we were finally in position, he disentangled his arm from mine, shaking his head. "No," he said. "This isn't right."

My shoulders, which were hunched and tense, frozen until that moment in an uncomfortable shrug, the curve of my clavicles nearly touching the angle of my jaws, relaxed, and I exhaled. My arm, rigid and sore, stopped quivering. I loosened my grip on the handle and lifted my finger from the trigger. So it had been a test after all, only a test, and by stepping with him to the very edge of death, by demonstrating to him and to myself that I was not afraid to look down at an unending drop, or was at least able to overcome my fear of the heights, I had passed. Now all that remained was for him to explain exactly how.

Instead, I sensed sudden motion. I felt the muzzle of his pistol against my chest. I looked down at it, wondering what it was doing there, and then up at him. His unblinking eyes were covered over with a depthless fanatical sheen, the brown irises as dark and empty as his pupils. I searched them, but that almost invisible residue of identity that somehow enables one thinking, intending, willing person to recognise another behind their surface was nowhere to be seen. He was absent from his eyes. Intensely absent. I

n a high-pitched tone of voice that asked *Where are you?* as much as it asked *What are you doing?* I said, "Zach?"

"Like this," he said. He grabbed my limp, hesitant hand and raised my pistol to his chest, so our arms formed parallel lines. I tried to pull it back, but his hand caught my elbow and held it straight. "*This* is how it should be done."

"But that's not suicide," I stammered. "It's murder."

"*Double* murder," he corrected. "It's *genius*. This whole week I've been meditating on a problem, a problem whose solution I've only now, right at this very instant, discovered." His mouth seemed to have hijacked his mind, and it moved as if his words were doing his thinking for him, pausing neither for breath nor clarity. "The problem is that suicide, intentional suicide, as I described it to you, is actually impossible. Think about it!" He was raving. Rain was dripping down his brow and cheeks and caromed off his lower lip as he spoke. " 'I kill myself' — it's a *reflexive* verb. With suicide, the person who does the killing is not the same as the person who does the dying, even if those two people happen to share the same body. Suicide doubles us, cuts us in two, turns us into pure subjects and pure objects at the same time. Doubles us just like language doubles things, by transforming them into referents. Suicide is always already murder, and so, still under the sign of natural death. To do it right it would have to be intentional *and* accidental *at the same time*. This *whole week* I've been in such a state of despair, Owen, *you can't even imagine*, every waking second, racking my brain, how to undo this paradox, how to solve this problem. But now I see! It's *so simple*. All you have to do is double the doubling! You have to will your death without performing it, while at the same time performing it for someone else who wills it. An authentic suicide, the only authentic act there is, can only be done with a partner, through a pact like this. I knew I wasn't wrong to take you along with me, Owen. My words will kill me, even though you pull the trigger, just as your words will kill you when I fire. We'll turn death into an *idea*! And ideas never die. Ideas live forever. Owen, it's genius! Pure genius."

"It's immor —"

"Exactly! That's exactly it!" he cried, though I doubt he understood what I was trying to tell him. "Now, I'm going to count back from three." He wiped the damp fringe off his brow with the back of his hand and repositioned his arm. "On zero, we fire." He cocked his pistol. "Three..."

My terrified eyes moved back and forth, wildly searching his, *Is he really going to do this?* unspoken on my dripping, trembling lips, begging him not to, the words frozen on my tongue. Moisture had entirely covered the inside of my glasses and I could no longer see his eyes, nor he mine.

He raised his voice: "Two..."

The rain was falling harder now, the sharp drops relentlessly striking the flat leaves of the trees and the muddy meadow, the stones of the abbey and the surface of the river. It sounded like the world and everything in it had suddenly turned into shattering glass. He really was going to do this; he was going to kill me. My thumb rolled back. I could feel the barrel of my pistol pressed against the button of his dress shirt and the inside of my forefinger slipping along the wet crescent of the trigger, as if my whole being had condensed into the line between these two points.

"One —"

A gentle pop. Barely audible above the rain. Opposite me, I felt his body lurch like a stalled engine. His right arm, the one holding the pistol, must have swung back as his chest absorbed the shot, because I felt a bullet whizz past my ear, off target. Letting go of my pistol, I sprang from my position and knocked him over the slope of the riverbank. He fell upside down, the back of his head hitting the ground not far from the edge of the water. My hands found his biceps and I pressed him into the mud with all my strength. The muscles of his right arm tensed as he struggled to free it from my grip, in order to turn the pistol on me, to finish what he'd started. I heard him grunt and gasp for breath, but the expression on his face was still invisible to me. All I could see was the blur of water on water, the rain now indistinguishable from my hysterical tears. I was breathing heavily through my open mouth, my chest heaving, a scream rounding the back of my bared teeth. I pressed harder. And kept pressing, long after I stopped encountering any resistance.

I don't know how long I held him there, but when I let go, wiped and replaced my glasses, he was still alive, barely alive. I saw his cheekbones rise, his eyebrows arch. His lips parted. Then they expanded into his cheeks, revealing red teeth. He tried to say something, to tell me something, of that I'm certain. But his last words, whatever they were meant to be, were lost in a gurgle of blood.

A WARNING TO THE CHILDREN OF THE SUN, EARTH, AND MOON.— Nothingness added to Being is not oneness, but duality. But as nothingness is chronologically primary to Being, Being has never been the One. Only nothingness is oneness, wholeness, harmony, and totality. Being is the name for the operation that irreparably divides the Zero in Two. Our desire to recover our lost wholeness is the desire for death.

How to tell you this, Vera says softly, with downcast eyes, shaking her head in slow dismay, as she reflects on the difficulty of putting into words all the thoughts she must have been gathering during the long, dense silence that followed my confession of the role I played in Zach's death. I just don't know how to begin, she tells me. No, that's not right. I know *how*. How is only a matter of willpower, of forcing the words out, even if they're not the right words. Where to begin, I mean, at what point to begin, how far back should I go, that's what I don't know. When, then, and not how. It's a different question. When asks: At what point in the past did you become the person who made the choices you made. When asks: What was the moment you could no longer make another choice and still be the person you are, whether you wanted to be this person or not, whether you're happy with the results of the choices you ended up making, unless this is too narrow a way of looking at it, because our lives may be like trees with billions of forking branches, but they are themselves a branching off, a branching off from a tree which is larger than us and grew before us — our choices are inherited from the choices that others have made, who in turn inherited their choices from others. To tell you what I am, what I have become, I have to look back toward the trunk of the tree from the tip of a branch that will no longer branch off, from the moment that whispered to me, *You are This and This you will be forever*, and while I can give a precise time to that moment, to get there, working backwards, wherever I end up beginning will not be far back enough.

These pearls, I could begin with these pearls. They are more than one hundred years old. They belonged to my great-grandmother, who passed them on to my grandmother, who passed them on to my mother, who passed them on to me. Four generations, four generations of women, passing on these pearls. Twice they were given as wedding presents, but one of the things I've never understood is why you'd give a bride a string of *black* pearls as a wedding present, it's perverse, ominous even, the kind of gift that is indistinguishable from a curse. What I do know is that the pearls were one of the things, one of the very few things, my grandmother took with her when she fled Europe before the war. What I also know is that unlike my grandmother and unlike her own mother, Mommy only received them when Oma died, when I was a young girl, seven years old. I don't remember my grandmother well, not just because she died when I was so young, but also because she and my mother had a very frosty relationship, they were almost estranged, and we didn't see Oma often. It had something to do with my mother's marriage I've come to believe, she didn't approve of my father, he wasn't good enough for my mother she probably thought, Oma was a real snob, from what I've gathered. I'm certain that if Mommy had a sister, instead of two brothers, Oma would have given them to this sister for her wedding, or at least left them to this sister in her will when she died. In fact, I've overheard that she willed them to my aunt, my mother's eldest brother's wife, but my aunt knew the history of the pearls, how they'd been passed on from daughter to daughter, and thought it would be wrong to accept them, and immediately *returned* them, I overheard, to their *rightful owner*. I believe Mommy wore them for the first time at Oma's funeral and now that I know what I know, I believe it would have been better if Mommy had buried her with them. But I didn't know then what I know now, so as a child I associated the pearls with my mother rather than with my grandmother, with my future rather than with my past, to me they were a symbol of what it meant to be a grown up, to be a woman. Because my mother didn't receive them for her wedding, she didn't wait for my wedding to give them to me, a tradition had been broken, or at least half-broken, because she passed them on to me anyway, I suppose, thus carrying it on in some respect. She gave them to me when I graduated high school. It was as if she was telling me, Y*ou're a grown up now. You're a woman now*. I was supposed to pass them on to my own daughter when the time came, whenever that occasion was, I would know, my mother told me. I felt like so much trust had been placed in me. So much responsibility whenever I wore them. And so I wore them rarely, on special occasions, for fear of losing them, or damaging them. Before Zach's funeral, the last time I put them on was on New Year's Eve, the day that turned out to contain the moment that whispered to me, *You are This and This you will be forever*. The moment that said to me, *What you are is a Monster*.

And then there's my brother, the other thing, you might say, I inherited from my mother. I could begin with him too. My beginning is his beginning, after all, his beginning is my beginning, we were born to the same forking branch, not two persons but one person, as I was telling you the other night, the I that is we and the we that is I, as he liked to say, something more than my other half, something less than my double. It can't be said that we didn't have our differences, however much we tried to ignore them, however badly we wanted to erase them. Differences we inherited. Differences that are older than us and proved to be greater than us, stronger than us. What I know now is that it was our differences, and our attempts to ignore them at first, and then our attempts to erase them, that made us the monster that we are, or that we were, in any case, the monster that we became. We were too close to each other and at the same time too far from each other. Zach must have known what these pearls meant to me, and now I wonder if he saw in them some manifestation of that difference, my distance from him, a distance we were born with, a small crack that grew wider with every passing year, the more adult we became. Do I need to tell you, in any case, what difference I'm talking about? Perhaps you already know, perhaps you've already begun to understand. I will tell you anyway. Because if no one has the courage to make the implicit explicit it stays implicit forever. It disappears. It gets ignored and erased. The difference I'm talking about is the oldest difference, the founding difference, the original difference, the difference between male and female, between women and men, sexual difference, the difference that makes and unmakes us all. I don't remember the moment I realized what sex was, though I know it was before Mommy and Daddy finally sat Zach and me down and explained it to us. Dr. Stein, whom I haven't told any of this, or at least not the main thing, observed that my sexuality, and thus Zach's sexuality, didn't develop normally. It was delayed, she says, *inflected* is the term she uses. Our parents, she told me, didn't differentiate us strongly enough or soon enough, perhaps they too saw us as merely one person in two bodies, even if our bodies, not knowing or caring who we thought we were or what we thought we wanted, did what all bodies naturally do, they went their own ways, changed, differentiated themselves, and in so doing, became complementary. Zach and I shared a room for what I now understand is an inappropriately long time, until the summer before our freshman year of high school, when Mommy and Daddy said enough is enough, though by then, yes, it was too late. In our room, there used to be two beds, but for us it was something of a formality, the second bed. Until we were finally separated we shared that too, at first because we didn't know any better, and then because I had nightmares when we tried to sleep alone, nightmares that Zach, by some miracle, was able to describe to me, to recount in their entirety, as if he'd had them too. He would wrap his arm around me and stroke my hair and whisper my dreams into my ear until I fell asleep. But when you share a bed with someone at that age, when you add physical proximity to mental and emotional proximity, you discover things about your body, things you forever associate with the person who discovered them with you. Zach's first wet dream happened on my thigh. Later, when I had my first period, I showed him the blood. Like all children, we heard things about sex at school, picked up information from our classmates with older siblings, inferred things from the films we saw, from the paintings we saw, images we saw before we were ready to see them, but which, given what our parents do for a living, were everywhere around us growing up. We had the images before we knew what words to give to them, which, of course, is the exact opposite experience from the one most children have, our classmates had to give us the names for the images our parents carelessly left out before us. Our classmates, it should be said, treated us differently, differently from them, I mean, precisely because we refused to acknowledge our own difference. At the age when boys and girls naturally split themselves up, share different lunch tables, play different games at recess, during what Dr. Stein would call our latency period, we did not split up, we went everywhere together. Zach sat out sports with me at the girls' table, and I never went to sleepovers because obviously Zach was never invited to them. For many years we were isolated by our classmates, from our classmates, like untouchables, as if they had some intuition, already at that age, about the monster we would become. We weren't even known by separate names, as Zach and Vera, they called us the Foedern Twins, except by our teachers, of course, we were always referred to collectively, and our classmates' opposition to our being together simply drove us closer together, threw us back on ourselves. Perhaps you are wondering why our parents didn't intervene. They did. But it was too late, as I was saying. I lied to you the other night, or I didn't tell you the whole story, just as until now you have been lying to me, withholding the whole story from me. The reason we were separated that summer, the reason I was kept here in the city and Zach was sent up to New Hampshire, was that one evening Mommy caught us kissing each other. *Just practicing* was how we tried to explain ourselves to her, under the guise of one of those childhood games we were at that point already too old to be playing. We got the talk, the talk that every normal American child gets at some point, Daddy and Mommy made explicit to us what we already sensed implicitly, they explained what sex was, and told us what every normal child is told, *Sex is a healthy and beautiful and meaningful activity and When we were old enough we could have safe, consensual sex with anyone we wanted to — except each other*. Zach was sent home early from camp that summer, that much of what I told you was true, but when he came back, all of his things, including the bed we never used, had been moved to a different room. Mommy and Daddy's excuse was that the room was no longer large enough for both of us and our things, and that's how we spent high school: under the same roof, in exile from each other.

During those years we tried to differentiate ourselves, or rather I did, I tried to separate myself from him, I was always more obedient than he was, more conventional. Other people's opinions, whether they were our parents' opinions, or our classmates' opinions, or Dr. Stein's opinions, mattered

215

much more to me than they did to him. I always felt them more strongly, they weighed on me more heavily, a weight around my neck I always found harder to endure, unless it was because I didn't resent them like he did, or perhaps because I didn't feel that it was my duty to ignore them or erase them, let alone contradict or rebel against them. Zach made it difficult for me, those four years, sensing my confusion and my ambivalence. A person with certainty and conviction will always overwhelm a person who is pulled in multiple directions, whose desires are many and therefore contradictory and therefore must be negotiated, single-mindedness always triumphs over vacillation, to vacillate is to be vulnerable, even if it is, in the end, also what it means to be moral. But I'm forced to remind myself that he would not have seen things that way. However crazy this might sound to someone who is used to regarding themselves as one person rather than two people, a person who identifies another person entirely with himself will regard her vacillation as his own, maybe Zach was trying, just as much as I was, to root out an inconsistency within himself. But I only understood this later, when I had the feeling myself, the feeling of jealousy, I mean. As I tried to bring other people, other boys, into my life, his love for me took a negative turn, expressed itself in hostility, through various forms of emotional sabotage and blackmail. At first he tried to scare off the boys who were interested in me, by spreading rumors about me, or humiliating my dates when I invited them to dinner, defending himself later, when we would fight about it, by saying this one was *too stupid for me*, or that one was *uncultured*, or another was clearly *using me to meet Mommy or Daddy* in order, the implication was, to get summer internships or college recommendations, which is actually not as outlandish as it sounds, given the shameless ambition of most of the students at Gansevoort, especially the ones who, at sixteen or seventeen, already thought of themselves as artists. You would think that this interference, this attack on my autonomy, would have inspired some resistance in me, and in fact it did, I resented it deeply at first. When I was sixteen and seventeen, I dated a boy who, when I look back on it, really was not for me, Zach was right about him in fact, but I dated this boy for over a year just to show Zach I wouldn't be intimidated or coerced. This boy was nothing more than my pawn, and now that I use this metaphor, I realize how foolish it was to do this, because Zach, as you know, was a ranked chess player who knew better than anyone how and when to force a sacrifice. This boy, then, this innocent bystander, was nothing more than my pawn, and a piece of his broken heart probably has my name still written on it, poor thing, because one of the awful things I've learned is that we never recover from the loss of our first love. I professed to love this boy, and he believed me, but really I didn't even see him for who he was, as an autonomous person, a person who stood in no relation to Zach. Zach stopped speaking to me, that was his first strategy, how childish it was, to give someone the silent treatment like that, but then we were children, we have always been children, perhaps we never stopped being children. Nevertheless, I found it agonizing, indescribably painful, it gave me the first taste of his absence, my first insight to what he himself was feeling, the cruelty I was inflicting upon him, even if, as I rationalized it then, it was actually he who was inflicting this punishment on us both. But I did not bend under this pressure, not yet knowing that people who do not bend under a small amount of pressure break more easily under a greater amount of pressure. You can guess, I'm sure, what I'm talking about, what pressure I'm referring to, Zach did what anyone in his position would do, I see that clearly now, what an obvious counterattack it was, he started dating a girl, a girl I particularly hated too, a girl who was my opposite in every way, he chose the girl who would most humiliate me and degrade me, he brought her home with him, to teach me what jealousy was, to show me how jealousy felt, to make me admit that I was jealous of him, to make me realize that the pain of jealousy is the deepest expression of attachment and love. One day he brought her home with him and he made sure that I knew it, that I knew it was her, he took her into his room and locked the door behind him. I should have left the house right then and there, but I had an exam the next morning, it was finals week, I remember, senior year, a few weeks before our graduation, a few weeks before I would receive the pearls from Mommy. In all honesty, I was incapable of leaving, as soon as I tried to stand my knees buckled under me, I was paralyzed by the thought that Zach was in our house with someone else, a thought that, no matter how I tried, I could not banish from my mind, even trying to banish it from my mind only reminded me of it, even trying to convince myself that what was happening was not happening only reminded me that it was in fact happening. I dragged myself down the hallway because I couldn't stand up and walk, I crawled to his door, that's when I found out it was locked, I pressed my ear to the door and listened to them, she was very loud, on purpose maybe, maybe she knew why Zach had brought her there, maybe Zach was a pawn in a game of her own, a game whose goal may have been to hurt me, or to hurt someone else, that was possible, I knew, because it was a game I had played myself, and why should we expect other people to be better intentioned or more considerate than we are. I listened outside his door while she moaned and whimpered, while she shouted obscenities and told Zach what to do to her, *that* I didn't even have to imagine for myself. I was collapsed and curled up on the floor outside our bedroom, tears were running down my face, snot was running from my nose, my throat gagged on each breath, a sudden need to vomit prevented me from speaking, from shouting, from begging them to stop. I dug my fingernails into my arm, to get some relief, I needed relief. But when this did not make the noises stop, when it did not make her obscene narrating stop, I pressed the fingers of my other hand between my legs, to get relief, I needed relief so badly, I held my hand there, pathetic and weak, imagining myself in her place. That was when I began to understand what I was feeling, when I was able to give a name to the pain I was feeling, the name of the pain was jealousy, and at that moment, the pain was so strong it overwhelmed the other feeling, my feeling of shame, my feeling of intense self-disgust. And I understood, even if I didn't admit it to myself until later, until the next morning, when I promised Zach I would no longer see other people if he promised me not to see other people, when, essentially, I gave in to him, though you could also say I was giving in to myself, or simply giving in, then and only then, as he held me in his arms and ran his hands through my hair and whispered into my ear, comforting me as he had comforted me when I had my childhood nightmares, only then did I understand that whatever feelings I had for him as a child, when I didn't know how disgusting those feelings were, when I was innocent of any shame, were feelings I had not grown out of. It was as if the nightmares I had as a child had now moved across the border into my waking life, where there was only one person who knew how to make them disappear, only one person capable of giving me the relief I needed.

In college we were given another chance to separate, to differentiate, maybe it was our last chance, our last chance to learn how to be apart, so that when we finally came to be apart, the pressure wouldn't destroy us, because, as I said, things that cannot bend under small pressures invariably break under great ones. But we didn't take it. The pendulum between distance and proximity, between tension and relief, between shame and desire, between absence and presence was already swinging and could not be stopped. The college assigned us to different dorm rooms, as a matter of school policy, there were no coed dorm rooms, even for siblings, Zach was assigned to a single in a dorm across campus from mine, where I had a double, with a roommate. This was our chance, our chance at separation, to keep our separate rooms, but now that our parents couldn't watch over us, Zach reasoned, there was no reason for us to be separate, no reason that things shouldn't return to the way they were when we were children, before we had to separate, to differentiate, to be apart. Zach persuaded my roommate to switch rooms with him. That wasn't difficult actually: by chance he had landed one of the most coveted room assignments in college, and when the RA discovered our violation of school policy, we paid him not to report it. No doubt it doubly pleased Zach that he had to break the rules to get what we wanted. At first we lived chastely as a monk and a nun, we went everywhere together, but we never pushed the border further than we already had, that was my wish, it was my idea to place some kind of border between us, so that we could survive the torture of our impossible love. Zach didn't object, at least not explicitly, he didn't pressure me any further, and the border between us stayed firm for two years, stayed firm until a few days before Zach went off to Oxford, went off on the advice of Dr. Stein and the insistence of our parents, went off with extreme ambivalence and anxiety on both of our parts, as I was telling you, when we cut each other for the first time and, in so doing, weakened the border we would totally erase as soon as he came back home for winter break.

When he came back home for winter break, after months of not seeing each other, in which our only contact was through language, through letters, through our invented code, I picked him up at the airport. To say I was happy to see him would be an understatement. I was ecstatic to see him, positively ecstatic, I threw my arms around his neck when he came through the doors of the terminal. Everyone there must have thought we were boyfriend and girlfriend. But at that moment I hardly cared, I thought, *So what! Let them!* and kissed him on the lips. New Year's Eve, the night that contained the moment, the moment that said to me, *You Are This*, he stayed here, with me. Katie was in Los Angeles, visiting her family for the holidays, we had the apartment to ourselves that night, the night that contained the moment that whispered to me, *This you will be forever*. That night it seemed like this apartment was the whole world, even though we could hear sounds from the street, people getting drunk, playing music, lighting firecrackers, celebrating, it was as if the world outside these walls didn't actually exist. We stayed inside, dressed in our finest clothes, I put on the pearls, the pearls I only wore on special occasions, because I sensed, without knowing, unfortunately, how right I would be, that this was a special occasion, and besides, they went perfectly with the dress he picked out for me. I picked out a suit for him, *that* suit, the one you're wearing now. He opened a bottle of champagne, I put on some music, we drank and danced, in the living room, like two people dancing at the center of the center of the world. We drank and talked, told each other about the months we had passed alone, expanded on what we had recounted in our letters, he had even written about you, he told me that he had noticed you, and though he'd never spoken to you, he sensed you were the only person at the college that he might be able to have a real conversation with, the only person he might be able to open up to. Then, when he was opening the second bottle of champagne, he asked me to see the scar, to see how it had healed. Instead of rolling up the sleeve, what was I thinking, I was probably thinking that I didn't want to tear or crease the fabric of the dress in my drunken state, instead of rolling up the sleeve, I unzipped it from the back and took it off, letting it fall to the floor, stepping out of it and hanging it over a chair, not thinking or probably not caring how provocative that would have looked, to be dressed in only the pearls and my underwear and the scar on my arm. Holding my arm, like you did, he rubbed his thumb over the scar, like you did, and asked me, almost offhandedly, as if it were a perfectly normal thing to ask, as if he was just wondering aloud, *When I cut you it excited me* and *Was it the same for you?* It was, as you know, I've confessed that to you already, it *was* the same for me, but in that moment it felt less like a confession of a secret shame than a confirmation of our connection, which had not diminished during the time we had spent apart from one another, a confirmation that Zach knew what I had been thinking, what I had been feeling, as he always had, and I felt close to him, closer than I ever had to him, as I asked him if he wanted to do it again. He didn't answer, he went into the kitchen and took the knife from the drawer, there's no way to say this without simply saying it, he cut me again, put a red line right beneath the white line where the other cut had healed, then he handed me the knife and started to unbutton his shirt. We could have stopped there, that was the moment to stop, that was the moment I could have said, *No, this has gone too far*, just as you could have said, but didn't say, *This has gone too far*. It was the last moment I could have said that, although the last moment one can say something or do something is always at least a moment too late, the last moment is really something we can only see in retrospect, when we try to trace things back to their origins, when we try to answer the question, When. At that moment, that too-late moment, I was watching him speechlessly, hypnotized by the taste of the champagne and the sight of blood, hypnotized and, yes, aroused, I was watching him lift my arm by the fingers, it felt like it was floating of its own free will, he lifted it to his lips, ran his mouth over the cut, licked the blood off my arm. Then I did the same to him, cut him and licked the blood off his arm, realizing at that moment that the way his blood tasted was exactly the way my blood would taste, warm, slightly metallic. I thought, *This is wrong*, and I re-member being excited by that too, by the *wrongness* of it. I remember thinking, for a moment, before things went too far, before we were kissing each other, before I lay on my back and unhooked my bra and felt his mouth on my breasts, as I held him there, my fingers threaded through the back of his hair, his lips pressed to my heart, I remember thinking, *There is no one in the world but Zach and me.* I lifted my hips so he could undress me, so that I could be naked with him, so he could be inside me, connected as no two people have ever been connected before. But in the next moment, the moment after the moment it was too late, I learned something awful, something horrifying, something which, from that moment on, I have wished I could unlearn. I learned that time never stops, and that the moment after the moment it seems to stop, the moment after the ecstatic moment, the moment after the moment where time itself seems fulfilled and completed, is free fall. Zach came quickly, the moment of our connection, of him being inside me, was only that, a moment, a moment that said to me, *What you are is a Monster.* While he was shaking, Zach reached out, as if to stabilize himself, as if he needed to prevent himself from free fall, he grabbed the closest thing at hand, the pearls. The necklace snapped. Then I did. I heard the pearls rolling on the floor, and as I heard them rolling on the floor, I remembered what my mother, our mother, told me when she gave them to me: *One day you'll pass these pearls on to your daughter.* My throat began to burn with acid, I felt sick, outside became real again, terrifyingly real, real with a vengeance, I could hear the sound of the fireworks outside, but instead of watching them from the rooftop, as we had planned, we spent the first moments of the New Year, naked, on our hands and knees, suddenly very cold, collecting the pearls from the floor, from under the couch, picking them out of the rug as if they were head lice. I was shrieking, in a panic, cupping the lost pearls in my hands, counting them up, there were thirty I knew, thirty in total, I knew because I played with them obsessively when I wore them, touched them all, counted them. We managed to find all of them but one, which I now know is the one he put in the letter to you, somehow he managed to hide it from me, put it in his pocket and took it halfway around the world with him, only to send it back to me, to send it back to its point of origin, back to the beginning, a beginning that was really the

223

beginning of an ending, his ending, through you, the person he thought would end with him, but you did not end, because time does not end, it does not stop, even when we try to end it, even when we try to put a stop to it. I was screaming, screaming at him about the missing pearl, *We must find it, What will Mommy think, What will I tell Mommy*. Screaming about the pearl, *It's lost, It's lost*, when both of us knew I was screaming about the other thing, about what we had just done, we hadn't used a condom, of course we hadn't, when you're going to fuck your sister, when you're going to commit incest, what's the point right, why even bother with something like that, who takes precautions when they throw caution to the wind. As I was screaming, *It's lost, It's lost*, as I was looking for the missing pearl, freezing cold, naked, on my hands and knees, the blood drying on my arm, the cut beginning to sting, I became certain, totally convinced that Zach had gotten me pregnant, that already cells were dividing inside me, cells that were at once too close to me and too far from me, cells that would divide and differentiate until they became the daughter to whom I'd promised my mother to pass on these pearls, all thirty of these awful pearls.

Afterwards, because there is always an afterwards, we were in the bathroom, I was leaning over the toilet, he was holding my hair, he was whispering to me, trying to comfort me, as if comfort were possible, as if he felt no shame whatsoever in what we had just done, perhaps he didn't feel any, perhaps he never did, perhaps that's another difference between us, one I couldn't ignore, one that couldn't be erased. For me, the pendulum had swung back again, shame had once again gotten the upper hand over anxiety and my fear of being without him, shame was the dull, acrid taste in my mouth, the taste of alcohol and blood and vomit, shame was the cold sweat on my forehead, a nausea that began that night and has been with me ever since. Zach fell asleep that morning just before the sun began to rise, he was able to fall asleep,

I couldn't believe it, I watched his face while he slept and, for the first time in my life, I found it ugly, he had an awful, placid look on his face, as if he were pleased with himself, as if he were somehow peaceful and happy, he didn't seem to feel my suffering, and, for that, in that moment, I hated him, I wanted to kill him. Later that day, the first of the year, around noon, when I couldn't stand to watch him sleep any longer, I woke him up, I slapped him across the face and threw him out, I wouldn't listen to him tell me to *Please, Vera, calm down*, I wouldn't listen to him attempt to explain why I was upset. I shrieked, *Get out, Out, I never want to see you again, I never want to speak to you again*, because in his face all I could see was my shame, the impossibility our lives had become after we had done what we had done, I screamed at him until he left, and, as if it were a curse, a curse I've inadvertently brought down on my own head, he left, and the words came true, I never saw him again, I never spoke to him again. Two weeks later, I went to the drugstore and got a pregnancy test and, thank God, what I saw there was a minus sign. Mommy didn't say anything to me when I brought the pearls to her to have them repaired, she didn't notice there was a pearl missing, when she returned them to me, and told me to be more careful next time, I felt as if I'd committed a crime and no one had noticed, that there would be no consequences, that no one would ever find out, that somehow Zach and I had gotten away with it, we'd been given a chance to start over, I told myself, not knowing that our chance to start over had long since passed us by. I called him on the phone to tell him this, but he didn't pick up. I left voicemails. I wrote him emails, apologizing for what I had said to him, trying to explain myself to him, trying to say that it was good for us to be apart, that we needed, now more than ever, to try to see other people, but he never responded. I began to miss him, desperately, but I wanted to force myself not to miss him. After he left, I fucked a new guy every week, I didn't care how ugly, or stupid, or uncultured, or dirty, or dangerous they were, the uglier and dumber and more uncultured and dirtier and more dangerous the better, I thought, I needed to defile myself, to be totally abject, so Zach would never want me again, so I could free myself from his love by being absolutely unlovable. There were dozens of them, dozens of these awful men, whose names I never learned, or have forgotten, and were anyway unimportant to me, because they were indistinguishable from each other, these men were just the sick minds attached to the hard cocks I was trying to punish myself with, to me they were pawns, just pawns, disposable pieces in a game they would never find out about, a game they could never begin to understand. I fucked anyone who propositioned me or flirted with me or offered me drugs or money in bars to come to the bathroom with them, or to come home with them, or come to their hotel room with them. I had one rule, only one rule, no sex, these men could tie me up or hit me or cum on my face or fuck me in the ass or take naked photos of me or lick my shoes while I told them what slime they were or watch me go down on their wives or their girlfriends while they jerked themselves off, but I never again wanted someone to be where Zach had been. You don't need to tell me how utterly stupid this was, how self-defeating it was, I recognized it myself. It was as if I were preserving part of myself for him, as if I were turning my cunt into some kind of shrine to the moment we had together, the moment that we were more closely connected than any two people have ever been connected, the moment that told me I was a monster, that he was a monster. I wanted to make him hate me, I wanted him to know that I was unworthy of his love, and so I wrote him a letter describing what I had done, what I had been doing, how degraded I was, I knew if I put it in a letter, written in our secret code, he would be forced to read it, he couldn't just delete it and pretend it was never sent. I gave this letter to Daddy, this disgusting record of what my life had become, I had my own father pass it on to him, that's how desperate I was, how unclearly I was thinking, and Daddy gave it to Zach when the two of them met in Berlin. *The scars are enough*, I wrote him. *We'll be connected to each other forever, but it is time, time to live our own lives, as separate people. It's time to fall in love with other people. What I have done to myself these past months is for my own good, for our own good. Otherwise, we'll never be happy. Otherwise, we'll scar each other forever.*

Otherwise we'll never be happy, she repeats, in an exhausted voice. My God, Owen. I guess he found a way to make sure of that, in the end.

THE CRIMINAL AND HIS AUDIENCE.— Not only is every great crime a secret confession, but the most exquisite pleasure of committing a crime ultimately lies in getting caught. Only a true ascetic would deny himself this pleasure by actually *getting away with it.*

Between the moment Zach closed his eyes for the last time and the moment I arrived at Claire's door, I flailed through decision after decision I wished I could take back. Each mistake made the one that followed it that much more inevitable, that much more irrevocable. I thought I was covering up for myself. Really, I was burying myself alive.

I wiped the pistol clean with my jacket sleeve and tossed it and the spent casing into the dark green water, but no sooner had they disappeared beneath the surface of the river than I wished I'd taken them straight to the police. As soon as I'd knocked at the Bevington Road, shivering and drenched, my trousers muddied and splodges of blood dotting my cheek and chin, my shirt and bowtie, I wished I'd first returned to college to clean myself up and change into a new set of clothes. And when Claire opened the door, looked at me with astonishment, and exclaimed, "You look frightful! What on earth happened to you?" I wished — at the very moment I was opening my mouth to lie to her — that I'd simply told the truth.

"You won't believe me when I tell you," was what I said. I dragged the toe of my right shoe down the heel of my left, peeling it off. Then, bending my leg to my knee like a stork, I removed it with a clumsy hop. I left the shoes on the doormat, rolled the hems of my trousers to my calves, and waited in the hallway whilst Claire went to fetch me a towel. On the table in the kitchen were four empty plates and four empty wineglasses. The warm smell of supper diffused through the flat. Bottles of wine and liquor were lined up on the kitchen counter.

"Well then?" asked Claire when she returned.

I took the towel from her and carefully dabbed my wet hair, doing my best, without the aid of a mirror, to avoid getting anything that might be taken for blood on the white cotton. She was looking at me expectantly. "I've been trashed," I told her, praying the nervousness in my voice would be taken for irritation and the involuntary chattering of my teeth attributed to the fact that I was sopping wet.

"You must be joking." Her fingers flew to her lips to cover a reflexive burst of surprised laughter.

"I wish I were. By accident, no less. It happened just now, as I was walking by St. John's, on my way here. Whoever it was must have confused me with one of his mates. The bloke who did it looked rather contrite, actually. Offered to pay my dry cleaning bill. God knows what awful mix of shite was in that bloody bin. I don't want to, that's for certain. What?" Claire was leaning forward, her hand on her heaving chest. She was taking heavy breaths. "It doesn't smell, does it?"

Tori appeared in the hallway, upset to see I'd arrived alone. She looked at me and then at Claire. "What's so funny?" Claire pointed at me, no longer able to contain her mirth, and repeated, through a loud chuckle, the explanation I'd given for my dishevelled state. But Tori barely acknowledged that her friend had spoken. She looked at my wet hair and filthy suit with total indifference, unless it was with disgust, and asked me pointedly where Zach was.

"I was just about to ask you that. I saw him as I was leaving college. He told me he had to run a few errands and that he wouldn't be able to collect me from the Exam Schools. I assumed we'd all meet here." Tori's arms were folded. She stared at me with discomfiting, flattened eyes, to let me know that she suspected I was not telling the whole truth. "Why don't you text him then?" I said, more defensively than I'd intended, wondering, utterly unnerved, what exactly she thought I could be covering up.

"I have," she snapped back, offended by the suggestion that she couldn't think to do that herself. "We both have. Several times."

They watched me fish out my mobile. With a lump in my throat I typed *where r u* and pressed send. I didn't know whether Zach had taken his mobile with him, whether it was not a drowned bit of electronics short-circuiting in the river. Somehow I doubted it. He wasn't the sort to die with a phone or even a wallet on his person, whereas it never occurred to me to leave mine behind. At that moment, his mobile was probably on his desk, the screen turning orange, buzzing once, going silent again. I should have texted him sooner than this. The coroner would be able to establish a time of death and I would be in need of alibis. Another blunder.

I tried to reassure Tori. "I'm sure he'll be here soon." I could feel the face I'd put on my face beginning to disintegrate. The trembling that had taken control of my jaw was spreading to the rest of my body. I desperately wanted to be alone. "Meantime, I'm a bit of a mess, as you can see. Supper won't have gone cold by the time I've had a shower, I hope."

"Frankly, I've lost my appetite," Tori said, looking as though she were also losing control of an emotion she was desperate to keep hidden from us. "Take the roast out of the oven in fifteen minutes and serve yourselves if you like. If Zach miraculously appears, tell him he can't sleep here tonight, I don't care how many times he apologises." We watched her return to her room in a huff, heard the door lock behind her. Before I disappeared into the shower, I asked Claire if we should be worried.

"Of course not. Let's celebrate *you* for a change. It's going to be a Distinction, isn't it? All right all right, I'll touch wood, but there's no need to be so modest. Go shower. And scrub yourself well. I want a perfectly clean pair of lips to kiss. I'll bring you your spare clothes."

When I walked back through the arched doorway of college the next morning — having divested myself, along the way, of my gown and dinner jacket, my shirt and bowtie, and the contents of my stomach, in that order — the Porter's Lodge was bustling with activity. The parents of classmates whose names I'd learned were proudly helping their bleary-eyed, tousle-haired children load suitcases, stereos, books, and computer monitors into the boots of vehicles parked in Pembroke Square and up Beef Lane. I squatted to retrieve the post from my pidge, which was on the lowest row. I stood up again, pretending to be examining the envelopes and flyers, watching out of the corner of my eye to see whether the Head Porter was paying any attention to me. As soon as Richard's back was turned, I nicked the envelope on which I'd written *Zachary Foedern* from his pidge.

Back in my rooms, I lay the post on my desk, took my letter to Zach from the top of the pile, and hid it in the inner pocket of my grey suit jacket. I collected the other envelope, the one that said *Owen Whiting* in Zach's handwriting, from the bottom, where I'd slipped it. It was only then I noticed something was different about it. I held it flat and studied the shape of the envelope. The paper rose slightly in the centre. I turned it lengthwise. The bulge fell to the edge of the white rectangle. With my thumb, I opened it and poured the unexpected object, a black sphere, no more than two millimetres in diameter, into my palm. I stared at it, my perplexity crowding out all other thoughts, until, some time later, the sudden blinking of my eyes awoke me from my trance. "Concentrate," I said out loud. "You need to concentrate." Right then, the object was not a mystery I'd time to solve, so it went into the jacket pocket as well, to be dealt with later. I breathed deeply and unfolded the letter without rereading it — I could barely stand to look at it — astonished to discover how much a single piece of paper could weigh. Arriving at the Porter's Lodge in a state of evident distress, I informed Richard of an urgent matter that should be brought to the immediate attention of the Master.

Richard accompanied me to Staircase XVI with his large metal circle of keys. I told him I'd gone there as soon as I read the note, but had heard no response to my knocking. Richard pounded on Zach's door with the side of his fist, shouting his name. He twisted the handle and, to our surprise, the door gave way, opening into an empty room. Next to Zach's mobile and his wallet, which had been left on the desk, as I had suspected they would be, were his keys. Richard rushed back to the Porter's Lodge and lifted the black telephone. A few hours later, I was standing in the Master's rooms, in the presence of the Master, the College Nurse, and two officers of the Thames Valley Police.

Like most working-class Englishmen, I have a-bred-in the-bone dislike for the working-class Englishmen who work for the constabulary, but these two I found specially loathsome. Inspector Giles Thompson was a series of wobbly circles stacked precariously atop one other. His speech was dull and damp, as if his thick tongue were coated in mayonnaise, every other sentence punctuated by the reverberating smack of his fleshy inner cheeks. His partner, Detective Constable Eric Leyland, was equally unpleasant to behold, a lanky squiggle of skull and bones with a pair of recessed eyes and a dramatic overbite. He loomed over Thompson's shoulder, pen and notepad permanently to hand, repeating aloud his boss's every word as he committed it to paper.

Doubtlessly they felt the same about me, who'd gone up to Oxford on scholarship, forgotten his station, put on airs, perhaps even turned a tad fairy in the meantime. Had he even noticed it, the Master, who'd spent his life in the company of the wealthy and the titled, would probably not have understood the look the officers and I exchanged when he introduced us, a mutually accusatory glare whose meaning could be summed up in a single word: *traitor*.

The Master, mindful of the potential scandal or lawsuit that might arise from a student's suicide, proposed that I make first contact with Zach's parents, rather than the college or the police, since I at least had met his father before. This, the College Nurse agreed, would help to lighten his inevitable shock. But their pleas were overridden by Inspector Thompson ("No that won't do, wouldn't be proper at all," echoed Leyland), who rang the number Zach had written on his registration form, the one to be phoned *in the event of an emergency*. Thompson waited, listened, replaced the receiver. "It went straight to the answering machine," he told us. "Someone called Vera Foedern. The lad's mum, in all likelihood." "His sister," I corrected, with an ill-concealed look of reproach. I took out my wallet and handed him the business card Bernard had given me in Berlin, wondering why Zach had chosen to list Vera rather than one of his parents as his emergency contact.

"Good morning, Madam," said Inspector Thompson to the person who answered the phone. "My name is Inspector Giles Thompson, Thames Valley Police. Is Bernard Foedern available to speak by any chance? I understand, Madam. Regrettably it's a matter of some urgency. Correct. Concerning his son. Yes, I'll hold." He pressed the receiver to his chest and told us what we might have already inferred, that Mr. Foedern's secretary had answered, and was now gathering Bernard from a meeting. "Yes, Mr. Foedern. Good morning. My name is..." Though I ought to have been paying careful attention to what the Inspector was saying — for me a great deal depended on the minutest discrepancies between what he knew and what he thought he knew— my mind began to wander. I had not been in the Master's rooms before. On the mahogany-panelled walls were portraits of the previous occupants, dating back to the college's founding in the early seventeenth century. Above Stuart ruffles, Regency cravats, Victorian ascots, and wide post-war neckties, pairs of brown and blue circles were staring down imperious noses and tightly pressed lips at me, as though they were underwhelmed by the sort of student now attending the college to which they had dedicated their lives.

Someone was saying my name. With an oblivious look, I turned toward the sound. The Inspector was extending the telephone. "Mr. Whiting? Says he'd like to speak to *you*, Mr. Whiting."

"Yes, Bernard. Hello." My voice shook; I was about to tell the worst lie I'd ever told. Tears were welling up in my eyes, tears which, because I could not hold them back, I hoped would be interpreted by the police officers as an admission of fear for the fate of my friend, rather than an unconscious confession that I already knew what it was. "I'm afraid so. Yes, I'm afraid so. The signature did look like Zach's. But we don't know anything for certain yet. I can't tell you how sorry I am to have to be telling you all this. I hope it all turns out to be nothing and you'll forgive me for having given you such an awful scare. Yes, Bernard. To you as well."

I nearly dropped the phone into the Master's outstretched hand and had to be escorted out of his rooms beneath the umbrella of the College Nurse. Trinity Term had concluded, but two new examinations had been scheduled for me: one with a representative from Counselling Services and one with Inspector Thompson and Constable Leyland, to whom I'd give my official statement.

From that moment on, events began to pile up with incredible speed. The next afternoon, whilst I sat, balancing a large clipboard on my lap, filling out a form for the NHS in the waiting room of a dreary office on Worcester Street, a tourist placed a call to the St. Aldate's Police Station to report the discovery of the body of a dead boy, washed up along the bank of the Isis, a few metres downstream from Godstow Abbey. The police, arriving at the scene, found the pistol.

Bernard caught the first flight to Heathrow, and within twenty-four hours was making a positive identification at the coroners'.

ON VIOLENCE.— Moderns regard violence as something internal to human beings: they often speak of the violence that originates in mankind, as if violence were a series of actions a man might perform, or — were he less ignorant, irrational, or superstitious — might as well not perform. This is why moderns are always surprised by sudden outbreaks of violence; it is why they ultimately cannot understand the phenomenon, even as our scientific and technological achievements multiply it exponentially. The ancients, however, knew better. Violence does not exist in man; man exists in violence. Man is merely a vessel for violence, the site where it occurs, the name given by violence itself to the instrument that enacts it. When the man in man is stripped away, he returns to his source and becomes his God.

So it was true what she'd said. What she'd said at the bar. Because he was disappointed in love. In love with his sister. At the bar she was talking about *herself*. The thought of suicide was not what freed him from moral inhibition, as he'd claimed when he proposed the pact to me; nor was his body the collateral he'd staked on his freedom, as he had led me to believe. It was his knowledge that nothing he'd do would be regarded as a greater transgression than the one he'd already committed. Compared to the taboo he'd broken, what we'd done together was merely a string of moral misdemeanours and dangerous semi-illegalities. Compared to incest, what was taking drugs, nicking typewriters, picking bar fights, lying to friends and strangers, or hiring a prostitute? What, indeed, was suicide? People did *that* every day.

When she first told me how they cut each other, it occurred to me that in some ways it was like our pact, a dress rehearsal for what he proposed to do in Port Meadow. Now it's clear that our pact was a repetition of one that had already come to pass. When I finally understood that the object he'd placed in his suicide note was one of her pearls, it occurred to me that he was trying to smuggle some message to her from beyond the grave, a message he didn't imagine I would live to discover, let alone transmit. Now it's clear that the suicide note itself, of which I was merely an unwitting co author, was addressed to *her* from beginning to end. He was telling her that what they had failed to do with love, he and I would do with death. All this time I've been looking at our pact from the wrong end of the telescope. I was nothing more than one of those sacrificeable pawns she had described, one of those little expendable pieces, which, once you understood how they moved, could easily be pushed around the board, pressed into the service of a game that was being played out behind my back and over my head. His last words were meant to be a *name*. A long vowel sound followed by a short vowel sound. Not Owen. Not Tori. *Vera*.

She goes to sit at the edge of the bed, as if in a trance, without looking at what is beneath her, and her body, finding too little flat space to support its weight, sinks slowly down to the floor. The mobile falls from her slackened fingers. With her other hand, she presses the letter to her heart.

During her monologue she had paced the room, slowly, looking everywhere — at the ceiling fan, at the floor, at the photos on the noticeboard on the wall — everywhere but at me. Holding her pearl tightly, I lit cigarette after cigarette with my two free fingers, letting the ends fall out of the open window. As she spoke, I was reminded of the impression I had when Zach explained his last-minute change to the choreography of our pact. The person behind the voice seemed entirely absent from it; her lips were merely the membrane through which her memories had become language, through which they diffused into the audible world. As on that occasion, I listened with fear. This time, though, the fear was so mesmerising I never once interrupted her or asked her to clarify what she had said; not once did I try to refute or cast suspicion on her story. This time my fear wasn't born of a sudden shock, but rather, from the opposite, from a dawning realisation that the wood from which I had built the bridge I was using to cross from ignorance to knowledge was too rotten and unsound to prevent me from falling into the bottomless space that lay below. Now that the circumference of the circle Vera and I had been drawing together was complete, the absent centre it defined looked nothing like it had when we started.

Now she turns her neck to the window, to me, to see how I have reacted to what she has said. Black lines are running down her cheeks and her upper lip still glistens, even after she runs her sleeve beneath her nose and inhales deeply. What my own face looks like — whether my mouth is hanging open or my eyes are bulging out — I cannot sense. Her interpretation of my expression is clear enough, though. In a voice scarred by speaking, in words that sound like she swallowed all the forking branches she had spoken of, she asks: Are you disgusted?

At first I'm unable to speak. Disgusted? No: something else. No: something worse. I feel *betrayed*. By him. And now by you. By you through him, or by him through you. Impossible to say which is worse. Impossible to sort it all out now. Zach was going to have me die. For what? For love, lowliest of motives. Most carnal, most natural, most pedestrian, most *causal* of motives. Said so himself! The thing must be done for the right reasons, he'd said. Done for freedom's sake. And for that alone. That was his theory. *His* theory. And he betrayed it.

To think: I believed I was the betrayer. To think: of the guilt I felt for not stopping it in time, for going along with it, for participating in it. To think: of my shame at my cowardice — for not going through with it, for allowing my instinct of self-preservation to overcome my faith in his idea.

Betrayed and *jealous*. But of whom? Of which one? As there is only one at whom I can direct my anger, only one who is present to hear the words that are now whirlwinding around my skull, it is she who will have to hear them. I stand from the windowsill and take a step toward the bed, my finger pointed straight at her chest.

When you were fucking me, you were thinking of *him*! I shout, finally.

Owen, she says, with infuriating calmness, as if this were exactly what she expected me to say. She repeats my name in a tender whisper as she gathers up her strength and rises from the floor, leaving the letter there, next to the mobile. Can't you see? You were doing the exact same thing.

The pearl is clenched in my sweating palm. With my other hand I make a fist. But at this threat she neither flinches nor cries for help. Instead she steps closer, tilting her chin toward me, a sneer on her lips, as if she were ready, keen even, to martyr herself on my knuckles. My shoulder loosens. My elbow locks. A dull, flat sound reaches my ears as a blast of painful warmth spreads across my fingers and shoots up the nerves of my arm.

Vera staggers back, back onto the bed, her hands fanned out before her face. Twice, quickly, she dabs her nose and her mouth with the tips of her fingers. There is blood on them, blood on her fingers, blood dripping over her lips, down her chin. Our eyes meet and, for a moment, it is unclear which of us is more astonished that I'd actually done what I had just done. I am on the verge of apologising, of prostrating myself before her, of clutching her knees to beg her forgiveness, but her stunned mouth comes to its senses before mine is able to, and she shrieks — with laughter.

A cruel laughter, metallic and harsh. A cold laughter, demented in its volume and violence. Hideous laughter that feeds off itself like a feud between delirium and frenzy, miraculously gaining strength as it continues, consuming and convulsing her entire body. Her neck whips from side to side, spotting the bed sheets with blood and saliva, as if she were having a seizure, as if she were possessed. The nails of one hand are sunk into her scalp, the fingers of the other tear at her necklace. Her chest pitches and heaves.

Vera. Stop. Stop it.

Yes, I had struck her, a line had been crossed, but rather than putting her in my power, the opposite had occurred. Her indifference to the blow, her knowledge that I had lost any standing to tell her to do anything, to ask anything of her, reduced me to pleading for her mercy. Although she couldn't know it, to my ears, her laughter was an echo. It reminded me of Zach's cruel, cold, hideous laughter in the brothel in Berlin. In her laughter I hear, as I heard then in his, the sound of pure contempt, a cracked eruption of disdain that made a mockery of the impotent fury he had provoked in Nadya and she had provoked in me.

Please, Vera. I'm begging you to stop.

But I may as well have been begging the laughter itself. With this madness in my ears, it's impossible to think clearly, the sound drives away all thoughts. All thoughts save one: *It has to stop.* I clap my palm over her open mouth, the palm with the pearl in it, holding my hand there, over her nose and chin, where the blood is drying brown on her skin. The pearl catches in her throat and immediately cuts her laughter short. She gags involuntarily and tries to sit up, to cough, to dislodge the object by sticking a finger down her throat, but I straddle her and press her back to the bed. Spread out behind

239

her, the sheets ripple like the surface of a river agitated by a thousand slants of falling water.

I lean toward her, my nose almost touching the back of my hand. I shout: Vera, stop. Stop for fuck's sake. You're not listening, are you? I'm telling you to fucking stop.

Her eyes widen, her dark pupils focus on me, the source of danger. The Vera who had seemed to vanish in laughter becomes recognisable again. She bites at my hand and claws at my face, attempting to free herself from my grip, a shrill whinnying of animal defiance escaping from her nose. With her dwindling strength, she tries to swallow, but her Adam's apple, like a spent casing that remains lodged in the chamber, will not budge. Her cheeks are turning blue. Now it is she who is begging me to stop, with her wide, terrified eyes, the only means of expression my hands have left her. Her pupils stutter, as if they were asking, *Why are you doing this?*

Don't you see? I whimper, answering the question she could not verbalise. Can't you see? It's what Zach would have wanted. Don't you understand? It's what he would have wanted...

On the pale green screen of the mobile on the floor are the three numbers she had dialled before we disappeared into her room to tell each other the truth about ourselves, to reveal the monsters we were to each other, numbers I recognise straight away from countless films and television shows. I press the call button and hold the mobile to my ear. Listening to the ringing, I think of the future that awaits me on the other end of the call. All the people I'll have to explain myself to. All the people I'll never be able to explain myself to. My parents. The Foederns. Claire and Victoria. The Master, the Inspector, the Constable, and the press. Barristers. Magistrates. Wardens.

New York, Nine One One. What is your emergency?

I'd like to report a murder. One Nine Five Stanton Street, Six C.

I press the red button.

On the bed, Vera's arms are sprawled back above her head, her unmoving eyes fixed on the slowly spinning ceiling fan. I close the lids with my palm, then curl up next to her, my cheek on her still, silent chest. I fold her limp arm around my waist, close my eyes, and await the arrival of the police.

FALSE GODS, TRUE BELIEVERS.— Three strategies are available to the believer who has been betrayed by his God. The believer can repudiate the false God, he can redouble his faith in him, or he can fill the void of his absence by attempting to take his place.

The presence of the two officers in the Master's rooms made me feel guilty. Not moral guilt, which had been instantaneous upon hearing the gunshot, but legal guilt, potential culpability. To my knowledge I had committed no crime. Although I had failed to report what I knew, a skilful barrister might have argued that I acted in self-defence. But the great advantage of the police is their ability to inspire the belief that you had done, merely by questioning you about it. Perhaps that's why they're called the filth, because their suspicion rubs off on you.

On my way back from my second session with the NHS psychiatrist, I stopped in to the college library, which, except for the librarian at the enquiry desk, was completely empty. I managed to locate the relevant statutes in a volume of the Parliamentary Record. Suicide, I read, had been decriminalised in 1961. Whilst suicide pacts were no longer considered murder, "*a person who aids, abets, counsels or procures the suicide of another, or an attempt by another to commit suicide, shall be liable on conviction on indictment to imprisonment for a term not exceeding fourteen years.*" Surely that refers to euthanasia, I thought, suddenly feeling rather queasy. At the bottom, the reader was directed to consult various related statutes. I flipped to the text of the Homicide Act of 1957, where, to my horror, in Part 1, Section 4, I read the following: "*It shall be manslaughter, and shall not be murder, for a person acting in pursuance of a suicide pact between him and another to kill the other or be a party to the other being killed by a third person.*" Consulting the sentencing guidelines did nothing to stop the feeling that the ground was slipping from beneath my feet.

I entered my staircase and heard the sound of two voices I recognised. The Inspector and the Constable were waiting for me outside my door. Our appointment was not scheduled for another two hours and it was meant to occur at the police station on St. Aldate's. What were they doing here? What had they found out? I let them in — what else could I do? — resolved to lie my way through as much of their surprise visit as I could.

Lying was something, once a rarity for me, that I was now becoming quite good at. With the help of some advice Zach had given me on the U Bahn in Berlin, I was able to recover my calm. Sinking into the paranoia induced by the pills we had ingested and the hash we had smoked, I was convinced that everyone, the *polizei* included, knew we were on drugs. *This is the secret of keeping a secret*, he said to me then. *You must have absolute confidence that no one will know what you know unless you tell them yourself.* These were the words that would help me survive Thompson and Leyland's interrogation. In order for me to escape punishment for what I had done to Zach, it was clear that I would have to become him, to think as he thought, and speak in his assured voice.

Inspector Thompson sat in my desk chair; Constable Leyland stood at his side. I was thus forced to sit on my bed, feeling rather disadvantaged by this arrangement. Perhaps that was their intention. According to what the telly had led me to believe is standard police procedure, the Inspector asked me to describe my activities on the night of 15 June, whilst his colleague transcribed my answers into the leather-bound notebook he'd flipped open.

"That's three nights ago? The night before I found..." I paused. "His suicide note."

They nodded in tandem. "Starting at six in the evening," said the Inspector.

"Well, let's see. At half six I would have just finished Prelims. Which I took at the Exam Schools on the High. Because he was a visiting student, Zach didn't have to take exams, so he met me outside —"

"How did he seem to you?" interrupted Constable Leyland.

"Are you referring to his emotional state? Nothing out of the ordinary so far as I could tell."

The Constable flipped through his notebook, looking for a piece of information. "The Head Porter, Richard... Hughes... told us he was wearing a dinner jacket and a gown when he left college. Didn't that seem a tad strange to you?"

"Not at all. Why should it have done?"

"He was dressed subfusc"— he air quoted the term — "even though *as you claim* he wasn't taking exams?" At first I flinched at the Constable's needless scepticism. Then I had to suppress a smile. The Constable was making a complete prat of himself, mistaking his ignorance of the minutiae of college customs for evidence of my untruthfulness.

I blinked heavily, as if I didn't understand what he was asking. Then I said, "Ah yes, I see what you mean. No, that wasn't at all out of character for Zach. Exams were being taken, therefore he was dressed subfusc. He never missed an opportunity to do a thing like that. Anyway, we were supposed to meet up later with Tori and Claire to celebrate."

"Tori and Claire?" asked the Inspector.

"Victoria Harwood and Claire Caldwell. Tori is Zach's girl-friend. Claire is mine," I said, emphasising the present tense.

Constable Leyland wrote down the names in his note-book, then looked at his colleague. Thompson was glaring at him, reproachfully it seemed to me, as if he were upset that this was not information they already had. "We shall have to have a word with Miss Harwood and Miss Caldwell, won't we?" he said. To which the Constable replied, "Yes, we shall." In my most helpful voice, I provided them with their college affiliation and their address.

"So you were supposed to meet up with Miss Harwood and Miss Caldwell," Thompson continued when Leyland had finished writing. "But you didn't. Or at least not straight away. Why not?"

"Zach said there were still things to get for the party before the shops closed. I assumed he meant to collect a few more bottles of champagne. I told him I was hungry and was going to get a bite to eat. And that I'd see him at Tori and Claire's in a few hours."

"And so you went for supper —"

"For a snack," I corrected. The Inspector was surprised I'd the gall to interrupt him like that, especially over what he clearly perceived to be an irrelevant distinction. If he was going to speak with Tori and Claire, though, such a difference would amount to a contradiction. I explained that Tori was cooking supper at the flat and I only wanted something to hold me over until then.

"Right, then. *A snack*. Where?"

I told him I'd got something to eat in the Covered Market, but now another problem presented itself to me. I had a missing half hour to account for. "Then I walked over to the White Horse," I said. "And had a pint. I think I lost track of time, because it wasn't until round half seven that I made my way to the Bevington Road."

"Then you went straight to see Miss Harwood and Miss Caldwell?"

"Correct. By my estimate I arrived a little after eight."

"And Zach never arrived that evening," the Constable stated. "Didn't you at least find that rather strange?"

"I did. We all did, in fact. We sent him texts all night, asking where he'd disappeared to." Once more, Thompson and Leyland met each other's glance. As they were in possession of Zach's mobile with our text messages on it, they could confirm what I said was true. "But Zach *never* answers his mobile," I told them. "Still, Tori, Zach's girlfriend," I reminded them, "was particularly hurt by it. They'd had a row the previous day. And so we all accepted that this was the reason he never came in the end, although I was suspicious of that, I should have guessed that he was lying to me when we met outside the Exam Schools. But things like that happened all the time with him. With them, I mean. I didn't even give it another thought until I found the note in my pidge the next morning."

Inspector Thompson asked, "Did Miss Harwood mention what the row was about?"

"She didn't. Claire told me about it, in fact, but she didn't give me any details. I assume it was about their relationship." I described their row over the Commemoration Ball. "But if you want to know what really happened you'll have to ask Tori herself."

"We certainly shall," the Constable said. "Now. Richard Hughes claims that when he saw you the next morning you weren't wearing your dinner jacket."

"That's also true."

He began to approach my wardrobe. "Let's have a look at it, shall we?"

"I'm terribly sorry, Constable. I'm afraid that's not going to be possible at the moment." With one hand on the wardrobe handle, the Constable stopped. With a suspicious look Inspector Thompson asked me for an explanation. "Because it's at the dry cleaner's," I said. "I dropped it off the morning of. The next morning, that is. On my way back to college. Just before I discovered the note."

"What for?"

"Why did I drop it off, you mean? Because it was *filthy*, of course." The two officers were naturally interested in this particular detail. Fine, I thought, I'll give you what you think you want. "Covered in mud, I mean. Specially the trousers."

"Mud?" said the Inspector, attempting to feign confusion, or surprise. "You say you walked from the Exam Schools to the Covered Market to Broad Street to the Bevington Road. How would you have managed to get the trousers of your dinner jacket muddy?" It was at that moment I knew for certain what I had suspected since I began answering their questions. They had already found Zach's body — that much we all knew I knew — but they hadn't definitively ruled out the possibility of foul play, or even outright homicide, with me as the prime suspect. "Mr. Whiting? How —"

I interrupted the Inspector's question with the same explanation I'd given Claire when I arrived at her door. Luckily, his colleague found it as amusing as she had.

"You're taking the piss," he said. He couldn't help himself. He began to sniff and wheeze with sickly laughter.

"Constable," Thompson said crossly, wondering what had possessed his partner to act so unprofessionally. "You're forgetting yourself." Leyland went silent. I could see embarrassment, in the form of a red rash, spreading up his grey neck. He looked like he was on the verge of apologising to me. The Inspector lifted himself from the chair and held out his hand. The Constable gave him the notebook. He flipped through the pages, and then closed it, indicating to his partner with a nod that it was time for them to leave. I also stood up and opened the door for them. "One last question," he said, turning to me, meeting my eyes. "We found your fingerprints all over the typewriter Zachary Foedern used to write his suicide note. Mind explaining that?"

I looked down at the floor as my lower lip began to tremble. I could feel my chest and throat tighten. I was on the verge of tears as I told them about the poems we had composed on it in Berlin.

It was shameful carrying on like that in front of the filth. When the Constable, perhaps to make amends for his earlier indiscretion, offered me a packet of tissues, I had to refuse it.

"We'll contact you if we have any further questions, Mr. Whiting," he said as he followed the Inspector out the door.

"Wait, Inspector!" I called after him. Thompson looked up at me from halfway down the staircase. "How long will I be needed here? I spoke with Mr. Foedern this morning. I was wondering if I'd be allowed to attend the funeral."

ACKNOWLEDGMENTS

It is with profound gratitude that I wish to acknowledge all those without whom the writing and the reading of this book would not have been possible. To my father for trusting me at a young age with dangerous books and to my mother for forcing me to submit and resubmit this one. To Helen Ison and Mairead McKendry for going on the adventure of youth with me and to Anna Durrett at whose address I spent some of its most memorable moments. To Dory Bavarsky, Pepin Gelardi, Peter Schwartz, and Matthew Cahill for giving an only child the experience of brotherhood and indulging a young writer in his aspirations. To Steve Masover, J. W. McCormack, Jane Mikkelson, Rosie Sherman, Natasha Vargas-Cooper, Sophie Lewis, Kate Zambreno, Dave Golden, Eva Jenke, Ben Mauk, Madeleine LaRue, Saskia Vogel, Maria Alexopoulos, and Amanda DeMarco, the writers, critics, scholars, and lovers of literature in whom this book had the good fortune to find not only its earliest readers, but also its ideal readers. To my friend and agent Melissa Flashman who began representing this book long before it was written, and whose hard work, patience, advice, and support are surely without equal in the history of her profession. To my visionary editor Libby Burton for rescuing it from the drawer and for always giving me permission to take it further. To managing editor Kallie Shimek, copyeditor Roland Ottewell, and proofreader Rick Ball for helping me bridge the divides in our common language. And to Lisa, who was there from the first "A" to the last "l," and to whom this book and its author will always be dedicated.

COME VISIT US AT
WWW.LEGENDPRESS.CO.UK

FOLLOW US
@LEGEND_PRESS